Tracy Reed was b
now lives in Lon
novel.

YELLOWHEART

Tracy Reed

BLACK SWAN

YELLOWHEART
A BLACK SWAN BOOK : 0 552 99664 5

First publication in Great Britain

PRINTING HISTORY
Black Swan edition published 1996

Set in 11/13pt Linotype Melior by Kestrel Data, Exeter

Black Swan Books are published by Transworld Publishers Ltd,
61–63 Uxbridge Road, London W5 5SA,
in Australia by Transworld Publishers (Australia) Pty Ltd,
15–25 Helles Avenue, Moorebank, NSW 2170
and in New Zealand by Transworld Publishers (NZ) Ltd,
3 William Pickering Drive, Albany, Auckland.

Reproduced, printed and bound in Great Britain by
Cox & Wyman Ltd, Reading, Berks.

YELLOWHEART

1

Like most people, I do enjoy receiving personal letters through the post. Except, of course, when they happen to contain dark threats, vile insults, sexual swear-words and crude drawings of female breasts and genitalia. These I do not enjoy at all. I don't send such things and do not believe I deserve to receive them, but try telling that to my postman. Postmen going about their work are as irresponsible as hit men, and these are the kind of letters which began shooting through my front door one gloomy January morning.

I smoothed that first one out on my lap and studied it for a long time. I stared and fondled and sniffed. I held the cheap file paper at arm's length, as if disgusted, and then I brought it up close enough to kiss. I read the lines and then between the lines, and then I read the lines again and again, carefully, intensely, my eyes snuffling amongst the words like two dogs trying to pick up a scent.

None of this was any use.

The southern town named in the postmark meant nothing to me. The handwriting was unfamiliar and the paper smelled only of paper. Slag, bitch, whore, the words repeated over and over but, although they did feel particularly tailored to suit me, I had to admit that such insults could actually have been chosen by *any* man and draped over *any* woman. An hour passed. My fridge hummed an electric tune and my mind buzzed, stalled, buzzed. Finally, I put the letter down and gave up, having learned nothing definite about who had sent it or why, nor anything else much at all, except for the obvious: that there was probably some trouble coming.

Outside my flat, January was getting on with its business as if nothing had happened. The factory that makes bleak days was churning out more of the same old stuff: an endless supply of cheap, scratchy winds, mass-produced drizzle-drops and flimsy clouds in wishy-washy shades that no-one wanted. On my window-ledge, a London pigeon cooed or coughed. On the road, traffic revved and peeped, as cars of many colours complained in a variety of accents. And then, on the street right outside my house, there was another sound, a nice sound: a man whistling a ditty so cheerful and pretty that it seemed to make the mean morning suddenly quite ashamed of itself.

Eddie. It was my Eddie. It was my lover, Eddie.

There was a surge of joy and then a scramble of panic as I shoved the letter back into its envelope and thrust the envelope into a nearby cupboard. Eddie must know nothing about all of this, I decided firmly, slamming the door on those foul words, shutting them up. I loved him and he loved me and he'd only worry. And besides, I was beginning to suspect that this letter might have come from Martin, one of my many other lovers, whom Eddie must also know nothing about.

'Hello,' he said at the door, stooping to kiss a tight, pale cheek. 'Look at you. You look beautiful.'

I raised my hands to my face defensively, as if caught out in a lie. My eyes were smudged underneath with old make-up and new worries. Too much early concentration and coffee and smoking had made ash of my complexion and, unwashed, my gingery hair had turned the colour of a cigarette's insides.

'You're beautiful,' he repeated, insisted. Eddie always was one to overestimate me. My name is Angela. He calls me Angel.

2

Eddie was a big man. Eddie had a big body.

I loved Eddie's body. I loved it.

I'd loved it when I'd first seen it, when I'd first watched him walking across a room towards and past me, padding like a great blonde bear, pausing and pawing at a doorknob, then bumping a furry head on a low wooden jamb.

'Ouch,' he'd said.

'Are you all right?' I'd said.

He'd turned round.

His face had looked grumpy and his head had looked sore and I'd half expected him to roar, but then his voice was soft and amused as he'd told me, 'No.'

'Oh.'

'Are you?'

'No, not really. But I can usually get through doors without too much pain.'

'I can't. I'm always doing this.'

'It's good to have a hobby.'

'Did I look stupid? Did I look stupid when I did that?'

'No. Don't worry about it. You're just too big, that's all.'

'Nah,' he'd said then, ducking back in through the doorway and looking down at me with a grin. 'It's the world that's too small.'

I loved his body now, as he stretched out beside me. I loved the long bones that just would not accept from the world any less than their fair share of space. The swelling muscles that gathered like righteous armies on the rise of his shoulders and arms and thighs. The nakedness that never quite looked naked enough, on account of this fat skin that he wore like a furry, all-over coat of armour, fastened at the belly with a small pink button.

February. It was February. We were in my flat, in my bed, in the late afternoon.

There had been some passion and a lot of sweating, and now there was a bit of breathing and swallowing and sighing, as we both lay very still, trying to get used to the idea of being two separate people again. The blood that had gathered for a good time in our private parts began to wander dizzily back to where it should be, like revellers leaving a party. The air that lived over the bed settled quietly around us, resting heavily against our bodies, as if tired out by its recent jostling. Slowly, bashfully, the room opened its eyes and came back into focus.

My room. My flat. Soon Eddie would be wanting to get up and out of my damp little flat. He didn't like it here, was always complaining about the unhealthiness of the conditions I lived in. I knew that he was right. The air in my rooms was so moist and chilled that you wouldn't have been surprised to hear the furniture sniff and sneeze. The wooden window frames were rotting and the bathroom wall regularly dribbled and there were some very nasty, speckly rashes on the kitchen and living-room ceilings which just wouldn't seem to clear up no matter what I did. I would redecorate these rooms two or three times a year, plastering on thick paint in soothing shades, only to find those black spots breaking out again a few months later, as raw and sore as ever.

I don't know where all the dampness came from. The

heating and overall ventilation seemed adequate, and we weren't near any water.

For a while, I had wondered if it was coming from me, for that musty, musky odour did not seem unlike the rich scent that I recognized as my own body smell. I only really discounted this possibility when, during a power cut, I had occasion to call in on my neighbours in the flats above, below and next door to me and, noticing that the air in their rooms was similarly moist and heavy, decided that I was probably not responsible for the bad atmosphere of this many homes.

Eddie sniffed pointedly. I ignored him. He sniffed again, and now I sat up and tried to change the subject.

'It's February,' I said.

'What? Yeah. Yeah. The beginning of February,' Eddie said.

'February. It's a lovely word, that.' I lay back against the pillows and repeated it. 'February. February.'

The sound made a picture in my mouth that was nice, like a girl with flushed cheeks and soft, brown hair. February. Feb. Febbie.

'I always expect to feel different when a new month begins. I do feel different. Optimistic. Maybe this one will be better than the last.'

'Maybe. But it doesn't look like much has changed out there.'

We looked out of the window. Eddie was right. The new month had brought only more of the same old weather. The frowning sky, preoccupied with dense cloud and thoughts, had no time for girlishness. The rain that prickled the pane was dark grey, rough as stubble, and the afternoon air seemed hard, as if it could take your best punch without flinching. Although still young, you could already see that February was planning to be the kind of month that would hang low over this city, pressing down on its people until they

12

stooped a little. I thought of flowers hiding underground, of families sheltering in sealed houses, of everybody keeping their heads down. I thought of the letter that had arrived for me two mornings before, another terrible, menacing letter from some terrible, menacing man, and that put an abrupt end to my fluffy cheerfulness.

'February,' I said again, but this time, I spat it like a swear-word. February! It shouldn't call itself February. Even March had the decency to hint at the grim determination that will be needed to get through it.

We dressed quickly, and then Eddie drove me to work.

These days I made my living as a cleaner.

It had been a friend's idea. I'd been rubbing up a furious shine on a chair that she'd been sitting on at the time and, instead of suggesting counselling, she'd quietly handed me the small ads page of the local newspaper and a way of making my obsession work for me.

I'd got that job, and then another, and then another, and then I was a proper full-time cleaner, and happier than I'd been in years. It suited me. I enjoyed the hard work. I liked the feverish feeling of doing my own small bit to combat the overall mess and muck of the world, and decided to postpone the cure for a time when I didn't need the money or the neurosis so much.

Eddie stopped the car on an ugly street in Camden Town, then scowled across at my place of work: a small, plain and functional office block, one of those buildings that are quite content to be clever and don't see why they should have to be pretty as well.

I walked confidently through the glass doors of the main entrance, flashed an important-looking pass at a new security guard, then strode on by the executive conference room and into my own office: a dark, damp cupboard, unpretentiously decorated in grey and stains and full of carefully filed dusters, cloths, mopheads and toilet bleaches.

I put on my apron and some more lipstick. I rolled up my sleeves and felt fine. I really did enjoy my work, you see, and this Camden Town job was the one that I enjoyed most of all.

I liked the people. That's what I liked. The people.

It was mostly men who worked here. Many men. All kinds of men. All kinds of interesting and distinctive men, although, strangely, even the strongest individuals quite tamely allowed themselves to be separated within the company into two distinct categories, and ever after conform to type. There were those who worked upstairs in the office and those who worked downstairs in the warehouse and depot. There was some animosity between these two groups. Those above couldn't stand the stubborn loutishness of those below and those below resented the smarmy bossiness of their smarmy bosses. And as for me, well, I just liked them all.

I liked the starched sexuality of the office-workers. The hairy mannishness trimmed back by manners. The desire that caught and staled like sweat beneath the sealed white cleanliness of shirts and office decorum. They seemed to like me too, and many of them waved or smiled as I passed them by that evening, even though they were in the middle of intercoursing with some computer or telephone or radio headset at the time. One or two of them were so pleased to see me that they seemed to crackle. I don't know why. Perhaps it was the way I moved around the room that did it: quietly, gently, soft as a duster, or the way that I was always so careful to show no sparks of personality whatsoever. Perhaps that was it. Perhaps pressing electrical equipment to their bodies all day had affected these men's own energy flow; had built up a high-flyer's, high-powered charge that could only be safely released against a person of compatibly low status and voltage.

I finished the office and went down the backstairs and along the cold corridor that led to the depot. Several men sent warm looks through the chilly air as they heaved loads in and out of lorries, slammed doors, dragged chains and then stomped into the tearoom saying fuck, fuck, bastard and fuck, their rough work having raised swear-words to the surface like blisters. I didn't mind. I rinsed the sink and didn't mind. The way they spoke was one of the main things that I liked about the downstairs men. The ring of hard accents against hard concrete. The talk of cocks and cunts. The bare-knuckle slang and the thrusting rhythms. I liked the way these men penetrated the politeness that usually covered people's private thoughts and parts, the way they fucked with language.

I even liked Bob, the man whose job it was to move between these two floors and worlds, adapting his vocabulary and personality a hundred times a day, depending on which level he was on at the time. Of course, the proper way to do it would have been to remain himself wherever he was and whoever he was with, but I didn't know that at the time, and was in no position to offer advice.

'Hello. An' how are *you*?' said Bob when I met him on the backstairs that evening. He paused to finger his clipboard and his trouser pocket. Caught between the two floors like this, his manner was both lascivious and polite.

'I'm fine,' I told him.

'Are you?'

'Yes. I'm fine.'

'Yes, you look fine.'

'Do I?'

'Yes. You certainly do look fine.'

'Thank you.'

I smiled at Bob. I didn't care what everybody said about him. I was not like those others who instinctively sidled away from his slippery character and his slicked-back hair and his oily changes of gear. I liked him. I sort of loved him. No. I fucked him, that's what I did, I fucked him that night, right there on the backstair after everyone else had gone home. Well, now you know. Now you know about me, don't you; what I like and what I am like.

The next morning, it snowed. Whoosh, and the grubby goings-on of the evening before were wiped out, whited out, easy as that.

They had come during the night, those snow-fat clouds; had come to lurch and stomp and then crouch over the city like a crowd of pregnant ladies, unable to hold themselves in any longer. Now, relieved of its load, the sky flattened again suddenly and a small, wan glow of sunshine or satisfaction came into the skinny white. Looking down, it seemed pleased with what it had made. It had made something beautiful, precious. I had never known London to seem so precious. It was as if someone had covered it over protectively while they went away for the winter, draping cotton sheets over the things on the streets; making antique furniture of a postbox, a litter-bin, a bench.

Oh, I knew it wouldn't last. I knew what a place like this would do to tenderness like that. I knew about the traffic that would come trampling its lines like firm opinions down the middle of the roads, lines that would widen and deepen with every minute, cynicism that would spread and spread until roadsides were yellow and simplicity was slush. Salt would be thrown like acid into a beautiful face. Grey would start to seep through everywhere, appearing in patches like old insecurities, and black thoughts would nibble away at the edge of every white Green. All of this would happen. But it hadn't happened yet. It was still early. London was still spellbound by the softness of the new friend it had met during the night. For now, the city allowed itself to be loved.

Eddie and I were walking and dog-walking in the park.

Eddie had a dog called Burroughs. It was a large, furry, burly animal with a soft underbelly, and they made a good pair.

We stopped to rest on a cold bench. An old man with snow or white hair on top of his head passed us slowly, his walking-stick leaving a distinct line of O's on the soft ground, alongside the slur of his stuttering feet. Nearby, there were a lot of black dots jiggling about against a white hill: Dalmatian. Burroughs went off to have a smell-conversation with the other dog, then came back to tell Eddie all about it. I was kissing and hugging Eddie at the time, but the animal didn't care about that. It nosed me roughly out of the way, climbed up to lap at Eddie's puffy breath, and then tried to wrap its coat around his shoulders. Eddie laughed and stroked the thick fur, while I sighed and sat back and felt cold.

'He hates me.' I said sulkily. 'Your dog hates me.'

'Ha ha ha. No he doesn't,' Eddie replied, ruffling his two pets fondly. 'He's just jealous, that's all it is. The poor old boy's jealous.'

'I think it's more than that.'

'He knows how much I love you, you see. That's what it is. He's sensitive, that's all.'

'Mmm.'

'Dogs are very sensitive creatures.'

'Mmm. They can smell fear, can't they?' I said. 'I've heard that.'

'What?'

17

'I've heard that you shouldn't hold your open palm out to a dog you're nervous of because they can smell the fear in your sweat and it drives them wild.'

'Really.'

'Yeah. I've also heard that you can kill a dog instantly by pulling its front legs apart. Outwards . . . like that!'

I demonstrated the movement. Eddie chuckled. Burroughs did not.

'Apparently, they've got no joint or muscle accommodation for this stretch, see, so everything kind of tears and it just sort of rips their heart right open.'

Eddie watched me intently as I screwed my face and waved my arms in the air, painting vivid pictures onto the white background.

'It's worth bearing in mind. It is. It might save your life one day. Stop laughing at me. Any dog can turn on you, you know.'

'Are you planning to turn on me, lad?' Eddie said, pushing Burroughs to the ground and rolling him roughly over with his boot. The animal lifted his head out of the sprawl and panted up adoringly. His pink tongue lolled stupidly out of the side of his smiley mouth. His furry head was planning nothing except how to get its next pat.

'I'm telling you, any of them can turn on you!' I repeated, suddenly loud and emotional. 'You've got to be careful. You've got to be careful! My dad taught me that.'

It was true. My dad had taught me that and lots of things like that. My dad believed that it was very important to know how to defend yourself; thought that you should be ready for all kinds of attacks from all kinds of attackers at all times. As you can imagine, this made him a well-prepared but rather tense man.

Even when he was relaxed, my father was tense. If you'd watched him watching TV, you'd have laughed

18

to see how he'd jump at some surprise gunshot or scream. At other times, while he was sunbathing or washing the car or chatting to neighbours, you could spot him rolling and rolling his great shoulders around in small, tight circles, trying to shrug off the cloak of tightness that he wore there in all weathers. Occasionally, you could catch him doing odd hand exercises too: wiggling and waggling his large fingers, then stretching them out as far as they would go, gently unclenching them from the fists into which they'd instinctively curled.

At night, he would double-check treble-locked doors. In the mornings, he'd awake very early and suddenly, as if sleep were a trap that he'd just escaped from. As soon as he got downstairs, he would pull his big boots on and he would keep those big boots on, laced up high and tight, right through until it was bedtime again. I suppose there must have seemed little point in taking them off. In shoes or socks or Christmas carpet slippers, his stout toes always remained fixed in the same pose: taut and rolled and compact, as if set for a fight. I have never heard of toe-fighting, neither as a sport nor as a form of self-defence, but should it ever have been necessary for my father to prove himself in this way, you can be sure that he would have been ready. Ready for that, for this, ready for anything.

I turned my head now and noticed that Eddie was staring at me very hard. No; he was staring at the space right in front of my face, where the word 'dad' still hung in the thick white air. Eddie was surprised to hear me mention my dad. I was surprised too. He'd been very dead for almost a year and a half and I just had no reason at all to ever talk or wonder or remember about him. Well, not until now.

'What made you think of that?' Eddie asked, but I didn't reply. I couldn't tell him about the letters, and that's what had started all of this, stirring me up with their threats and their curses, setting me off worrying and wondering and remembering like that. Feelings. I suddenly had all these feelings, and not just fear, but also sadness, grief, guilt, joy, depression, excitement and love. That's just the way it is with feelings sometimes, you see. That's the trouble with feelings: they hold hands inside you, and when you tug on one, all these others come along too.

'What else?' Eddie asked, trying to make a conversation of it, but he was too late. By this time, I was concentrating all my energy on packing ice around my dad's face, freezing the memory of him out, numbing the place in my mind which held it.

'What else did your dad teach you?' he persisted, and now I got angry and the whole day got spoiled.

'Nothing. Leave it. Come on.'

Soon, Eddie would kiss me and offer to buy me a coffee and a bun, but I would push him away, saying that I felt neither hungry nor sexy. Soon, when no-one was looking, I would pinch Burroughs' soft side very hard with my gloved fingers, but even this would not raise my spirits above a low chortle.

'Come on. Come on!' I snapped now, marching off down the path, feeling my black mood spill over onto the clean morning like blood onto snow.

3

Some time passed. The snow went. All lingering memories of February melted as the air turned soft and surrendered to the pounding rain and the military grey of March. A new metallic gloom entered the air of the city, and then another hate letter arrived at my house.

It came, as the others had, on the first Saturday of the month, and this time I was ready for it. I scooped the envelope up the moment it touched my mat, carried it swiftly upstairs, and then shoved it straight into the kitchen bin; pushed those filthy words and rubbishy emotions deep, deep down into the dirty, dirty bin where they belonged.

I'm just not interested in anything he has to say, I told myself, as I let the tap run very hot, then vigorously washed my hands of the whole affair. I am going to calmly make my breakfast now, that's what I am going to do; I'm going to make breakfast and be uninterested and stay calm, calm, calm.

Defiantly, deliberately, I prepared some cheerful food. Carefully, hummingly, I brought the food over to the table. I licked my lips ridiculously. I sat down slowly. And then I stood up again suddenly and dashed across the room. At the last moment, it turned out that my curiosity was actually far stronger than my pride or my hunger, and now I found myself back by the bin, gracelessly scavenging the soiled envelope from the jaws of an empty egg box, then greedily scouring its contents for any clue as to what was going on here and what I could do. It was no good, though. I soon found that the letter had nothing fresh to offer. This latest letter came out of the bin stinking of fish oil and cigarette ash and the same old stuff.

Here is what it said:

ANGELA. OH GOD YOU ARE IN TROUBLE NOW. YOU ARE A SLAG BITCH WHORE AND I AM COMING FOR YOU YES YOU DESERVE ALL YOU ARE GOING TO GET WATCH OUT FOR ME BECAUSE I WILL DESTROY YOU BECAUSE YOU HAVE ASKED FOR IT YOU KNOW WHAT I MEAN? WHAT IS GOING TO HAPPEN WHEN IS IT GOING TO HAPPEN YOU ARE THINKING BUT YOU DON'T KNOW ONLY ME. ALL I WILL TELL YOU FOR SURE IS THAT BY THE END OF THIS YEAR YOU WILL BE DEAD YOU FUCKING WHORE AND IN THE MEANTIME I WILL ENJOY SEEING YOU SWEATING AND THEN I WILL COME AND I MIGHT RAPE YOU OR I MIGHT NOT YOU ARE SO DIRTY. ARE YOU SWEATING YET CUNT BITCH YOU SHOULD BE I WILL SEE YOU SOON AND THEN YOU WILL SEE. THINK ABOUT ME I AM THINKING ABOUT YOU ALL THE TIME. WATCH OUT. LOOK OUT. REMEMBER THIS AND DO NOT SLEEP.

Well, that's not very nice, I thought as I slumped back to the table and tucked into soggy, depressed cereal and toast that had cringed at the edges with waiting and distaste. All of this, it wasn't nice. It was a worry. It was enough to put a less calm woman right off her breakfast.

*   *   *

Halfway through March, I made a new friend. It's not what you're thinking. It's a girl. My new friend was the new girl who had moved into the basement flat of my house.

She'd actually arrived some weeks ago. I'd seen her one morning, by herself, dragging drab boxes into the drab apartment, but I had not thought to go down and give her a hand or to go into my kitchen and whip up a chummy cherry-cake welcome. It did not seem appropriate. I was not a cherry-cake sort of a person, and this was not a welcoming sort of a house.

We finally met one day after a cheeky breeze had nipped in through my bedroom window, unhooking some underwear from where it was trying to dry on the ledge, then tossing it down into her bit of backyard.

'Hello. Can I have my knickers back, please?'

'Yes, of course. Come in.'

I had been painting on a small canvas in my bedroom that morning, trying to invent a new red, and had the notes to my experiments jotted untidily across my face, hands and clothes. As we stalled in her living-room, I saw this girl looking at the paint intently, but more as if she were considering the colours themselves, rather than what they were doing all over me. I liked that, and in return stared quite openly and rudely around her flat.

At first, I saw mess.

The chairs in this main room were all placed randomly and at odd angles, grazing roughly against the grain of the polished wooden floorboards. Small cardboard boxes, groaning to spill their load, sat before a large, empty cupboard whose door stood wide open, like a rigged trap. Elsewhere, fat bundles of documents, nipped in at the waist with rubber bands, lolled uncomfortably on the top of a desk, instead of being allowed to bed down neatly in its drawers. Mess. That's what I thought first: mess.

23

But then, slowly, I began to straighten the room with my eyes, and then, curiously, I began to notice beneath the disorder a strong sense of bareness. This wasn't clutter. There was no litter here, no waste, none of those endless papers and trinkets and bits of rubbish that us tidy people like to gather and file and keep. This girl hadn't pressed rugs onto the floors or pasted new paper and pictures onto the walls, or done any of those other tricks by which we stick ourselves to a place. I noticed suddenly the way that the wooden packing crates and ornate suitcases had been given the most prominent positions in the room. One was being used as a coffee-table, another as a lamp stand, while a third propped up a small, efficient-looking clock. All seemed more like furniture than luggage, and I realized then that here was a person and a set of belongings that could be packed and ready to go anywhere within half an hour, maybe less. This was not a display of untidiness, but of unsettledness.

The girl and I went out into the small back garden. We were becoming interested in each other now.

The reaction to an awkward silence is a good measure of most people's character, and so the two of us stood together without speaking for some minutes. I looked at her. She looked at me. I had that unexplained flash of vermilion on my cheek. She had fascinatingly cold blue eyes and killed a few weeds with her boot as we both waited for the other to break and speak.

'I don't like people much,' she said finally, suddenly.

I considered this for a moment. I hadn't asked for this information. It made no sense in the context of the only conversation we'd had. It's some sort of code, I thought. One that I know.

'I'm scared of dogs,' I replied, and at that we both relaxed and smiled warmly, as if we'd just recognized each other. We had some tea. We had some laughs.

You'd have thought we were lifelong friends if you'd seen us giggling in Caroline's kitchen that afternoon, although it wasn't until our second or third meeting that we actually learned each other's names. I liked that too.

The importance a person places on names and titles and other definitive adjectives is another good gauge of character.

Psychiatrists, for example, have, in my opinion, a very disturbing fondness for them. You can see it by the steely glint they get in their eyes whenever one comes to mind. They just love these words, just love them and their sharp precision and their ability to pin and hold people in place, like butterflies in a case. Oh, they have their reasons and excuses for doing this. They say that it helps in their study of you, that it helps them to understand and cure you, but I say what use is that if you're already dead by then?

I knew a psychiatrist once: Mrs Morris. I'd been forced to get to know her and to let her know me; ordered to see her after a bit of art-college violence had got out of hand.

Mrs Morris had names for me, I know she did. Sometimes, as I sat beside her, I would feel her trying this term and that on me, to see which she thought suited me best. I called her office The Changing Room. She'd smiled hard when I'd told her that; seemed pleased. I think she'd taken it as a compliment on her powers to transform, but that's not how I'd meant it at all. Eyes watching you undress; that's more what I'd meant.

While she was still smirking, I'd asked Mrs Morris if the strait-jacket that she was measuring me for was ready yet, and then her face had fallen suddenly. That's a very interesting comment, she'd said earnestly, and after that there'd been no more humour between us; just those funny words that she tagged onto my notes at the end of each session, like punch-lines which she understood and I didn't.

Outsiders, outcasts, drifters, loners, travellers, eccentrics. These people do not often show much concern for names. They belong to no local club which demands of its members reassuring specifics about history, status, identity, sanity. I don't think I ever really got to know what Caroline was like. She was this and she was that and, sometimes, something else. She was a strange girl, people said, and always bound to become a good friend of mine.

'I want to shoot you,' Eddie said one late March morning, gently stroking my head and then leaping suddenly out of bed, as if some great idea or temper had just taken hold of him.

'What?'

His words jolted me out of a dream about crashing aeroplanes. I landed in the bed with a heavy thud and then sleepiness turned immediately to stiffness as I flashed my eyes open and tried hard to focus on where I was and who I was with and what was going on.

'Don't move!' Eddie shouted.

'What?'

'No! Don't move!'

I turned slowly around to see a small black hole squinting up at me from the end of the bed.

'What? What?'

'Ha! I've got you now. Ha! Got you!'

Eddie grinned and chuckled triumphantly. I realized what he was up to and sighed resignedly; let my head flop back down onto the bed, let the pillow cover my eyes like a blindfold.

'OK,' I told him. 'OK. Do what you like. Just do what you like. You're a bad man, Eddie.'

I heard heavy breathing. I heard the slow cocking of a camera shutter. I felt my lover releasing on me the full force of his affectionate gaze.

Eddie was not a bad man. He was a photographer.

At the present time, he was working in a commercial West End studio three days a week, which was a repetitive and uninspiring job, but did at least provide him with the time and the facilities to develop his own work.

For a while, he had been with a more up-market studio, where he'd been paid lots of money to take flattering photographs of rich people and their children, but this hadn't worked out. Eddie could be gentle with the truth, but he could not lie, and so you can see the problem. Some of these people had spent a fortune on the right clothes, cosmetics, teeth and noses, and quite reasonably expected their portraitist to enhance the illusion that they had created, not to see straight through it. If Eddie thought that someone seemed deeply unhappy, then he would create a picture of them looking so exquisitely sad that they would want to burst into tears and tell him their troubles the moment they saw it. If an overdressed and overly well-mannered child appeared before him, Eddie would usher their parent out of the room and start to have some fun with the kid, chatting and chasing and giggling until he finally got one shot of them looking untidy and uncouth and wonderful. One day he did harsh things with his lights and pictured a bitchy society wife looking like a bored, hungry vampire, and that had been that.

Before he'd discovered photography, Eddie had wanted to be a psychologist. He'd actually studied the subject for a number of years, and had been a brilliant student by all accounts, but then one day he'd suddenly decided to transfer to the art college across town instead; he tells me it was on account of the way he was always off trying to capture the spirit of some deserted warehouse or graveyard, when he should have been in the library staring at diagrams of dead people's brains.

But you could do important work, his tutor had told him when he'd left. The human mind, the whole of human experience just waiting to be observed and understood; stay with us, you can do it, this is the way to do it. But Eddie had a camera now, a third eye, a new way of seeing into things.

A way of seeing me more clearly, he'd said at the beginning of our relationship when, to my delight, he'd started filling rolls and rolls of expensive film with images of me, just me, just as if my eyes, smile, fingers, second-hand clothes were valuable things which deserved to be preserved.

These days, now that the novelty had worn off, I no longer posed for Eddie's camera, barely even noticed it any more, which only seemed to make him keener than ever.

This morning, I pulled a magazine from the bedside table and became absorbed in an article about tortured monkeys. Oh, that's such a cruel thing, I thought when I'd finished, and then I came back to the room to find that Eddie had been sitting at the other end of it for the last half an hour, covering my sad face with his click click little kisses.

Now I turned away and covered my face, ashamed. I was quite upset, and I never got upset. I just never ever got upset, only this particular animal experiment was just so very cruel, you see. They were testing the monkeys for love, that's what they were doing. First they made the monkeys lonely and then they let them build intense, loving relationships with their keepers, and then they wired the human 'friends' with electric-shock pads, in order to find out how many times the little animals would come back and try to hug the

28

people who were hurting them. A love experiment, you see. Well, those scientists had been surprised by the results. How many times did the monkeys come back? Lots and lots of times, lots and lots. One of the creatures had actually perished in one embrace, and many others only stayed away when they had lost the feeling in their burned fingers and hands. When it was all over and the monkeys were returned to their cages, every one showed signs of a depression far deeper than before the love experiment had begun. The article did not say how the scientists or the keepers had felt afterwards. Just 'surprised' apparently.

Now I put the magazine down, but the feelings that it had started did not stop. I was definitely upset now, and not just over those poor, stupid, singed monkeys.

I lied, you see.

Sometimes, I was not calm at all. Sometimes, I felt bad, really bad. Sometimes, I'd look around me and wonder how I could do the things that I was doing to Eddie. How could I do that? I'd think to myself. *How* could I *do* that? And then I'd remember.

'What are you doing tonight?' Eddie asked suddenly.

'Oh, I'm going out sketching,' I told him casually. 'I'll have a bit of tea with you, but then I'll be going out, all right?'

'All right.'

'Won't be too late, OK?'

'Yeah. OK. No problem.'

That's how I did it. It was easy, see?

I had a date with my postman that evening.

I'd got chatting to him one morning about the possibilities of tracing threatening letters and we'd stayed friendly and now we had a date.

As promised, I went round to Eddie's house

29

beforehand, and we had a nice meal together. Well, I think it was a nice meal. I can't really be sure because I hardly tasted a thing as I nervously bit and chewed and gulped the food before me. Eddie was probably nice that evening too, probably sweet and warm and nourishing, but I don't remember him too clearly either; he blurred before my eyes as the time sped past and my mind focused on six-thirty.

It was an eerie thing, experiencing someone losing their fleshiness right in front of you like that. And Eddie had so much fleshiness to lose that you'd have thought it would have been quite a job, stripping him down in this way. But it wasn't, you know. It was easy. It was just a knack I had, I suppose, and by the time Eddie got up from the table, he was barely there at all; I had so diminished the man that I now felt I could walk right through him and barely feel a thing.

Eddie floated off to the kitchen. His shadowy dog followed, but then changed his mind and came back to sit under the table at my feet, sensing in his supernatural way that I was too nervous to eat much and might have some furtive scraps to spare.

I fed Burroughs the remains of my tea and then, to use up a little more time and nervous energy, started a chase game with him around the room. He hesitated at first, suspicious of my sudden friendliness, but I persisted and then persisted some more, until finally the essentially doggy side of his nature proved too strong to resist the sight of a jogging human being with a toy, and the animal smiled furrily and started to play.

I ducked and twirled in and out of the furniture. Hooray! Come on, then, come on, wheeeee! Ha ha. Excited, excited. Six-twenty. Come on, boy! Up, up, that's it, well done! Six twenty-five. OK, OK, get off now. That's enough now. Calm down, dog, calm down. Sit!

Burroughs settled obediently at my feet as I brushed my hair in front of the mirror. He panted amusedly as me and my reflection pranced about, posing and whirling and preening and getting ourselves ready.

I turned a fine, precise pirouette in the centre of the room. And then another. And then another. And then, I got careless. In my spinning giddiness, I got clumsy and knocked a large glass of blackcurrant juice over and onto the carpet. Oh-oh. That wasn't supposed to happen. Oh-oh. I snatched a breath and watched in horror as the leaf-green rug took in the drink, absorbing the water but spitting the nasty artificial colour back up onto the woollen surface, making a great long purple streak with several guilty splashes pointing in my direction.

Oh-oh. Look at that. Look at that and look at the time. It was my fault, but it was also six-thirty, and if I owned up and cleaned up now, I would maybe miss the date I had with the man who'd whipped up this frenzy in the first place.

The stain glared up at me vividly. It was the kind of purple that could spoil a mood just like that. Eddie came back into the room, came back into sharp focus.

'What's happened here?' he said.

I said, well, I said something.

Burroughs was still smiling when Eddie marched over to tell him off.

'Bloody hell. That's my best rug. Bloody hell. Look what you've done.'

Burroughs did look. He looked at me, at the stain, at Eddie, then back up at me. He sniffed the blackcurrant juice, pawed it, then tried to lick it up, but only made it worse and worse; took his punishment of an hour in the kitchen quite well really, considering.

When I called into that room to collect a bag on my way out, the dog was rolled up meekly in his basket, with his fat head resting heavily on a furry paw. He looked up at me slowly and suspiciously. He looked sad and puzzled. He looked as if he were trying very hard to work out what had just happened here; knowing that something funny was going on.

Fortunately, his master was an altogether more trusting creature.

'I'm off, then. Bye, Ed.'

'Oh, yeah. See you, lovey. Have a nice time. Be careful. Have you got all your stuff?'

'What? Oh, yeah,' I said, tapping my bag. 'Pencils, brushes, water pot, pad. Yeah, yeah.'

Lipstick, hairbrush, perfume, condoms, I silently added, as I threw the bag over my shoulder and went off to get on with my hobby.

At around nine o'clock that night, my date was over and I was heading hurriedly back home to Eddie.

The date had not gone well in the end; had all been a bit of a mistake, really. I did not mind the fact that my postman was unintelligent and uncouth, but he would insist on being strangely inattentive to me all evening too, which is in my opinion the very worst thing that a man can do. Of course, I'd had sex with him anyway, because that's the way it goes with me, but don't think that I enjoyed it or anything. I did not enjoy it, and told him so immediately afterwards, and then I'd had his full attention suddenly. He'd started to swear a bit. He'd pulled a face, made a threat. Perhaps one day soon, my postman would be delivering to my door hate letters of his own, but there you are, that's just the way it goes.

I found a tube station, galloped down its escalator and into a tiled tunnel, wrinkling my nose and sensibilities as the stale air whooshed up behind me, carrying me along in a rush that was as fast and foul as the flow of a toilet pipe.

Back up on the street again, the air was no fresher. You'd have thought that the earlier shower would have rinsed the city clean, but instead it had just left the streets sloshing and stinking like dirty bathwater. People everywhere put their heads down and hurried along in straight lines, keen to get out of the filthy evening and away from that terrible smell that could not be ignored or stepped around. Even one of the drunks that I passed on the pavement seemed to have noticed the extra-strong fumes that were around tonight; I saw him sniff himself and then sniff the air and then shrug resignedly and hold the bottle that could blot out anything a little closer to his face. Only the drains seemed to be enjoying themselves tonight, as they gargled happily with the London rainwater, but then the drains were disgusting creatures who would drink anything, even the man with the three coats and the two bottles of meths could tell you that.

The dirt got into my eyes and into my clothes and into my hair. I shouldn't keep it so long, I thought now, as I moved forward, feeling my hair filtering the filthy breeze which blew through it; trapping street pollution in its thick strands and leaving the air behind me clean again for a moment or two. I should cut it all off, I will cut it all off! I decided suddenly, but I could tell that I didn't really mean it. I knew that I would not be me without my hair. Eddie liked my hair. My lovers loved my hair. My dad had been rather fond of it too, I remembered now.

He used to brush it for me every single morning when I was a child; early mornings, five o'clock, before he went to work. Previously, this had been my mum's job, but her thin, fine fingers had a surprising lack of artistry in them, and she never had been quite able to control

33

the pattern of a plait or even the even placement of a simple bunch on either side of my head. Well, it seemed to upset my dad to think of me going off to school looking all unbalanced like that, so one day he'd taken charge; sat me down and waved a confident comb and become boss of my hair. A very good boss, though. A very kind and rare and gentle boss; stroking and manipulating those wilful strands until they were all curled and obedient in his hands, and more than willing to do what he wanted.

From then on, he'd made a space for me every single work day in his precious, private morning time. Now his early routine was: tea, fag, toast, fag, radio, fag, Angela's hair. It was good, that. It was good. He seemed to like all that soothing and smoothing and tidying, and me, well, I just loved being intertwined with his day in this way.

When I grew too old or self-conscious for his lap and his tickles, my hair had continued the contact between us, unfurling before his chair each day like a golden bridge between his body and mine. Above me, there would be the sound of a family asleep over our heads. Behind me, there would be my dad, singing and smoking and concentrating. And I would just sit there making no sound at all, as fondness and a little pain warmed my scalp, running like electricity up each copper strand that he touched.

My dad loved my hair, I know he did. It seemed to please him deeply to see that, although our blue eyes and sweet smiles were the same, my shining locks were and always would be so unlike his own dark, coarse stuff. Why should this delight him so much? I don't know. Perhaps he thought it meant that I had inherited only the best of him.

I turned a sharp corner and a sudden, slapping breeze brought me out of the day-dream and back into the night. My feet stomped hard along the pavement, and my cheeks burned with irritation as I realized that I'd been doing it again; remembering again! This was no good. This did not feel good. These days my thoughts were getting more and more out of control, going off their own way, hurtling along lines that were like veins: fast and blue and always leading back to the same, hot place.

Well, my heart was pounding very hard as I ran up Eddie's stairs and burst into his living-room and got energetic with the smiles and the hugs and the Hello lovey, how'd it go, fine, miss me, kiss me, love you and all that stuff. I laid my coat across the chair. I took my shoes off. I grinned a lot, and then I got out of there as soon as I could.

Calm, calm, I told myself as I ran a bath, folded my clothes into a neat pile and then lowered myself slowly into the mad, splashing, untidy water. Calm, calm. All that excitement is no good for this heart. Your blood is pumping hotter and faster than the hot, fast water from this tap, and your chest is as packed and set for overflowing as this full bath-tub right here. Relax, relax, it's over now, it's all right. Your worries are floating away from you, dissolving like sugar lumps, let them go, there they go; evaporating into sweet steam and dispersing harmlessly into the quiet air.

Soon, the yellow water was lapping up around my body in smaller and smaller waves, and then I started to feel better. As my body became smooth and still, my mind began to calmly ripple and think and plan. I ran through all the questions that Eddie would innocently ask in the next few minutes. I wiped a hand over my face and practised the innocent expression that I would use as I made some answers up. I lay there for a long time, plotting my alibi and retracing my movements, attending to the relevant details with such care that you

35

might have thought I'd just been out to kill someone rather than to have sex with them, and I suppose I couldn't blame you. I suppose that the same basic rules apply to all the major sins; infidelity, murder, genocide, it's all the same really. First, you must keep your eye on the details, then you must refrain from squeamishness at the critical moment, and then you must always, always remember to clean up well after yourself when you've done.

I opened a new pack of green soap, had a good rub, felt fine again.

'Supper's ready,' Eddie called.

So was I.

There. That's better. Top layer of skin and scum gone. Body lotion and talc and my fragrant love for Eddie seeping back into every pore. Discarded guilt whooshing away down the dark drain, along the mucky rivers of the land and then out to sea with the rest of the sewage, where you won't have to notice it any more; where you won't have to look at and think about the pollution and the mistakes that have been made.

The odd month ended oddly. It got warm. Too warm for March. Surprised people and flowers pushed tentative heads out of their hiding holes to see what was going on and birds sang suspicious songs in blossoming trees. Everywhere, spring was prematurely getting into its swing, and as this fertile season began, I decided that I was pregnant. I was sure of it.

It was the last day of March, and I was late. I was on my way to the doctor's, but it was taking me longer than usual to get ready, and now I was late.

I had got stuck in front of the mirror, that's what had happened; I'd just got stuck there, sure as if my skin were suckered to the glass. It was my face, you see. I could not seem to stop looking at my washed, early face; had been sitting there staring at it for a full half an hour now, doing nothing, thinking nothing.

It wasn't as if there weren't things to think. I could've wondered what the doctor would tell me. I could have wondered what I would do about what he would tell me. I could have wondered how this had happened and whom this had happened with. Oh yes, there were thoughts to be thought and considerations to be considered, but for now my mind stayed as still and folded as the hands in my lap.

My make-up sat on the table before me, its colours jumping impatiently. It was waiting, it was ready; ready to paint pigment and meaning onto the pale, clean skin. Soon there would be a kind pink or a cruel crimson mouth. Soon, blue eyes would be brought out and made to sparkle with a little peach eye-shadow, or pushed back to hide behind thick black lashes. Soon, the edges of eyebrows would flick up or down like an emperor's thumb. Soon enough, I said to myself, and then I stared some more at that face, and it stared right back; blank, open, unfinished as a foetus.

Well, it was not such a big decision in the end. I chose a medium red lipstick, cool foundation, neutral eyes, and set out for the surgery with the certainty that I would either have the baby or I would not.

If I didn't, then everything would be simple, I told myself, as the glass doors of the medical centre closed behind me with a discreet Ssshhh. And if I did, well that would be simple too. I would have no hesitation in electing Eddie for daddy, no matter how many candidates there might be, nor would I have any fear of losing my nerve in the coming months of moral and hormonal panic. I had, in the past, seen certain pregnancies trigger certain astounding confessions, but I just considered these outbursts puzzling and unnecessary.

It was as if people believed that the growing swell of a dubious baby must push out all other secrets; as if there weren't actually room in the body for a thousand lies of any size.

Baby, baby. Well, as it turned out, there was no baby. Missed periods due to weight loss or stress, that was all that had happened here. It's a false alarm, the doctor said to me that day; false alarm, false alarm, although alarm may not have been quite the right word. You know me. I had remained perfectly calm throughout.

4

Well, I was not so calm a few days later.

Another violent letter jabbed itself through my door, and this time I tore the envelope right open, raked impatiently through the familiar threats, shivered, stamped my foot, sweated, swore several times, then shivered again.

This was starting to get to me a little now, I admit.

Recently, I had noticed myself becoming more and more paranoid while out walking on the London streets; feeling as if every casual drunk's curse or woman's scream was personally directly at me. I had started looking over my shoulder. I had started listening to footsteps. In the last few weeks, I had even taken to carrying a knife around with me, just in case; a razor-sharp Stanley knife that could conveniently transform itself into an offensive weapon or an inoffensive artist's tool, depending on who tried to stop me and look in my bag or clothes.

'Who are you?' I shouted loudly into the quiet hallway now. 'Who are you? What do you want? Where are you from?' but the envelope said nothing useful at all, its postmark showing only the name of another insignificant southern town, the word stamped in nasty red and curving up at me like a smug smile.

'Fuck. Fuck! Who is it?' I demanded, getting frustrated, getting rough with the letter, but the handwriting wore its disguise firmly, and the mask of deliberately childish felt-tip scrawl would not be peeked under or shaken off.

'Martin? Martin?' I whispered finally, quietly, holding the letter close to my face and pausing for a long time, as if I genuinely expected a reply. 'Martin? Martin? Martin? Is that you?'

I should tell you about Martin.

You should know that I had met Martin almost a year earlier, when I had gone round one morning with my references and my lipstick to clean his house.

Martin's was a big house. It was a posh house, with curvaceous living-room furniture and bedroom carpets that took your footprints like pastel snow and air everywhere that was soft and expensive and warm. Of course, that was back in those days when it was still a family house.

Part-time domestic help wanted, the advert had said. Hello. Here I am, I can help, I'd said. I can take away the dirty floors and the washing-up so that you and your happy family will have more time to spend together, to spend being happy together. Go on. Let me help. Let me do it. I want to do it.

'Hi. You must be Angie. Come in, my dear, come in,' Martin said at the door that first day, pushing at me an accent that was soft-Scottish and a manner that was friendly without borders. As I slid past him and into the hallway, I noticed that he had a little hairspray in his hair and a lot of sex in his eyes. Oh yes, I noticed this latter feature straight away. I couldn't prove it, but I could see it; his eyes had sex in them in the way that other people have streaks or speckles in theirs.

'It's Angela,' I corrected him pleasantly, then smiled and chatted as he took me in and introduced me to his stiff, polished wife and his dull, bright children.

'I'm sure you'll get along with us, Angie, once you

get to know us,' he said as we weighed each other up in the kitchen.

'It's Angela,' I repeated.

'I work from home a lot, Angie,' he said as he guided me around the lounge, study, bathrooms. 'So it'd be just you and me most days. You wouldn't mind that, would you? I'm not so bad, am I? Aye, you seem like the kind of girl who knows how to get on with people, oh aye, oh aye.'

'I'm Angela,' I told him once more, said it quietly and firmly, as if to convince us both that he'd got me all wrong.

'So when can you start, Angie?' he asked now, putting a sturdy arm around my waist and leading me upstairs, and this time I couldn't be bothered trying to correct his mistake. Instead, I smoothed a bed cover and said, 'Well, I'm available Tuesdays and Thursdays if you want me.'

On Tuesday, Martin and I kissed in the kitchen.

It was a sudden and awkward thing. I couldn't touch his face like I wanted to, because my hands were all fluffy-wet with popping soap bubbles. His own hands felt soft and strong against my cheeks, hair, breasts.

After just a few minutes, though, he pulled abruptly away from me and left the room, and I was sure that this meant that the fun was over for that day; that he had gone off to work or feel bad in his study for the rest of the morning. I needn't have worried, though, because when me and the vacuum cleaner reached the top floor and the main bedroom, there Martin was, lying on top of the floral duvet, smiling and waiting; shirt off, turned on.

We soon got into a routine. Martin would meet me at the door on Tuesdays with a cloth or a black sack in his eager hands, then he would dust and empty bins while I washed and vacuumed the house. It was a very efficient arrangement, which meant that the cleaning and the sex afterwards would all be well out of the way by the time his wife came home for lunch.

'You really are very efficient,' Mrs Robbins confirmed one day, slipping off her coat and glancing around the sparkling lounge. 'It's lovely. Thank you.'

'That's OK,' I said, embarrassed and fidgeting.

'She loves her work, don't you, Angie?' Martin added, standing in the background somewhere, blowing kisses at me and laughing at his wife.

Well, that wasn't a nice thing to do.

That's when I first began to realize that Martin was not a very nice man. He had a very cruel side and, as time went on, I started to see more and more of it and to love my job less and less. Our sessions behind the drawn bedroom curtains seemed to get darker every time. After one month, Martin was already showing me the illegal collection of violent, imported pornography that he kept locked in his garden shed. After two, he was telling me all about his own grubby, home-made sexual desires. A month or so later, we tentatively started to act out these fantasies, and in no time at all we were doing unpleasant and rather dangerous things to each other every single Tuesday morning, in the dim light of that locked room, at the top of that otherwise lovely and fragrant family home.

Now, in itself, this was OK. It was OK right up until the day that Eddie caught me wincing with pain and I found myself hurriedly having to explain several great big black and yellow bruises away. This was not OK at all, and this is when I had to finally admit that my present affair and job were really going nowhere.

Quite soon after this, Martin's wife found out about us, and she was not pleased.

Oh, he'd had affairs before, and she'd always forgiven him, but fucking the cleaning lady, well, that turned out to be the final straw. She was a snobbish woman and I was only worth four pounds an hour and her cornered pride left her nowhere to go but out of the door, taking with her the children, the cat, the best car and a lot of things and leaving Martin alone and with nothing.

He couldn't believe it. He was furious. He was also devastated, panicked, lonely and contrite, but mostly he was just furious. I don't blame him. His wife hadn't found out about his infidelity by accident, you see. Someone had told her. I'm afraid it could have been me.

'You little bitch!' Martin screamed in my face when I went round to try and tidy up for him one last time. 'What are you doing here? What have you done? What have you done to me, you little bitch!'

'I'm sorry.'

'Do you know what you've done? Why did you do it? Why did you *do* that?'

'I don't know.'

'I don't believe this! Aye, so you think you can just wreck my life, do you? Is that what you think?'

'Let go of me, please.'

'You will regret this, you little slut. You're not going to get away with this, do you hear me?'

'Goodbye, Martin,' I said.

'Slag! Whore! Bitch!' he said.

That was the last time I'd seen Martin. That was last November, and since then I'd hardly thought about him at all. It was over, you see. As far as I was concerned, it was just all over. I'd never liked the man and I certainly didn't miss him, although it now looked as if he still had some very strong feelings for me.

I had some strong feelings of my own later that same day. I put April's letter away and then I went out

43

shopping with Eddie, and then I went a bit mad in a market.

Well, I was tense, you see. That's what did it. The letters were beginning to make me really quite tense now, and that's why I did what I did to that girl that day.

The shopping trip had started well enough.

I was pleased to be with Eddie and I was pleased to be out of my flat; to unhook the address that I carried like a target around my neck; somewhere for someone to send the bad letters and wishes that came flying like poison arrows across this city. I was also pleased to be at that busy little outdoor market, letting its hustle and bustle sweep my mood along, jostling and crowding my senses until there was no space for thoughts of anything but cheap cabbages, second-hand candlesticks, fat rag-rugs.

Soon I was darting breathlessly from stall to stall, pinballing between trinkets and books and toys, finger-ing this and trying out that, greedy to add more and more pleasure to the afternoon. I wanted everything. I wanted *everything*, but in the end I settled for a modest vegetable pastie and a small bottle of lemonade, although I did insist on expensive buns to take home with us, to be sure of extending this extravagant mood to teatime at least.

'Calm down,' Eddie said, as if to a small, giddy child, but I could tell that he felt good too. It was just that his happiness was allowed to settle inside him like warm, nourishing food, not fizz up like frothy bubbles all the time, going to your head, making you dizzy.

We shared a joke with a rosy fruit and veg man. We let an old woman witter on to us about the war or royalty or something. We had a rough game of two-a-side football up the street with a bruised plum. It was nice. Just really nice, see. And then we turned a corner.

Eddie was gazing up at the yellow sky, but I was looking straight ahead and I saw the girls in front of us. Teenage girls. It was a couple of teenage girls, wearing hard make-up and crippling shoes and dancing lamely to some lightweight, portable music. I smiled nicely at the two girls, because that's the kind of mood I was suddenly in that day. As we approached, they fell expertly into a wall-slouch and stared hard at Eddie, and now they were smiling too; only not in a nice way.

One of them giggled as we passed. The other muttered something to our backs.

'What did they say?' I asked Eddie.

'Nothing. Leave it.'

'Were they laughing at us? Were they?'

'Leave it, Angel. Just leave it,' he said firmly, and maybe I would have, maybe I really would have, if only those silly girls hadn't suddenly turned up the volume of their shrill laughter; if only they hadn't gone and started accompanying it with the exaggerated drumming sounds of loud shoes on quiet pavements.

Fatman, they said. Elephant, lardy, fatman, they said. They did, and this time everybody heard it.

'Come on. They're just kids, come on,' Eddie insisted quietly; a bit hurt, but planning to get over it in a moment or two.

Eddie had taught me a lot already.

He was the first person who'd ever made me consider that goodness, honesty, humility, might possibly be strengths rather than weaknesses. Just by watching him breeze easily through his days and life, I felt that I was learning about important things. I was learning about when it is appropriate to take a stand, and when it is easier on yourself and the world to just roll over and not care. I was learning to entertain the possibility that the only proper struggle is the one to free yourself from struggle. I was even beginning to consider that maybe, just maybe, anger and violence are not necessarily the same thing. I was learning, you see, I was; although back then, on that particular April afternoon, I probably still hadn't entirely gotten the hang of it.

'What did you say? You! What the fucking fuck did you fucking say?'

Through the dark clouds in my eyes, I saw the taller girl's smile freeze and her face flush white as I thundered back across the road and bore down on the two teenagers.

'I'm talking to you.'

'Nothin'.'

I grabbed hold of a soft arm and squeezed it.

'Nothing! NOTHING!'

Under my icy stare, the girl's stupid, rubbery face turned brittle and then broke, so I turned instead to her wiry companion, who was eyeing me loosely and maintaining the wide stretch of her chewing-gum grin.

'You. What's funny? Go on, tell me. Go on. I like to laugh, me.'

Slowly, the girl unstuck herself from the wall. She pulled herself up to her full height and snapped her pink mouth back into a tight, hard line. I watched fascinated as small, white teeth came out and bit down on a cherry lip to form the first, delicious, elongated letter of,

'Ffffuck off.' And then, slowly, slowly: 'I said he was a fat, ugly bastard. Because he is.'

Cold fury numbed me instantly and I'm sure that, if someone had come along and slapped me hard about the head right then, I would have barely felt a thing. For a moment, I thought that this is what had happened, because there was a sharp, smacking sound and my eyes blinked hard from a sudden impact, but then they opened again and saw the girl before me holding her face, and when I turned up my palm, I found that it had the red tingle of her cheek all over it.

'Fucking hell! Fucking hell!'

'Shut up.' I slapped her again.

'Fucking HELL!'

'Shut up.' I slapped her again.

'OW! GIVE OVER! FUCK OFF, WILL YOU!'

I raised my hand once more, and wondered if this would go on for ever; wondered how long it would take her to realize that I would not stop until I had perfect silence.

The noisy girl and the portable stereo on the wall beside her whined on. All around me, there was a fuzz of white, high-pitched screaming, like the sound of trapped electricity. Shut up, shut up, shut up, shut up. I had a fist in my hand and was ready to throw it.

I can't tell you exactly what happened next, except that, instead of lunging forwards, I was suddenly walking backwards. Eddie was leading me back, blowing the storm in my head away with his gentle whispering, and it was all Calm down, calm down, it's all right, it's OK, until the roaring in my ears started to move off into the distance and some blue began to come back into my eyes.

'It's all right.'

'Yeah.'

'It's all right, Angel.'

'Yeah. Yes. Yeah. It's all right. OK, OK. It's all right.'

Well, it might have been all right. It might easily have been all right, if only that stupid girl hadn't stupidly gone and started up her stupid racket and insults all over again, just as we were walking quietly away.

What did I do? Well, I did good, considering that I wanted her dead and that I had the nerve and the knife to do it.

'FFFFFFFUCCKKKKKOFFFFFFFFF!' went her mouth as

she saw me coming back. CLOMP! CLOMP! went her shoes, battering the pavement in a show of terror or bravado. HISSSSSSS . . . went the tape machine on the wall and the electricity in my head. And then there was another sound, a nice one, like bells tinkling, and then my eyes tuned in just in time to see my half-empty pop bottle smashing on the street at her feet. Glass splinters jumped up onto bare skin. Lemonade made sweet blood trickle down a brown ankle in pink, wiggly lines. That was good. It looked good; pretty.

The girl was shrieking, dancing again, as Eddie dragged me off down the road, scolding and fretting and wondering out loud what could be done with me, as if I were the one in the wrong here.

By the time we got back to his flat, I felt fine again, but Eddie didn't. He kept lurching around miserably from room to room, avoiding my eye and my tickling fingers. At four o'clock, we sat down to eat our sandwiches and buns in silence and, as I finished up and threw away the crumby remains of what should have been a smashing tea, I felt a wave of resentment that my punishment should be going on for so long.

'It's not fair!' I said. 'I did it for you.'

Eddie looked at me properly for the first time in hours. Judging by his expression, he did not like what he saw.

'Don't be like that. Ed! What they said; it hurt you, I know it did!'

'They were kids.'

'What? Yeah, I know. I know that. I just got mad.'

'You went mad.'

'Yeah. OK, OK. I'm sorry, all right? I've just been feeling a bit tense, lately, that's all. All right? It won't happen again. Honest, Eddie. It won't happen again.'

He shook his head and gave a small, humourless laugh. He didn't believe me. He thought that it probably would happen again, because he knew that it had happened before.

The first time that I'd hit him, Eddie had been so surprised that he'd fallen right over. His bullish body must have barely felt a thing, but somehow the sudden impact of my small fist had crumpled him deeply, and he'd gone straight down, bumping his side on a table as he went, then steadying himself finally on one knee, staring back up at me in confusion and horror.

I remember that he'd been wearing his reading glasses at the time, and that they'd come off. I'd knocked them off, and now they lay like an upturned, wiry insect on the floor. He'd put out a hand and gathered them up protectively, turning them gently to see if they were OK, and I couldn't have been more horrified if I'd poked out his eyes and then stood watching him scurry around on the carpet after them.

Of course, I'd said sorry. I'd said sorry, sorry, sorry for a whole hour or so, but the damage had already been done. They were ruined, those fragile spectacles, and no amount of fiddling could put them right. When Eddie had balanced them on his nose that night and looked over at me sadly, strangely, wonkily, well, you could just tell that he and me and they would never be the same again.

I did not bother trying to say sorry now, as I turned my attention back to the present tense and the ruined Saturday before me. It is a weak word that I have never liked and rarely meant. Instead, I looked cute and asked Eddie if he couldn't just forget about my recent moment of madness with the teenage girl in the market, or at least postpone his anger until Monday when I would be at work and out of his way, but he said that No, he couldn't bloody fucking do that, and then he swooped away from me and back into silence. Well, that was that. It was no good talking to him because his face had closed against me like a door. It was no good pleading or stroking or squeezing him; I could see that I would get no more love out of his big body today, and this was a terrible thing because I needed love, I needed a lot of love.

'Fine!' I shouted, grabbing my coat and stomping away down his stairs. 'Fine! Just fine!' but I did not feel fine at all; I was starting to get tense all over again.

So I had sex with a man on my way home.

He asked me for a smile and I gave him one, and then he asked me for a cigarette, and again I obliged, and it just sort of went on from there; he just kept on asking and I just kept on giving.

He told me his name, although there was no need, and then he told me that he worked in a fast-food mobile down the road, which I had already guessed. He had grease in his hair and cap, salty sweat above his top lip and sharp, vinegar body odour coming up from beneath his arms. He had me in a disused alley-way, in broad daylight, behind the back of a biscuit factory. I remember newspaper litter blowing past me and his pale, chippy fingers dipping into me, and that's about all that I can remember about this. It's not important. It meant nothing to me. It was just a quick and unsatisfying snack, no more than that.

Back at my flat, I marched straight into the bedroom, threw off my coat and then sat down in the corner to paint. I thought this was a good idea. I thought that the thick oils in their ointment tubes might soothe me, only it worked out the other way round and, instead, I upset them; pushing the paints around, stirring them up into bubbling swirls on the glass palette and then daubing them roughly onto the braced canvas. I usually worked like this, like a vandal with a lot of resentment and not much time. Consequently, my pictures usually turned out like this; more graffiti than art.

Half an hour later, sweating and sighing heavily, I sat back to look at what I had done. I had made some bony shapes and some beefy ones and some that were as stubby as fists or swear-words. I had forced together a green and a red of equal strength so that I could enjoy the show as they clashed and screeched and fought out their differences before me. My best little brush had cracked under the pressure. My arm ached. Now I shook my head tiredly and thought of how typical this was of me. Wasn't it enough that my working life was rough and that my sex life was exhausting? No, apparently not, because here I was again, filling my precious leisure time with activities that were every bit as hard and bruising and ugly.

My dad had been just the same.

My dad had never had any actual hobbies as such, but he did collect enemies in the same way that other people collect foreign coins or stamps.

Oh, most of them weren't very valuable: just a neighbour or a stranger here or there who had run up against our dad's temper and, backing away, had made bold threats and solemn promises that they would clearly never keep. But he did have others who were more impressive. Some of the most cherished would stay with him for years, in equal parts hated and prized for their ability to justify our dad's view of the world and the expense of three locks on each door.

We children came to know of the enemies through the bedtime stories that our father told us.

My brothers and I regarded it as a great treat to be allowed into our parents' room for these stories. Bathed and pyjama'd, we'd crowd around him under the covers, warming ourselves on familiar blood, and then jostling amongst ourselves to get a little closer to the middle of the bed and our dad's chest; each wanting to curl up in the very heart of the home.

'Well, I was walking down the street, minding me own business, see, when this big bloke comes up to me,' our dad would say. This is how his stories usually began. This is how we liked them to begin. 'I'd done nothin', said nothin', but here he comes, looking for trouble, you could tell he were looking for trouble, see.'

We nodded in the dim light. We could tell, yes, we could tell.

' "What're you looking at?" the bloke says. Me, I just carry on walking, but then he steps out into me path, tells me he needs some money for a drink, keeps saying that I should buy him a drink, on and on, on and on. Well, I'm still ignoring him, and he's thinking now that I'm soft, but o'course, I'm just giving him a chance to back down, so that when I hit him I know I'll be in the right, see. It's important, that.'

He paused seriously at this point. We children started to nod enough to make our heads fall off.

'What did you do, Dad? What did you do?'

He waited a little longer, until our ears and eyes were very wide.

'What did you *do*?'

'Well, what could I do? He's pushing at me now, wouldn't leave it. What could I do?'

We don't know. We don't know, my brothers and I thought, holding sweaty hands under the bed covers.

'I did what I had to do. Decked him. One shot; straight down and he didn't get up again. All over, no messin'. Saw him again a few weeks later, and he were as nice as pie. Knew he'd picked on the wrong fella, see. I'm not a violent man, but I'll do what I have to, and he knows that now and if he tries it again, he'll get the same again, that's all.'

Our dad patted our bodies happily. Our faces grinned and our hearts cheered with love and pride as we congratulated ourselves on having a father who was so strong and brave and wise.

'There are friends and there are enemies,' he would tell us when he was feeling theatrical and philosophical. 'And no person can be both at the same time.' Although, apparently, they could change their status, and sometimes with remarkable speed.

One evening, a jolly, cheeky friend made a jolly, cheeky joke about our mum. She laughed, and so too did us kids. We didn't really get the joke, but it sounded funny, like those seaside postcards that we liked to giggle and puzzle over. Ha ha ha. He was a funny man. We liked him, we were glad he was here. But, suddenly, he was gone. Our smiles turned to idiot grins as we watched our friend being led away by the neck, as we heard our dad stomp back into the room, shouting about how the jolly man was actually a dirty bugger, and that neither him nor his name would be allowed in the house again.

'Aye, I allus thought he was sly, that one.'

'But we liked him, Dad.'

'Aye, and that just goes to show that you know nothin'. Listen to your old dad. You can't trust nobody, *nobody*, all right? That's the way it is, and you might as well start getting used to it.'

Well, kids are nothing if not adaptable. We got used to it. We learned, and the next family friend did not find us children such easy, naïve company. We knew now that jokes were not funny until they had first proved themselves harmless. We had got into the habit of first checking all our spontaneous responses with our dad. Sweets were accepted shiftily and eaten quickly, as if they might have to be given back.

Some people complimented us on our quietness and obedience. Others became visibly unnerved by our increasingly solemn and watchful behaviour, and I suppose that you couldn't blame them. After all, these days we were mostly just waiting for our guests to reveal themselves as weak or disloyal or devious or dirty; already braced against that moment when they would have to leave suddenly and not come back and good riddance to bad rubbish.

Our dad was right, you can't trust anybody. We'd seen this with our own eyes, had watched our dad proving himself right. He liked to be right, my father, and so hunting our enemies was, for him, a fitting and satisfying pastime, although there were disadvantages too. I have since learned that enemies, like the secrets and the cigarettes which were his only other indulgence, are not, in the long run, very good for you.

Eddie came around to my flat later that afternoon to try and patch things up; to say, Come on, sorry, it's silly, let's forget it, eh? Which would have been nice if I'd been there. I was not there. I was at Martin's house; had stormed off in a fury to confront him and warn him and maybe kill him. It was turning out to be that kind of day.

I marched down his street scowling and swearing quietly, with my knife jogging encouragingly in my bag, and little anger and fear pains stabbing away rhythmically in my chest. I was going to have it out with Martin, that's what I was going to do; fight it out with him if I had to. Maybe I would come away bruised and battered, yes, but I could deal with that. It was all the waiting and the worrying that I could not handle; waiting and worrying day after day like this seemed to be causing me far more pain than I might get from any quick blow of his.

Now I reached Martin's house. Now I gathered my

courage. Now I curled my small hands into small fists, and then stormed up his front steps.

Well, it was all a big let-down.

The house was empty. Empty, after all that! I muttered, with a hollow laugh.

Peeking through the letter-box, I saw a drift of junk mail up against the front door, pale squares instead of pictures on the walls, no furniture, no curtains, no pets and no signs of anyone at all. Martin was not here, probably hadn't been near the place in months. Still, just in case, I put my mouth to the letter-box and shouted, 'Fuck off,' into his hallway. I was doing what I'd come here to do. I was saying what I'd come here to say, that's all, although I have to admit that it did not feel nearly as good as I'd imagined; the words swooping and fading harmlessly and frustratingly in the quiet air, like a missed punch.

5

May. It was the first Monday in May, and I was not well. I was at the local medical centre again, waiting patiently in the waiting-room; feeling bad, surrounded by people who looked terrible.

I didn't much like it there.

The room was small and warm and uncomfortably cheerful. The walls were painted a supple, rosy pink, the carpet was springy and firm and the toys and magazines on the sturdy table were all in great condition. The chairs looked soft, but had a way of gently insisting that you sit up properly and the lights overhead were similarly kind and bossy; the fluorescent strips pouring vigorous white brightness down into the spaces which you might prefer to fill with quiet and gloomy thoughts. I suppose it was good that someone had made such an effort with the room, but the effect of all this peppy decor was really more sarcastic than sympathetic, and in the end most of our eyes settled on the feeble pot plants in the corners, which alone told the yellowing truth about the struggle of life.

Amongst the listless babies and the limpy, lumpy, old folk, there was a man in there that I recognized. He was a big fellow, but stooped, with untidy grey hair and features, and he was coughing in a wet, rolling, infinite way. More than his face, it was that terrible blizzard cough which was familiar and fascinating to me. The look of it upset me. The spray from it disgusted me. The sound of it worried me, although admittedly slightly less so in these surroundings than where I heard it usually: at the cigarette counter of my local, unhygienic off-licence.

Right beside him sat a tall youth with orange hair, black stitches and brilliantly coloured bruises, and next to him I saw that a man with my Uncle Jack's swollen, alcoholic features and belly was squirming and sweating and shaking very hard in his seat; afraid perhaps of today's abstinence or of tomorrow's binge.

Poor man, I thought as I met his nervous, twitching eyes.

Poor people, I thought.

And poor doctor, too.

It must be very hard to be a doctor when you have patients like these, I decided; patients, people, who just won't learn their lessons and give over damaging themselves.

'Angela?' called the receptionist.

'Yes. Yes. Here.'

'My veins ache,' I told the doctor.

'Mmm.'

'It's hard to explain.'

'Yes.'

'And I have these pains in my chest.'

'Right. What kinds of pains? Can you describe them?'

'Knobbly ones,' I told him.

'Knobbly.'

'And sometimes spongey.'

'Spongey.'

'Yes.'

They had a colour too, but I didn't want to irritate him any more than I already had.

Well, I was nervous. These places made me nervous.

It wasn't the idea of being diagnosed with some awful disease which unsettled me so much as the quiet intimacy of the situation. It filled my head like a nice drug. Being there in a doctor's surgery, like being high, offers a terrible licence for you to do or say anything. To cry or confide or undress. Leave your secrets at the door. Come in. Be yourself. Bare your body and soul and let's have a look at what's wrong with you. I found all of that very unsettling.

I took a deep breath and let my mind drift off around the room. Followed a black fly on its forlorn hunt for shit or rubbish amongst all this antiseptic and glass. Tried to find some meaning, a code, in the scrambled letters of an eye chart. Pictured myself lying down on the hard leather bed beside us. A cool, firm bed. A cool, firm body. Me, gazing peacefully up at a white ceiling, a white coat; breathing deeply in and deeply out, all relaxed and ready for inspection. The doctor sighed and I came abruptly back to my chair.

He doesn't like me much, I thought suddenly. Paranoia, I added immediately, but that didn't stop me from feeling hurt for a few seconds, didn't stop my throat from tightening or my attention from returning to the bed and the part that it could play in *making* him like me. Stop it, stop that; not *now*.

'My family have a history of heart disease,' I told him quietly, reluctantly, keen to break the silence, but disgusted by the sound of my own words and unluckiness.

'Yes. Well,' the doctor said now, loudly, brusquely. 'You're right to mention it, of course, but you know it would be stupid to think that . . . well, anyway, let's have a look, shall we?'

He opened my file and glanced through it calmly. I gripped the arm of my chair and glared at him furiously. He'd called me stupid. He thought I was stupid. My face went pink. How dare he. How *dare* he. My knuckles were white. He's the stupid one, I thought, scowling at the lowered head before me. His face was handsome, but unintelligent. His gestures were confident and professional but obviously over-rehearsed. With those perfect, photogenic bones and dopey, film-star eyes, he suddenly looked to me for all the world like a competent but vain actor in a props department white coat, auditioning for the part of a doctor. Another exaggerated sigh. I wouldn't have given it to him.

He went for a swivel in his chair, spraying out melodramatic impatience in my direction. I glared back, unamused by his performance, resentful at having to deal with such an amateur, and for some moments we just sat there, batting our silent grievances backwards and forwards across the large wooden desk.

'Well, your last check-up shows your cholesterol level to be good and low,' he said finally, referring back to his notes; reading his lines.

'But I have these pains.'

'And your blood pressure is not at all high.'

'But I have these pains.'

'Your general health seems good. You exercise regularly. Lost a little weight recently, but nothing too severe.'

'But these *pains* . . .' I argued.

'Yes.'

The doctor looked lost and turned again to my file, dug deeper into my file, deeper, deeper.

'Ah,' he said eventually.

Ah what?

'I see.'

See what?

'Right. I see.'

What? What did he see? He didn't seem inclined to explain, so I leaned forward a little and tried to find out for myself. I worried that the unedited file might give him the wrong idea, that it might not tell the whole truth about me. I also worried, of course, that it would.

'Tell me, have you been feeling stressed recently?' the doctor slyly asked.

Damn!

'Erm, how do you mean?'

I sank back a little.

'Upset. Worried. *Stressed.*'

'Erm . . .' I stalled, pulling my jacket around me and hearing May's hate letter crackle or cackle in my pocket.

'Well, yes, I suppose so.'

'Ah!' he said, with a quiet, triumphant smile and the happy prospect of Next please already on his lips.

'That's probably it, then. Tension. It can build up awfully around the shoulders and neck, you know. Perhaps it's even the odd panic attack that you're having.'

'Panic attack?' I said, trying to slow the conversation down, but he was unstoppable now.

'Yes. I suggest that you practise some relaxation techniques. You're lucky; there are some good self-help groups in this area. I'll give you details of an information line you can call. OK?'

'Oh. Right.'

'Come back if it gets any worse,' he said cheerfully, still hamming it up.

'Right. Thanks.'

I straightened my jacket, prepared to leave.

'But you're sure that my blood pressure isn't high? My heart beats very fast sometimes. There couldn't be a mistake?'

He gave me a stupid smile, swept back his stupid blond hair ready for the next scene; handed me a piece of paper with a few numbers and his stupid autograph on it.

'No. It's normal. I'm sure there's nothing to worry about.'

'Oh. Right. OK.'

I still wanted more. Wanted to hear more and to say more. I wanted to make a bit of fuss and noise, but I could feel my body purring quietly at the doctor now and knew that there was no point in arguing; not today, and not with him. I zipped myself up and went quietly away.

Well, how could I argue with him? He said I was normal, he said he was sure. What would I tell him: that my body had a genius for deception and that he looked as if he could be easily fooled?

'Talk to me, Eddie.'

It was after supper, before bedtime and I was restless.

Eddie had dipped away into a book and kept shrugging me off with One more page, just one more; stuck in a serious novel, in the adult world and refusing to come out to play. There was nothing much on TV or the radio. Burroughs was in the room, but still not talking to me. I had drunk half a bottle of red wine.

'Come on. Put it down, eh? Come on, come on, come on,' I said, buzzing around Eddie in an irritating way.

'Bugger off,' he said good-naturedly, waving me out of his face.

'Where shall I bugger off to, Eddie?'

'I don't care. Anywhere. Outer Mongolia.'

I giggled at the encouragement, swooped over to the bookshelf and searched out a world atlas.

'Eddie . . .' I whined after a few minutes. 'It says here that in Outer Mongolia the people are as scarce as the trees. Which are very scarce indeed. I've changed my mind, Eddie. Eddie? Eddie! I don't think I want to go there after all.'

'You'd get lonely, wouldn't you?'

'Yep.'

'No-one to talk to.'

'Nope.'

We laughed and then he did his one more page bit and then I couldn't stand it any more and swung suddenly across the room and into ill humour.

'Oh, I'm fed up. Might as well go home,' I said unreasonably, stomping my way back to the settee and the wine. 'Fed up. You've been ignoring me all night. I wanted to do things. Messing about and stuff. Put your book down, eh? Go on, go on. Now.'

'I will in a minute.'

'Aw. Now.'

'No.'

'Now!'

'No! Give over! What's the matter with you?'

The sound of his irritation snagged in my ears and triggered another mood change. My sullen features straightened abruptly and set into seriousness and I looked back at him like an adult now, with different, grown-up things on my mind.

'I'm lonely, that's all. Just lonely.'

Eddie softened his eyes, sighed. Put his book down.

'Some more?' I said, heaving myself up from the sofa and over to the bottle on the coffee-table.

'Nah. I've had too much.'

'Me too.' I poured until the bottle was empty and my glass was full. 'Too much, not enough.'

Eddie watched me drink.

'What's up?' he asked.

'Nothing.'

'Tell me.'

'Nothing to tell. I'm all right. I am all right. I went to the doctor's and he said that I'm all right, so I must be, eh?'

Eddie came over to me, came over all concerned; made me go through all my symptoms and made me suddenly sorry that I'd said anything.

'So you think there's something wrong with you? With your heart? What is it? What's wrong with it? Tell me. Tell me. *Tell* me.'

'No! It's nothing. Come on, Eddie! Ssshhh! Leave it, eh?'

The wine was making me weary and bad-tempered and honest. It was an uneasy combination and I sensed danger. Put the wine down. Put it down. Reach over and lower your glass carefully to the table and don't touch it again. It's explosive stuff. Danger, danger, watch out! A few more sips and you might just blow up and tell him exactly why you are anxious, and what you really think is wrong with your heart.

'What's on your mind?'

'Nothing.'

'Something's making you sad. Is it your dad?'

I glanced at him curiously, surprised by the question. Well, yes actually, my dad was probably around there somewhere; over in the shadows by the window maybe, disapproving of the alcohol, shaking his head sadly and saying, 'Watch out, watch out!'

'No,' I snapped. 'Why should it be my dad? Of course it's not my dad, I never think about him. I'm OK, I've told you!'

I tried to settle back into Eddie, but he insisted on keeping me uncomfortable; kept fussing and pecking and nagging on at me about what the problem was and how much he loved me and why were there so many things that I wouldn't tell him?

Finally, I leapt to my feet in bitter frustration and finished my drink in two huge, sour gulps. Why wouldn't he just shut up? Just SHUT UP! Just leave me alone and stop trying to make me talk. I didn't want to talk; once people start talking, there is always the danger that something will get said.

'Come here.'

'No!'

'Come on.'

Eddie grabbed me from behind, wrapped himself heavily around my body, pinning my arms by my side; holding me tightly, tightly, in a hug from which there was no escape. From habit, I fought back, but after a few moments fatigue washed over me and suddenly all I could do was stand there, squashed in Eddie's grip, watching as the struggle turned mushy-liquid and drained down and out through my shoes.

He kissed my neck and hair, pushed his cheek up against mine and then, I don't know, maybe it was just the last of the bloodish wine going to my head, but suddenly I thought that perhaps I could tell him. Maybe I can. Maybe, maybe. I mean, look at him. Look at how much he loves me, at how much he wants to know. I could just tell him something. Just that I love him, but like other men. How would that be? A little bit of truth for starters, how would that be?

I arched my neck, curved my gaze around to meet his encouraging eyes. Could I do that? He kissed again. Oh. Oh. I think I could. I think I could.

The telephone rang like alarm bells.

'Hello?' Eddie said. 'What? Oh yeah. Yeah. Right. Well. OK. OK, mate, OK. Yeah.'

Oh. Well. Right. It didn't matter now. All of that would have to wait now. Tomorrow, Eddie's brother was coming to stay.

Eddie and I didn't exchange words or glances, but a moment of shock ran backwards and forwards between us as we first spotted Jimmy coming towards us through the barrier gates and the dirty air of the railway station.

He looks ill, Eddie thought. Yes, ill and thin, I silently agreed. Pale, drooped, sickly, rough, drawn, worn out, ill and thin. Almost ugly, I realized. Now there's a thing. There's a young man that you'd have thought would stay handsome until the day he died, and maybe for a short while after that. I had known Jimmy almost as long as I'd known Eddie, and I had never known him not to look good, great, only here he was today turning no female heads, getting no second glances from anyone but Eddie and me, who were doing double takes to make sure that it was really him.

He came closer. Seemed to bring a cloud of train dust with him; stayed quite grey and untidy around the edges. A little closer and we could see that he had one tatty bag, that he was smoking a long, sagging fag and that his skin was the colour of an old man's coat. Closer. Closer and closer. Close enough now for us to pick out the finer details, the small bits of familiar beauty within this new ugliness; the lively eyes and quick smile that he flashed like an identity card, allowing us at last to recognize him and say without awkwardness or doubt, 'Hello, Jimmy.'

Eddie moved forward. He was not much taller than his brother, but right then it looked as if he could lift him cleanly off the ground if he wanted to; pick him up and spin him around and around: Hello, Jimmy mate! Whoosh! Whizz! Wheeee! Eddie did not do that. Instead, he patted Jimmy affectionately on the shoulder, and did even this quite gently, aware of his own strength and not at all sure of his brother's.

We laughed and chatted for a while, but Eddie is a straight man and could not stay bent around the obvious for very long.

'You look rough, mate,' he said over hot tea in the

station café. 'Really rough.' The steam from the mug he held before his face did nothing to soften his direct words and tone. 'Really bad. What the fuck's up?'

'Ha.'

'You look horrible.'

'Thanks, brother.'

'Well, you do. What's happened?'

'Oh, you know.'

'Not unless you tell me, I don't.'

'It's a long story.'

'Go on.'

'Well, you know.'

'What?'

'Ah, it's complicated.'

The smiles disappeared. They didn't wither, they just disappeared, as suddenly as only fake ones can, and then there was a long pause. Eddie stared hard at Jimmy and drank noisily from his mug: sip, sip, sip, SIP, SIP, as if to suck words from the mouth of the brother opposite. I looked over expectantly too, drawing deeply all the time on a cigarette, hoping to add to the drag in the air. Jimmy sighed heavily, wearily, and then finally sprawled loosely forward, succumbing at last to the pull of our friendship.

'I've had a bit of trouble. Needed to get away. You know. Not been so happy lately.'

He left these sentences in the air and then leaned back in his chair to look at them properly.

'I've been unhappy,' he corrected after a while. 'I've had a lot of trouble.'

More minutes passed silently. Jimmy rested his head back against the wall.

'I had to leave, you see. I've left my clothes, my flat, my car. I had to leave suddenly, you see.'

Long legs were unfolded under the table. Tired eyes closed for a minute.

'There's just some things to sort out in my head. Some heavy thinking to do. You know.'

His chin and shoulders drooped a little more now, as if to prove the weight of the things on his mind.

'Hard to say what exactly. Like I told you, it's complicated.'

A slack smile and another yielding sigh.

'See . . . see . . . I . . .' he said slowly, searching for the right words, running a hand through long, tangly hair, as if he might find them there.

'It's hard to say. You know.'

'Yes,' Eddie said.

Yes, I thought. It was hard. You could tell that it was hard. I could tell that it was hard, and so I tried to make it easier.

'Have you had a fight with Fay?' I asked.

There is a line of elastic which runs through the body and up the neck and down along each limb and, at the sound of my words, the stretch on his contracted so violently that you could almost hear it snapping back into place.

'No, not really,' Jimmy said tightly. 'Sort of, but she's OK. I am too. Just needed a break. I'll be fine after a bit of a break. I'm just tired, that's all. Just a bit tired.'

And, with that, he finished his tea and what he had started and would say no more that day about his girlfriend or his unhappiness.

'Jim?' Eddie persisted.

'I'm fine.'

'Come on, mate.'

'What? I'm OK.'

'Are you?'

'Yeah. Yeah. I'm pleased to see you, Ed.'

Well, at least this last part seemed true. It had only been fifteen minutes or so and already Jimmy had more colour in his face and more straightness in his spine.

He looked to be visibly growing in his big brother's presence and by the time we left the station he was seeming a lot more like his old self. His deep, striding voice had regained some of its swagger. His heavy-booted feet met the ground more and more surely. A pretty young woman to our left glanced around to watch him walking away.

Now I should tell you something. Now I should tell you that the fact that I regularly failed to dodge trouble does not necessarily mean that I always failed to see it coming.

'How long do you think Jimmy will be staying for?' I whispered to Eddie as we made a quiet supper in his kitchen that night.

'What?'

'How long? Days, weeks, what?'

Shrug.

'Months? You don't think it could be months?'

'I don't know. As long as he likes. As long as it takes.'

'Oh.'

I thought about this for a while.

'But, you know,' I said next, dripping oil smoothly, slyly into a pan. 'I'd have thought that he might've wanted to stay with your parents. They've got plenty of room, haven't they, not like us. He should have gone there. They'd love to have him, wouldn't they?'

'What? What are you talking about? I told you, he wants to stay here.'

'OK. Sorry.'

'It's right that he's here.'

Eddie buttered bread furiously. I seemed to have made him mad. Perhaps I shouldn't have said that about his brother. Eddie loved his brother very much.

Eddie loved all of his family, every member. He was proud of them too. A nice bunch of people, he said of them. A remarkably successful medical family, a book in the library had said, although there had also been locally famous artists, clever politicians and noted musicians included in their number. They had flourished in many professions, over many generations and in many parts of the world. Talent, it seemed, was not limited in any way amongst this clan. Just a good bunch of people, Eddie had said again, as if this were the key to all that unbounded success, and perhaps it was.

They were all proud of each other. They must have been. I imagined their gatherings, imagined them confidently discussing the youngsters and the things that they would do, and respectfully reviving the dead ancestors by remembering the things that they had done; the marks that they had made in the world by plastering the family name over some disease or by securing it to some movement or by scrawling it deeply in the bottom right-hand corner of some fine oil-painting.

Apart from Jimmy, I had never actually met any of Eddie's relatives. I didn't want to, that's all. Instead, I got to know and love them through my lover and through their things. There was a book on Eddie's shelf in which I could look up his grandfather's thoughts. I could hear his second cousin on CD or cassette any time I wanted to. There was a piece of a dead aunt hanging on Eddie's bedroom wall and, in his encyclopedia, a photograph of a bravery badge that had been won by some great-uncle during some great war.

'Ha ha. It's not a badge, Angel! It's a medal,' Eddie had corrected me once.

'All right. Don't be pompous.'

'Ha ha ha. And you don't "win" them. It's not like bingo, you know.'

'Eddie, fuck off please.'

'A badge! She calls it a badge!'

'Did he kill a lot of people then?'

'What? Aw! Come here, Angel. Give me a kiss.'

'No. Go on, tell me. Did he kill a lot of people? I'm really interested. Did he?'

'All right, I'm sorry about the bingo thing.'

'It's a terrible thing to take a life, don't you think?'

'I think that we should—'

'He might have gone to hell for it, your Uncle Hero chap. Don't you think so, Eddie? Don't you think that he might have gone to hell for it?'

Eddie's body stiffened a little now and his cheeks flushed very slightly as his blood rose in defence of the dead man's honour. I watched him coolly as he went on to detail his relative's war record; watched his eyes go all funny as he glanced backwards through time to focus on courageous acts that he hadn't actually seen but felt able to claim as his entitlement; as his own. Eddie knew that his antecedents were good people. He knew that he was a good person. He knew that his family name had been handed lovingly down through worthy generations, not passed like a buck.

'Come and meet them,' he'd asked one day. 'Just my parents. Come on. It'll be good.'

'No thanks.'

'Come on, Angel. I want you to. I really do.'

'Another time, eh?'

'It doesn't matter if you don't like them. But I think you will. And they'll like you, they'll love you. Make you welcome, make you part of the family, if you want. Come on. Come and be part of my family.'

His voice as he said this was very soft and rich. His offer was so tempting that it almost made my mouth and eyes water. Before I knew what was happening, Eddie had packed a bag and me into a car that was heading for his home sweet home.

'Do I look all right? Eddie? Do I look all right?'

'What? Yeah, of course. Beautiful. Where'd that dress come from? It's a bit tasteful for my taste, but yeah, beautiful.'

'Pleased to meet you. Pleased to *meet* you. Does it sound OK?'

'Ha ha.'

'Hey, what do I call them? Eddie! What do I call them? I mean, I don't want to be too formal, but I don't want to offend. What are their names? Liz? That sounds a bit chummy, though, doesn't it? Oh I don't know. What's your dad's name again? Dick? You're kidding me. You are kidding me.'

'Ha ha ha.'

'Yes, I am an artist,' I said aloud, practising framing myself for them. 'One day I hope to have a small exhibition, yes, yes. Oh, just modest, pretty pictures mostly, you know: landscapes, flowers.'

'Ha ha ha ha ha.'

'That's a thought. Maybe I should take your mum some flowers. Should I take your mum some flowers? Eddie? Eddie, please stop laughing.'

'Ha ha ha ha ha ha ha!'

'Stop it. No, stop it. Stop the car, Eddie. Stop it!'

It wasn't really my nerve that had gone, it was my confidence. I knew that I was good at fooling people who felt with their eyes, ears, heads, but I was suddenly not at all sure how I'd fare against the sensitive instincts of a mother's belly. She would talk to me cheerfully and shrilly, listening all the time. She would feel her womanly way discreetly and rudely around my edges and curves. She would stare and stare and stare at me with wide, shining, animal eyes, trying to see through me, trying to illuminate the single tiny gesture that would confirm her gut reactions. Well, the best of girlfriends would sweat under such a spotlight, and I was not the best of girlfriends. No, I would not meet them, because they would not like me.

'Of course they'd like a visit. 'Course they would. They'd love it, but I don't think it's going to happen.'

'Pardon?'

I looked at Eddie sharply, startled and scared by his apparent ability to follow my thoughts.

'My parents. They'd love it if Jimmy went up to stay with them.'

'Oh. Jimmy. Yeah. Hang on, though. Why won't it happen?'

'Oh, he's not seen them for years. Two or three, I think.'

'I didn't know that. You never said. Tell me about it.'

'I don't know much. I've asked Jim, but you know what he's like. He just frowns and says it's too complicated, then he starts going on about cars or money or girls; things that he knows how to handle.'

'But what do you think it's about?'

'Well, he's always found them difficult. He has this ridiculous idea . . .'

'Yeah?'

'It's crazy, of course.'

'Go on.'

'Well, basically, he keeps away from them because he thinks that they don't like him very much.'

'Really. Really.'

Jimmy came into the kitchen, smiling boyishly. I handed him warm food and smiles and sympathy.

'Welcome,' I said, and that's how Jimmy and his complications came to set in on us.

Towards the end of May, we had a dinner party. It was my idea. It was to be held in Caroline's flat. She would be cooking a three-course meal for five guests and at six-thirty I went down to see if she was all right.

72

I shivered as soon as I walked through her door. Despite the pleasant weather outside, Caroline's home was still remarkably damp and cold, even damper and colder than my own, which struck me as quite an impressive and frightening achievement. Her shadowy nooks and corners just seemed packed with crouching chilliness, as if Winter had crept in through the holes in her walls to hide and bide its time away here, in these rarely visited basement rooms. Those same holes also gave access to strange, spiteful draughts which whispered about you all the time and, on bad days, could slam a door right in your face. When she'd first arrived, Caroline had made some efforts to fill the holes that she could find, but it had never really worked; you'd block up one gap and the draught would just come in at you through another, only with twice the force this time; pressed into an icy rage by the attempt to exclude it.

I stood in the living-room and looked around. The atmosphere was depressing, there was no doubt about it. The walls in here badly needed redecorating, on account of the fact that the previous tenant had been mentally ill for a long time and had probably had things other than wallpaper-hanging on his mind in the years leading up to his suicide. Caroline's own timid contributions to the decor had brought little cheer, and now a recent tidy-up had made things even worse. Chairs and tables and packing crates had been spread far apart, in a subtle undermining of their solidity. The soft, labrador-coloured boxes which had lain around like excellent pets by the skirting-boards had all disappeared, and a small plant that I'd bought for her a few weeks earlier was also gone; hidden or given away or destroyed. Caroline seemed to have removed anything that could snag the eye or the interest in any way, as if she'd worried that a small guest might get caught in a complicated corner, and never leave. The only proper colour that I could find in here now was contained in the curtain by the door I'd just passed through; a long, draught curtain in jubilant Indian oranges that danced around the jamb like a celebration of exits.

'I've never done this before,' Caroline told me now, in the tone of one about to break commandments. 'I mean, I've fed people, if they were hungry. But never all *this*.'

I followed her into the kitchen. Stood and watched as she agitated seething vegetables, worried a delicate soup.

'Ouch! Ouch!' she said suddenly, pushing a lump of cheese against a grater and forgetting to stop at her fingers. 'Look. I'm just not used to this.'

'I know, I know,' I said kindly, as I began to unpack the crockery and glass and cutlery that I'd brought with me. 'I know.'

Caroline took a sharp breath and held her head high, but she couldn't quite keep her hands from shaking as she took the cups and saucers. I lowered my face and tried to seem sympathetic, but I couldn't keep from smiling at the sight of this woman who had travelled a colourful world alone now standing in her own kitchen, trembling at the challenge of pale plates, white wine and English cheddar.

We set the table for six; for Caroline and me, Eddie and Jimmy, a new girlfriend of Jimmy's and a man called David.

'So,' I said as she laid the sixth place.

'So?'

'So.'

'So . . . what?'

'So . . . who is he then?'

'Mmm? Sorry? What?'

I smiled at our game. She wasn't bad at it, really. Her voice was light, her expression casual, and I myself couldn't have improved on the I-don't-know-what-you're-talking-aboutness of her eyes. It was only her hands that let her down, too small hands articulating her secret as clearly as any amount of long words could do. She realized this too, and suddenly tucked them away into her pockets, but not before I had seen the way that those fingers had whispered over this guest's cutlery, touching the knife and fork and spoon he would soon use as gingerly as if she sensed electricity in the moment, in the metal.

'David,' I said.

'Oh, David. Oh, he's someone I met.'

'Work colleague? Friend?'

'Friend. Yeah.'

'Just a friend?'

'Yeah.'

'A good friend?'

'I suppose.'

'A boyfriend?'

'Boyfriend? What do you mean? He's a friend, that's all, just a boy who is a friend. That's all.'

'OK.'

I grinned, and then stopped my teasing. Caroline blushed or paled and hurried off back to the kitchen. I found her in there a little later, stirring a sloppy sauce and repeating the word 'boyfriend' to herself once or twice; rolling the word around her mouth as if testing its taste.

At seven o'clock, a car pulled up outside. There was a ring on the doorbell. Noises. Voices. People.

My interest rifled through the heads in the doorway like a licked finger, and then stopped when it reached Jimmy's girlfriend. Jimmy's girlfriend. It's Jimmy's new girlfriend. Well, let's have a look at her, I thought, then

I pulled her out from the pack, which wasn't difficult because she was a big girl. She was big in a way that eyes can measure and rulers can't.

She had an enormous frilly purple flower behind her right ear and a fat orange one behind her left. Her corn-yellow hair had been raked away from her face and pulled into a long plait, up which bright strands of embroidery cotton climbed like snakes or vines. She wore a vast cloak, green and velvety, which made a hillside of her shoulders and back and, underneath, a fluttering dress that contained the sort of vivid, clashing colours that might have worked had she been a bouquet. On her feet, the girl wore only the flimsiest of open-toed sandals, as if she expected at any moment to return to the garden she had been plucked from.

Well, you might have thought that any personality would pale beneath this garish attire, but no, not this girl's. As she entered the room, she put the outfit firmly in its place; tossed her cape open and her hair back and let these things trail after her like students.

'Hi! Hi!' she said in a high voice, then she sashayed across the room to a central chair, waited for us to get comfortable, and began telling us all about herself.

She told us where she was from and how lucky she was to have been born in such a *wonderful* city. She told us of the places she'd visited recently, and what an *amazing* time she'd had there. She told us about the places she was going to next and where else she could have been tonight. She told us how much she *loved* nature and *hated* pollution and how *exciting* her job was and how *marvellous* her friends were and then, in between breaths, she glanced around to make sure that we were all listening properly; that we were properly understanding what a really *fantastic* person she was.

I watched her haughtily, incredulously. Normally, I had no difficulty with people who liked being creative with the truth. It was just that this girl was so very *bad* at it.

She didn't have the first idea about how beautifully the lines between fact and fiction can be blurred and, consequently, the picture she presented of herself was full of ugly, hard-edged contradictions. Her larger exaggerations were so glaringly synthetic that they appeared almost fluorescent, and this was a tone that sat very badly beside the mud-brown that her sloppy phrasing was elsewhere making of even the simplest fibs. The name-dropping and boasts and high-coloured hyperbole that came out of her mouth just seemed utterly untouched by any kind of sensitivity or skill and, although her eagerness did contain a certain raw vitality, it was also, like the excited application of straight-from-the-tube pigments, clearly the mark of an amateur.

Just as I finished thinking this, the girl stopped gushing. Just stopped. Just like that. I don't know why. Perhaps she had noticed the look of disdain on my face as I considered her cheapening of this art form. More likely, she'd suddenly remembered reading in a magazine that people might like you more if you allow them to speak now and then.

So the monologue ended and the questions began.

'Angela. You're Eddie's girlfriend, aren't you? Eddie, you look very different to Jimmy, don't you? Isn't it chilly in here? Caroline, you're Angela's friend then, are you? And this is your flat? It's very bare, isn't it? Could do with a few flowers, don't you think, maybe a pot plant, eh? Were we on time? Something smells nice, doesn't it? Isn't it chilly in here?'

'Yes,' we said.

'Right!' she announced next. 'Right, you lot! Come on! Why don't you tell me all about yourselves? Come on now! What do you all do?'

As questions go, this was not a good one to use on this group of people. Even if we'd liked her, we wouldn't have liked her question.

'I'm a photographer,' said Eddie flatly, avoiding the girl's flashing eyes, looking around for a change of subject.

'Really? Oooh! Tell me about that. Do you do fashion spreads? Have you photographed anyone famous? What are you working on at the moment, anything exciting?'

'No. Not really.'

Eddie was not a man in the habit of discussing what he did. Even I didn't know what he was working on at the moment. A 'special project' is all that he would say. That was all that he would ever say. Sometimes, if you were lucky, when he had finished something he would show it to you; would flick open a portfolio or a magazine, still without giving or expecting too many words, and then he'd nod, flick the book and the subject closed again, and go straight into not talking about his next project.

'Mmm, that's interesting, Eddie,' the girl was murmuring now, tilting her head photogenically at him. 'I've done a bit of modelling, you know.'

When her posing and our embarrassment subsided, the girl turned to me.

'And what do you do, Angela?'

She had a way of making 'what do you do?' sound like 'who are you?' and when I replied 'cleaner' she heard 'nobody' and pretty much left me alone after that.

'And you, Caroline?'

Caroline shrugged. She didn't want to talk about it either.

Caroline worked with numbers. She worked here, at a flimsy desk, at a small computer that folded up like a suitcase. She apparently had quite a genius for numbers, although you'd never find her boasting about

78

this. She was glad to be intelligent. Intelligence is solitary and portable and she was glad of its ability to purchase for her the lonely lifestyle she required, but she would no sooner discuss this mundane exchange than she would relate the details of her daily visit to the bread shop.

'I'm a statistician,' she said now. It wasn't entirely accurate, but it was her usual reply when asked about her occupation. It was a difficult word to pronounce and she found most people prepared to let the subject drop right there, for fear that they'd have to attempt it themselves should they continue.

'Oooooh, you must be brainy!' shrieked the girl. 'Me, I like a person who's good with their hands!'

She fondled and nuzzled Jimmy crudely, ridiculously. He grinned privately. I wondered, unkindly, if he'd brought this person along tonight for her amusement or ours.

She didn't ask Jimmy to talk about what he did for a living. Nobody ever asked Jimmy what he did, where he got his money from.

He was a 'buyer and seller', that's the most anyone ever knew for sure. 'A buyer and a seller.' He'd said this to me once a long time ago, when I didn't yet know him well enough not to ask, and his sharp tone of voice had wrapped around the words like barbed wire, discouraging me from going any further.

'It must pay well, this buying and selling,' I'd said to Eddie a few days earlier, just after the unhappy little brother had cheered himself up with the purchase of a brand-new big car. 'What does he deal in then? Disposable lighters? Second-hand records? I think not.'

Eddie had looked uncomfortable at that. Told me that he didn't know. Told me that it was none of his business. Told me that, yes, it might be drugs, but that as long as he kept his room clean, Jimmy could stay.

'And what do you do?' Eddie asked Jimmy's girlfriend politely now.

'Oh,' she said, making dramatic gestures with a flower that she'd just untangled from her hair; a gaudy, fluttery flower that, like her, had turned out to be made of pretty, flimsy plastic. 'Me, I'm an actress.'

'Oh.'

'Can't you tell? I'm an actress. I act.'

'Oh, right. Right. Yes.'

We all doubted it, and didn't doubt it.

Eight o'clock arrived, and David didn't. I caught Caroline watching the door, sending it looks that would strip wood.

'He's probably hit some traffic,' I said kindly.

'I'm starving,' said Eddie frankly.

'Yes,' said Caroline finally. 'He's not coming. Never mind. Let's eat.'

Looking back, I can see that Jimmy had probably not actually intended to try and seduce Caroline that evening. Not quite. Not really. It was just that he was a compulsive charmer, and that she was the only person in the room who didn't already adore him.

Eight-thirty, nine o'clock, ten. Hours later, she still didn't.

'Your flat's interesting,' he would say.

'It's not meant to be,' she'd say.

'So do you go out much, then?'

'Clubs, you mean?'

'Yes.'

'No.'

'And where are you from originally?' he tried at one point, blowing blue cigarette smoke over her as if it were a spell.

'The south.'

'And you're a statistician?'

'Sometimes.'

80

'How do you mean?'

'Hmm?'

'Do you mean that you work part time?'

'I mean that sometimes I work with my head and sometimes I work with my hands.'

'Depending on . . . ?'

'Yes. Depending on.'

She waved the smoke and attention away with a sharp, sleight gesture that had a magic of its own.

'So how old would you be then? Have you been to Brighton? Where did you live before?'

'Twenty-eight. No. Here and there.'

'Australia,' I said, trying to keep this bit of dialogue flowing, while Eddie went over to open a conversation and a new bottle of wine with Jimmy's girlfriend. She had quietened considerably by this point. Throughout the evening, her mood had turned hot then cold then hot again as she'd watched her boyfriend trying to make a new friend, and these temperature extremes clearly did not suit her. Her chatter had dried up. Her colours were fading. Jimmy's warm attentions were pouring down onto another face suddenly, and now this girl started to droop like a flower with the sun gone.

'Australia? Really?' said Jimmy.

'Yeah,' said Caroline. 'Does anybody want some more coffee?'

Australia. I can see her in Australia, I thought, as I watched her moving around the room, dodging questions and bodies, her flat far too crowded for comfort with the five guests in it. Australia. A big, big country. A small, small population. I could see how she'd like that.

'And you're twenty-eight,' Jimmy went on. 'If you don't mind me saying so, you look a bit older than that.'

'Do I?'

I looked at my friend. Her hair was still sun-bleached, frizzy, unruly as a bush or The Bush. Her complexion was more sand and sunsets than peaches and cream and she had sharp, early creases around her eyes and mouth, which added a certain crisp dryness to her expressions and words. The country had left its marks on Caroline, and the marks suited her.

'I like to travel too,' Jimmy was saying. 'You know, just take off in my car. That's why I like to have a fast car, you see; you can be anywhere in a flash.'

'Yes, I've noticed your car,' Caroline said. 'It is very flash.'

'Caroline's rude, isn't she?' Jimmy said to me a few minutes later, with her away at the table doing to the crockery what she could not do to the guests; gathering, stacking, clearing.

'Or maybe she's a bit dim. I can't work out which. She just won't talk to me. I don't know. Maybe she doesn't like me. I've given her no reason not to, have I? Have I?'

'No,' I smiled. 'You haven't. Don't worry about it.'

There was no need for him to take it personally. Caroline was always like this in company; always those words as slippery in her mouth as she was in the fingers of the world; always that voice trailing away into nothingness, with even the most promising sentences withering away before they had a chance to take root and grow into a healthy little conversation. It was just her way. She preferred to keep her words, like her belongings, always minimal and unsettled, as unwilling to commit to a precise meaning as to a place; refusing ever to assert that formidable I Am Here! on which great speeches and towns are built.

I tried to tell Jimmy this, but he wasn't listening.

'Maybe she just doesn't like me. I don't know. Maybe she simply doesn't like me,' he was muttering, lowering his head and studying this idea as if it were a brand-new possession.

Well, all in all, the evening was not a success.

The girlfriend got drunk and wilted unattractively in the corner. Eddie got sick from too much sweet pudding. David continued not to come and Jimmy continued pestering Caroline right up until the moment he left, finally forcing her to come right out and admit that, Yes, he was quite right, she simply did not like him.

'Really? How odd,' Jimmy said on the doorstep, his dark eyes twinkling with moonlight, his handsome mouth falling into a slow, lazy grin. 'Oh well. Never mind. Good night.'

Yes, how odd, I thought, as I watched Caroline snorting and sneering and casually slamming the door on Jimmy's beautiful smile, quite immune to the very best that this very charming man could offer. Like I said, Caroline was a strange girl. Like I said, my friend was smart. Smarter than him, and much smarter than me.

6

June. Hot. Sweaty. Sensual. Summer.

After a lot of flirting and teasing, summer had finally come.

For months, we Londoners had been watching the sky to see what it would do, and now we all glanced up and said 'Ah!' and prepared to prepare our reactions.

I heard the hot sun calling thin people out of their rooms and clothes. Felt it sending other people into a sweat and a small fat panic. Motorists turned their windows down and their radios up. Truanting teenagers lolled in baggy T-shirts on street corners, flaunting their youth and freedom, while businessmen hurried enviously by, tugging at their ties. Young women with the guts and the breasts for it left their bras in their drawers and old women dared sandals and one less cardigan. And children, well, they seemed to like it best of all. The sun beamed, and they beamed right back. White toddlers in pink shorts on green grass beneath blue, blue skies. Their sensuous trust had not yet been burned out of them, and now they ran straight towards the light, exposing their shoulders, arms, chests, to the fierce love from above.

It was morning. Eddie and I were in bed again, in his bed, lying together, breathing in sunshine and each other.

His bedroom was at the back of the house, facing south into good light. It was a large and airy room and a gaze from its main window travelled for a full thirty yards or so before being interrupted by concrete or red brick, which, in this part of this town, passed for a rather splendid view. There was a good garden below, but unfortunately this belonged to the people in the basement flat and, excepting a twenty-foot leap from the ledge, we had no access to it. Never mind. We still managed to enjoy the presence of this and the other gardens. You cannot put a fence around grassy smells or birdsong, and these things carried out and up, beyond the parameters of exclusive tenancy agreements.

Eddie had been watching me and now he reached over and traced his forefinger down the centre of my forehead. Along the bridge of my nose. A bobble over the lips and chin, down the neck, between the breasts and then further, further; continuing the line beneath the bed sheet and along to the warm end of my body.

Something in me twinkled.

'This is nice,' one of us said.

I closed my eyes and heard a couple of plump clouds bumping bellies. The top leaves of a tree tittered and shook, and then this set off a gaggle of giggling birds. Somewhere, an electric mower buzzed and a pair of shears snipped, barbering out tidy trims to unruly hedges and long-haired, layabout lawns, while further out, some dogs scrapped in a scrap yard and a toddler squealed a disobedient appeal, then was immediately overruled by the authoritative boom of an aeroplane. It was a peaceful morning. Such a deeply peaceful morning that even these latter warring sounds could not disturb it, because beneath them all you could clearly detect the unmistakable hum of well-being. Everything would be all right. You could just tell. No-one would come to any real harm this particular morning. No bombs would drop on this neighbourhood today.

'It's my birthday,' said Eddie. 'Today.'

'Eh? What? No it isn't. It's next Saturday.'

'No. It's today.'

'No, no,' I said, lifting my head from the pillow and shaking it patiently. 'No. Not today. It can't be.'

I looked at Eddie as if he were stupid. He laughed to himself over my ability to make an argument of even this.

'Well, I can ring my mother to check, if you like.'

'What? No. 'Course. You must be right. Shit. OK. Right. OK. Get up.'

'Eh?'

'Come on, let's get up.'

'No, it's nice here.'

'Up! Get up! Come on, come on. I've got to go now.'

'Where?'

'To get you a present, of course,' I told him firmly. 'I love you and you deserve a present.'

His elbow banged hard on the floor as I drew up my legs and shoved him out of bed.

Yes, a present, I repeated all the way home. He deserves a present. A good present. A proper present. Not just daffodils pinched from a park; no, not that.

I stood in my living-room for a long time, counting the money in my money tin; fondling notes and thinking about my lover and trying to add up what he was worth. Then I stuffed the whole bundle into my bag and set off.

I reached an affluent north London suburb and spent a few luxurious hours wandering around, indulging myself with tea and cakes in a sweet café, then ice-cream and ducks in a park. I browsed and dawdled, wasting time and money up and down the pretty high street, without feeling bad even once; I was here for Eddie, so I need not feel bad.

I walked past a good bookshop. And kept on walking. Books! I thought! Books! Books! No. No. Eddie had books, plenty of books; too many books. He had flimsy, silly ones. He had sensitive and humourless ones. He had some which were well-used and sprang open to show you all they'd got the moment you pulled them from the shelf, and others which were so uptight and smooth that it seemed as if they had never been touched. His big books, the ones on the top shelf of his bookcase, were my least favourites. Here Eddie kept his psychology books.

He had often tried to get me to read these. I think he imagined that I might find myself in there, under some neat heading of some tidy chapter. I had tried to get into them, for his sake, but it was no good; they always ended up snapping shut against me before I was even halfway through. Either that, or I would find myself slapping them, cursing them, and then throwing them roughly down onto the floor, only to have to pick them up later and have them tell me exactly why I had behaved so aggressively before. I didn't like those books. Just didn't like them, that's all; didn't like the way they talked to me or about me.

In the end, I found a specialist photography shop and picked a present for Eddie from there. I chose it very carefully. I made the assistant wrap the object safely and beautifully. And then I thanked him for his help, and then we agreed to have lunch together.

'Shall we have pizza?' he said, grabbing his jacket. 'A quick one. I only have an hour.'

'Pizza?'

'Yeah. Pizza.'

'Yes, great,' I said. 'I like pizza.'

'OK. Let's get a pizza, then.'

But in the end, we didn't.

We spent almost thirty minutes searching for a public toilet and then, when we did find one, there was more delay as we hesitated over which side we should use. I eventually insisted on the Ladies, persuading him that there would be more cubicles and less stench, and so we sneaked through that entrance and down the stone steps and locked ourselves into ten minutes of cool, dark dampness out of that warm summer's day.

I leaned against the wall and giggled. The young man stood by the door, blushing. He was very awkward. Well, after all, we'd only just met. The dialogue between us had so far consisted mainly of lavatories and public spending cuts and this wasn't romantic, like women were supposed to need it to be. He wasn't used to this; wasn't used to things and girls being as easy as this.

A few more minutes passed, and it looked as if we wouldn't know what to do, but then he suddenly lurched forward with open, sticky lips and it all came back to us. It was all right now. Once you have a person's tongue inside your mouth, there is no more need for words or awkwardness. It was good. It was OK. He was surprisingly gentle; took the camera-lens box very carefully from under my arm and placed it safely in the corner, by the toilet pipe.

I came quickly, with a small, echoing shudder; my bottom cheeks pressed hard against cold tiles, my eyes clinging to some obscene graffiti on the opposite wall, while, above us, the locals went about their sunny lunchtime business. With my orgasm still in the hands of this hasty young man, I closed my eyes and listened. I listened to polite laughter, to the pretty bells of teashop doors, to well-behaved traffic and the steady click of sensible shoes on even pavements. As I listened, I suddenly smirked and understood why there was only one public toilet in this area; I could see how the good people of a nice neighbourhood like that would not want to even accidentally accommodate a grubby pleasure like this.

There was some tissue-wiping, zip-zipping, watch-checking.

'Ready?' the boy asked.

'Yes.'

'I've got to get straight back, see.'

'Yes.'

'OK then. Bye, then. Oh, and thanks very much.'

'You're welcome.'

I straightened my skirt and my hair. Let my eyes and mood adjust to the bright day. Made sure I had all my bags and boxes with me, then bussed home to give Eddie his present.

Eddie and I had a nice late birthday lunch together, and then some fine conversation and then some lovely loving, and then he had to go off to take some photographs and I had to reluctantly hurry away to an afternoon cleaning appointment. It was turning out to be a busy day, a very busy day, although in the end I did manage to squeeze in a bit more sex before I was due at my next job in Camden Town that evening.

I hadn't planned it. I had not expected to run into Christopher, to have him come along in his car and pick me up on the high street that day.

'Hello, my sweetheart, my Venus, queen of the Camden streets!' he called through his car window, twitching his grey beard and large hands enthusiastically in my direction. He was wearing a yellow shirt, an orange waistcoat and a stripy cotton hat, and now he started peeping his car horn over and over, as if he wasn't already quite loud enough. Some people looked around and stared at the eccentric driver. I just smiled and got into his car.

Christopher was a bit of a strange man, but he was not a stranger. He was a friendly, middle-aged artist whom I'd met several times before. We had fondled once beneath a pub table in the West End and again in the front seat of his car, although so far we had never been in a position to actually have full sex.

'This is great,' I said, as he showed me into his house and his studio. It was a big studio and contained everything that an eager artist could ever need: stacks of pre-stretched canvases, shelves full of art books and new paints, wide wedges of good, natural light, a big kettle, a small fridge, two sinks and a bed.

'This is great.'

In the far corner of the studio, there was a crowd of Christopher's finished paintings. They were bright and beautiful. They were violet, raspberry, olive, beef, pea, tea, aniseed and blood. Their colours leaked out into the air, and drifted across the white room, pulling me towards the corner like a tempting smell.

'They're delicious,' I said, and Christopher seemed pleased and then we talked for a while about his work. Well, he talked. Talked too much. Talked and talked and talked, all the time using dismal tones and dull-as-dishwater words that seemed to bear no relation to the sparkling pictures before us.

'I'm trying to nullify myths,' he said. 'To elevate ambiguity until everything is possible. In my art, you see, there is no contradiction between the beautiful and the raucous, the explicit and the enigmatic, the pure and the . . . meretricious.'

'Really.'

He saw me frowning and explained, 'Meretricious means—'

'Yes,' I snapped. 'Yes.'

I understood the word. I just didn't like it, that's all.

The paintings started to sit a little heavily on me after a while. I watched bits of them congeal as Christopher spoke. He didn't seem to notice, though; just went on and on until even his freshest greens went off and the air around us started to smell pale and stale.

At some point, I felt queasy, and decided to put an end to things; pointed out a vital orange and told him that he had killed it. 'Sorry.'

'Well, if that's what you think.'

Pause.

'I'd like to see your work,' he said next, defensive now, as if I'd just challenged him to a colour fight or something. 'You do paint, don't you? You do. I can tell. Tell me about it. Go on. Go on.'

'No.'

'If you want to be a painter,' an art tutor had told me once, 'then you'd better learn to talk about your work.'

'What?'

'You have to make people understand. I don't understand you. This line here, for instance, what is that about?'

'I don't know.'

'And these shapes. Why did you put them in?'

'Dunno.'

'Does this picture elate or depress you? Does it have meaning? Memories? And this red. Why do you keep using this red everywhere all the time? What are you trying to say with it? What does red *mean*?'

I'd shrugged my shoulders then, and someone had snickered. A girl. A fellow student; one of those who knew exactly how she had come to be here and what she wanted and what to say in order to get it. I'd glared hard at that giggling girl's wide mouth, feeling my mood and my colour rising to match that of her gloating lipstick. Later, when we were alone, I would show her exactly what red meant.

'Look, Angela,' the tutor had concluded impatiently. 'If you have any serious sort of ambition, then you had

91

better start learning to explain yourself! All right? All right?'

'I have no ambition,' I told Christopher sincerely now, and after that he seemed happy again; gave me a cup of tea and a mouldy kiss.

'I want to paint you,' he said next.

'Oh yes?'

'To capture the colours of you!'

'Really.'

His yellow corniness was starting to make me feel nauseous all over again.

'I also want to make love to you. Perhaps I could do the two things at the same time.'

'That would be clever. That your party trick?'

'No, my darling, I mean that I could photograph you. Naked. With your legs open. I could have you both ways then.'

'Could you?'

'Are you shocked?' he asked, like a childish dare.

'No.'

'Good. I have a Polaroid camera.'

'I'm pleased for you.'

He skipped off across the room like a young man.

'Look. Here's the camera. It's a good one. There's some new film. What do you say? Yes! It'll be good. Let the artist do his stuff! You like me, don't you? Yes! No? What do you think? Angela? What do you think?'

I paused for a while, sighing and smiling a little, fiddling with my hair and uncertainly crossing and uncrossing my legs. In case you hadn't realized it, this was me playing hard to get. Now the middle-aged, mediocre artist paused and posed amongst his pictures, priming himself for criticism, bracing himself against rejection, but of course there was no need for all that.

'OK,' I said a moment later.

'Yes?'

'OK. OK.'

Christopher hurried off to arrange some lamps. I sat on the mattress and fondled his camera. Peeked through it. Rubbed the lens. Unwrapped the film from the foil where it lay sealed like a condom; airtight and hygienic and ready for the dirty deed.

As I lay down, I noticed a beautiful, small painting on the floor beneath the table. Beautiful colours. What beautiful colours: a slab of incredible red resting on chalky orange, cheese and lemon balls. What colours! What are these colours? Fruity? Savoury? Bitter? Sweet? No, I decided as I stared. No, those words aren't right at all. Now that I thought about it, I could see that food was not an entirely accurate analogy. My consumption of colours was not quite like eating, just as it was not quite like smoking or fucking; it was just that I couldn't find any other way to describe my desire for these things. Hunger. That's about the best I can do, I decided, as I opened myself to Christopher's camera and then to him. Hunger. Hunger. An instinctive appetite, an irresistible craving to take something inside you and be filled by it.

I did not enjoy cleaning that evening. Peppery dust made my throat tickle. Dry fly corpses on the window ledges turned my stomach. The hot weather and the busy day had weakened me considerably by this point; I was exhausted, really worn out, and instead of getting on top of the mess around me I suddenly seemed to be getting lost in it, pulled down, soiled, jostled and dissembled. When the last person left the office, I had a strong urge to sink slowly to the floor and float off to sleep in a murky sea of frothing litter-bins and paper cups and soft brown carpet fluff. Instead, I sat down by a computer, yawned, looked around and then looked down at myself.

I saw that I had ugly stains on me from where an earlier bleach accident had left splatters like white blood down the red front of my T-shirt. I had dry fingers and palms from the paper that I'd been handling; waste paper, used paper, which nevertheless seemed to think that it might yet be able to grow itself back into a tree, if only it could suck enough moisture out of me. I also had a bad iron burn on my inner arm, a cigar-shaped flash of peachy, raw flesh that gaped shockingly from the otherwise smooth surface, as if the white skin all around it were a piece of clothing that had just fallen open. Of course, this is to say nothing of the bruises and the sorenesses that I had gathered whilst performing my other duties of the day; the ones that I now kept modestly tucked away beneath my conscious thoughts and my real clothes.

Some quiet minutes passed. The mess waited impatiently. Sensitive, expensive office equipment shuddered dully beneath the indignity of cheap dust and full litter-bins sat obediently by each desk, watching me imploringly, like dogs waiting to be taken out. Finally, with a great effort, I got tough again; got up and got on with my job.

I did not mind too much about my marks and injuries. I was not too vain and I was all right about pain. Still, I did wonder briefly that evening, as I turned around and banged my shin hard on a bin, if life and work were really meant to be like this, as rough and as damaging as this?

My dad didn't like working, either.

I remembered that now. He did not like working.

Well, what was there to like? He had a rough job too. He was an unskilled labourer and when he set out at six o'clock on a Monday morning, he was never headed for a cosy desk and warm boredom. He was off to get deafened on some factory floor, or burned in the furnace room of some steelworks, or frozen to his foundations on an icy, open building site.

He was always in and out of jobs as we were growing up, often having four or five different ones in the same year. The repetitive harshness of the work he did was partly responsible, I suppose, although, he was a very strong and stubborn man and could mostly take that. What he couldn't seem to take was being bossed. He just couldn't *stand* being bossed; that seemed to be the main problem.

'Just because you have to do a shit job, they think they can treat you like muck.'

The bosses were bad people. It was his experience. They asked you to do things which weren't good for you. To handle asbestos without protective clothing, without even the knowledge that it was asbestos. To go up in a crane which had mildly electrocuted a man only the day before. To climb scaffolding which was only held together by weak rope and hope. He didn't trust any of them, not on any point, and even minor disagreements with a manager would mostly end up with our dad saying Stuff it, and marching off through the gates, just to prove himself a free man; picking up his cards on the way out.

The best and longest job he ever had was as a slinger in the dispatch warehouse of a large steelworks. It doesn't sound like much. It wasn't much. But at least it was semi-indoor work and the company employed so many workers that my dad rarely had to speak to anyone above foreman level. Also, he was good at it. It did require some level of skill. A badly slung, ten-ton hunk of metal on the back of a jogging lorry headed for the Continent is a dangerous thing, and this element of peril put my father's talent for being excessively careful at all times to some use at last.

So this is what he did. He did this for five, six years. I don't know if he liked it. I don't know what else he could have done. He must have had an idea or two himself, but I don't remember him ever telling anybody what they were, and I don't really remember anyone asking.

I do know that, as a boy, my dad had been excellent at football, English composition and drawing. He'd won a prize once at school, for a sketch of a cat. He'd got pencils and a bit of money, I think. A teacher had told him that he was very artistic and that he should consider carrying it on, but thinking about it, I don't suppose there'd have seemed to be much call for it in that rough pit village where he grew up.

His father had taken the money and chucked the pencils on the coal fire, just to make this point. It must have been a hard lesson to learn, but then, my grandad was a hard man. Labourer, amateur boxer, in and out of jail all the time for debts and brawling, and guilty of other things, that he would never be directly punished for. He drank away all of his opportunities, and many of his working hours, and when he did have to face up to the world, he did it with a set jaw and raised fists. He never had any money in his pocket, nor any joy in his heart, so this must have been the only thing in the world that he had to pass on to his only son, this lesson: life is tough, and you have to be tougher.

My dad didn't get into the school football team, because he didn't have any boots. Sometimes, he didn't even have ordinary shoes and then, for weeks at a time, he couldn't even get into school. That's just the way it was. This is the way it was: a fourteen-year-old man going off to his first job in second-hand wellies two sizes too big for him; tramping off to start a lifetime of digging and lifting and hammering and chaining and hodding sodding bricks until his young shoulders and mind were numb and his artistic fingers felt like the stuff that strong shoes are made of.

The job as slinger ended when the firm tried to force our dad into a small promotion. He fell into a peculiar depression for a while afterwards, and didn't work for months and months and months, and then we were really, properly poor.

I remember wearing old T-shirts back to front, so that the stains wouldn't show so much. My knee-length socks went grey, but there was no money to replace them, so instead, our mum bleached them all in the sink one day; only she didn't put enough bleach in or something, and it didn't really work, and for a long time I was the only girl at school with yellow socks instead of white ones.

We had home-made remedies for worn-out footwear too; cardboard insoles to stop the stones coming through and stabbing our feet. All of us kids would sit around the kitchen table helping our dad with this mending, drawing around our shoes, giggling and chatting and making a family evening of it. It was fun, that. Other times, we'd come home hungry from school and find that there was only bread and jam in the house for tea, but our mum would do her best to look cheerful and not hungry; would sit us out in the backyard with a blanket and tell us that it was a picnic, so that was OK too.

Then our mum found some part-time work as a pub cleaner. It was only a bit of money, but it helped a lot. Our parents would still have to sit down once or twice a week to do sums and shuffle little paper-threats around, but these days it was more likely to end in a cup of tea and a sigh than tears. Things were OK. Not good, but better.

Our mum wasn't really supposed to be working,

though. At least, not without my dad first informing the social security, so that they could do their own sums and subtract her earnings from his benefit, and make the whole thing not worth doing in the first place. Still, not to worry; someone else thoughtfully informed them on his behalf, and one day a man came to our flat and said, 'We have received an anonymous letter and have reason to believe that your claim for benefit is unlawful.'

The man wasn't very nice about it. He said some stuff about prisons and courts, and our mum started to panic and sob. He shook his head at her, said that it was her own fault after all and what did she expect? And then, he called our dad a thief and a liar. He did, he said that. Oh-oh. We all held our breath. Fancy that. Sitting on our settee, drinking our tea, making our mum cry and calling our dad a thief and a liar. Fancy saying that. To our dad. There was a bit of violence and the man turned pale, as if surprised.

'Your dad's going to jail, i'nt he?' said a fat girl at school one day, poking me in the arm; the same girl who'd laughed at my yellow socks.

'No.'

'He is. He's a scrounger and he hit somebody, di'nt he? He did, di'nt he?'

My dad got a big fine for the assault, but he did not go to prison. He had been provoked, his solicitor said. So had I. I punched that girl hard in the face, made blood come down her fat, nosey nose and run into her fat, mouthy mouth; got a whack for it from my mum later.

I left work early and went to a pub in Camden Town for a quiet drink. Soon, I'd hurry home to Eddie, to share a nice birthday meal with him and Jimmy and some friends, but for now I couldn't quite face that, and instead I found a dark corner and settled there and prepared to celebrate in my own way.

The pub was small, crowded already. The lighting was reddish, rich and smooth; poor for reading, but great for drinking in. Two big men at the bar were laughing and shoulder-slapping, each enjoying the other's company and body, while elsewhere, here and there, small groups of friends, out to get fall-down drunk, were standing around in uneven patches, already dizzy on the swirling Paisley carpet. In the corner opposite mine, a young man was brooding and sniffing, holding a glass of beer instead of the woman he loved. An old drunk bumped this young man suddenly, making him drop his cigarette to the floor, and now he stubbed it out roughly with his shoe; wisely reluctant to put anything that had been on that filthy carpet back into his mouth. In here, when the fags or the snacks went down, they stayed down; as, occasionally, did the customers.

I drank my lager thirstily, parched after the evening's cleaning. The stuff was fairly disgusting, watered down and maybe topped up with slops too, but right then I didn't have the energy or the dignity to complain. It was a cheap trick, but then I was cheap labour. After a while, the alcohol did start to go to my head, but it didn't help my mood at all; only sloshed my thoughts around in an unpleasant, seasick fashion, rather than washing them away as I'd hoped.

What was wrong with me tonight? I didn't feel good, but I didn't know why. Nothing unusual had happened today. I'd had an expected hate letter, a couple of regular cleaning appointments, several unpleasant memories and sex with two men that weren't Eddie. That wasn't so very unusual. What was new and strange, though, was the feeling that I'd had after the sex.

Up until now, you see, I'd always been sure that I was the one doing most of the taking during my exchanges with the men that I met. After all, their bodies were left quite emptied afterwards, while I came away with something that I hadn't had previous to our encounter; my own body stuffed like a shoplifter's pockets with the stolen gifts of their semen, their desire, their flattery, attention, gratitude, or even love.

But just lately, it had been different. Just lately, I had begun to see myself less as a clever and powerful love goddess, and more for what I was: a promiscuous little cleaning lady with stained sleeves and sad eyes and no pride. These days the penises which had once seemed to gush now seemed to suck; had started to feel like so many vacuum-cleaner nozzles being poked around and about my insides which, as you can imagine, was not a very nice feeling at all.

So why don't you stop, then?

What?

I said, why don't you stop?

I jumped a little in my seat, as if someone had just run across and shouted this idea into my ear; couldn't believe that it had come from me.

Why don't you just stop it? the voice repeated.

What; just like that?

Yes. Just do it. Just stop.

Well, yes. Yes. That is a possibility, I suppose.

It was certainly something to think about; something that I had never really seriously thought about before. All at once, I felt quite odd and dizzy, as I watched the concept swirl like cigarette smoke around my head and then slowly begin to form itself into firmer shapes, and then actual words.

You could stop tomorrow. You could stop right now. You could say Never again! and mean it, and then do it and not do it. Now I was quite excited. You could say no. Yes! You could say no. No, no, no, no! It's easy, see? What you have to do is easy and clear; look, look, look, for heaven's sake, you have the words right here! Only, suddenly, they were gone. I lost concentration for a moment and felt the resolutions immediately turn wispy again and then drift away to get lost amongst the churn of the other customers' heavy smoke and thoughts.

Something had distracted me. A man. I turned my head irritably and gratefully towards a big man who was staring hard at me from the bar. I felt him hook his gaze into my eyes, test the hold and then swing across the room on it towards me, like Tarzan on a vine. This mental picture made me laugh aloud, which in turn encouraged the man to stretch his own grin wide as he swooped over the carpet and landed at my side. He looked confident. He looked as if I were already his. I half expected him to raise his head and beat his chest, but instead he just quietly unloaded onto my table the drinks and the winks and the questions that he had brought with him.

'How are you? OK if I sit here? You got a name then, have you? You're so pretty, I couldn't stop myself from coming over, you see? Isn't it hot in here? Is your drink OK? Aren't you small? Would you like to come out for a bit of air?'

'Yes,' I said.

'Aren't you small?' the big man said again ten minutes later, in an alley-way, in me.

7

July. It was a feverishly hot July day and I was on a crowded bus, on my way to an early afternoon cleaning session in Hampstead.

The journey was not enjoyable. The air in the bus was chokingly dry around the silently sweating passengers. Clothes clung and time dragged and wasps panicked noisily at the bus windows, trying to get off, having long since missed their stop. As we moved into the posh suburb, the houses got finer and the pavements got cleaner and greener, but the air did not improve at all; the cool breezes seemingly no more attracted to this desirable neighbourhood than to any other.

We reached the busy main road, and then got caught up for ten minutes or so in a sticky traffic jam. The hot tarmac swelled beneath us. The heat pushed down. Cars pressed together unhealthily close, breathing pollution and impatience all over each other, and in no time at all a rash of arguments was breaking out all around, spreading quickly through the crowd of open-windowed vehicles. People and engines tutted. Exhaust pipes phutted. Nippy Minis smirked cheekily and tried to squeeze through small gaps in the traffic, while large lorries loomed and roared and tried to throw their weight around. Every now and then, the traffic would come to a complete halt, forcing fuming drivers in sporty cars to sit and watch as plump pedestrians sauntered past, showing off their fast legs.

Finally, we reached a good length of open road and our burly driver put his foot down, only to have to raise it reluctantly a few moments later as we reached a busy bus-stop. Now the vehicle paused quietly and dutifully as the crowd rushed up to the side of its heavy body, eager and jostling as suckling piglets. A few moments later, we were rumbling and grumbling off again, towards another bus-stop and then another and another. I watched the driver's face in the interior mirror. He was glowing with sweat and ill-temper, finding the constant stop–startingness of his work as annoying as interrupted coitus. Another shelter loomed up ahead, and I was sure that he would not stop this time, even though he had clearly seen the old lady sticking her hand out at him, flashing her pass as confidently as if it were a nice bit of leg. You could just tell that he did not want to be doing this. You could see that he bitterly wanted to be a taxi-driver, able to choose whom he would pick up, or one of those long-distance truckers who could just go on for hours and hours.

The smell of the man's soured sexuality and frustrated fury wafted along the body of the bus towards me and suddenly reminded me of the unopened letter in my bag. July's letter. July's hate letter. I peeked in and saw this item of unwelcome post waiting there for me, scrunched and glowering like an overdue bill; an irksome reminder of something urgent and unpleasant.

FUCKING HELL SO YOU'RE STILL ALIVE WELL I SAID I MIGHT WAIT OR THAT I MIGHT NOT IT'S UP TO ME ISN'T IT. I HATE YOU CUNT BUT I CAN TAKE MY TIME IF I WANT TO OR I CAN FINISH YOU OFF TODAY IF I LIKE YOU JUST DON'T KNOW BUT YOU WONDER ABOUT IT ALL THE TIME DON'T YOU. I THINK YOU ARE LOOKING PALE THESE DAYS AND HAVE

YOU LOST WEIGHT? SEE HOW I NOTICE THESE THINGS? I AM A SENSITIVE PERSON NOT LIKE YOU BUT I'M ALSO STRONG SO DON'T THINK I WON'T DO IT BECAUSE I WILL. I AM VERY CLOSE TO YOU NOW CAN YOU FEEL IT? I MIGHT BE WATCHING YOU RIGHT NOW THINK OF THAT. RIGHT NEXT TO YOU LOOK AROUND MAYBE I AM HERE WHAT DO YOU THINK OF THAT THEN? THERE'S NO HURRY I AM GOING TO HAVE YOU ONE DAY WHORE BITCH SO KEEP WAITING IT WON'T BE LONG DON'T WORRY.

I shoved the letter back into my bag and looked around suspiciously. It could be him, I thought, eyeing the thin fellow across the aisle. It might not be Martin who's doing this, it could be this chap right here; just because I did not recognize him did not mean that I had not known him intimately at some point. He looks like a sensitive fellow; it could be him, or him, or maybe him. My eyes frisked several other of the male passengers, but I quickly gave up, realizing that it could really be any one of a hundred or so people. My attachments to my casual lovers had been brief but very intense affairs and it wouldn't have taken much for me to inadvertently rub a sensitive type up the wrong way.

Now the thin man on the bus looked back at me, looked interested, but although his glance was not entirely innocent, I had to admit that it wasn't particularly guilty either. This was a shame because I wanted a face to hit. I wanted to be able to do something about this; a fair fight, that would be all right, but no, I just had to sit here and wait instead, with all the pummelling and the scratching going on uselessly and destructively in the confined space of my chest. I realized, of course, that this was probably my tormentor's precise intention; that he might be planning not to knife me or to strangle me but to worry me to death, and the thought of this subtle, prowling approach made me bristle anew with fear at my predator's particular cunning and at my own particular weakness.

By this point, I had reached the right Hampstead street and now I got out of my seat and rang the bell several times as I swayed slowly down the aisle. This made the driver tut loudly and swear quietly and send a shivery, killer stare along the spine of the bus towards me. The side-doors opened and I was about to call Thank you, and leave the unhappy man with a bit of a flirt, like a small tip, but before I had a chance, those strong doors were closing up again, firmly, resentfully, and I only just managed to hop out through them in time. A few seconds later and they would have snapped shut on some vital part of me. Phew! That was close, I thought, as I stood sweating and startled on the pavement, picturing myself being dragged wailing off up the street by a bus that sped gleefully away, like a wolf with a mangled lamb between its teeth.

When I arrived home that evening, I was surprised and pleased to find Jimmy waiting outside my front door. I breathed easily and swept up the steps towards his smile, delighted to be greeted by such a pleasant, friendly face after such a rough and hostile day.

When I reached Jimmy, however, I found that his smile was actually quite thin and worn out and, a few minutes later, in the privacy of my living-room, it finally gave way.

'I wanted to talk to you, privately, you know,' he said.

'Oh. Yeah. Of course. Sit down. What's up?'

'Well, it's just, you know, some stuff.'

'Yeah.'

'Some things that I can't talk to Eddie, or anybody, about. I don't know. I'm not sure why I came here. I just wanted to . . . Can I talk to you?'

'Yes, of course,' I said. 'Of course you can!'

I did realize that it wasn't quite fair of me to take other people's secrets so keenly. After all, I had nothing of my own that I was prepared to offer in return. Eddie had tried to pressure me into telling him my secrets once and now he believed that my mother was an alcoholic and that I had been molested as an infant by an uncle. Well, he had been rushing me. He'd panicked me. He'd forced me to produce these substitute truths, these almost-could-have-been-truths; lies, I suppose. Still, he'd seemed quite pleased with them in the end. Had even thanked me. They'd made him happy and they really had brought us a little closer together that evening, as well as providing some sort of rational explanation for my increasingly abstract behaviour.

Jimmy, I suspected, also only told the truth when he ran out of useful or interesting lies, so tonight should be fascinating.

'It's about Fay,' he said.

'Oh yeah.'

'Yeah. It's . . . No. Hang on. Oh, I don't know.'

'Go on, Jim. Go on.'

'Wait. I'm not sure. OK. Right. Well . . .'

He ruffled his hair and opened his mouth again, but no words came out this time. He was trying to speak, but he just couldn't. Just. Could. Not. Well, I knew that feeling myself. I too had one of those hands inside me that reach up to cover your mouth whenever you try to be honest, grabbing the daring words out of your throat and back into the pit of your stomach where they belong.

I looked at Jimmy with sympathy. With curiosity. With interest. Jimmy looked very handsome that evening. Very, very, handsome; so impossibly handsome that I found myself just staring and staring at him, as if trying to work out the trick of it. What was it? How did he do it? What was it about him?

His eyes were brown-black. His clothes were blue-black and his sloppy hair was a lovely wet black-black, and yet for all his darkness, I felt his beauty as a red, as a deep and painful red. I realized suddenly that Jimmy must have been in my head as I'd stirred and stroked the paints in my bedroom that morning. Yes. Now I knew what it was about him. It was crimson; a sharp, jolting crimson that caught behind the eyes like cigarette smoke at the back of a throat. Yes, yes, that was his colour; I'd mixed it myself that very day. Crimson like Jimmy. Crimson like aching beauty. Beauty like a curse.

He'd cut off all of his lovely hair once. Eddie had told me about it.

Jimmy had been a young man at the time, thirteen or fourteen, and just starting to notice the effect that his looks had on people; the hearts and the possibilities that they opened up.

One evening, some girl had cut herself over him. No, not just over him but all over him. She had begged him to love her. She'd held her wrist in the air. And then she'd cut the young white skin with her father's old razor-blade; cut once and cut deep so that when Jimmy had looked up, he'd seen a slit opening like eyelids, splashing his lovely face with its little wet sobs of pain. Jimmy had taken the girl home. Her parents had cried and apologized. He had run back to his own house and sat in the bathroom, staring at his reflection, all night long.

In the early hours of the next morning, he'd taken a

blade to himself. He'd gone into a darkened room with scissors and no mirror and he'd started hacking away wildly at his thick hair; chopping and snapping and tearing as if to blunt and limit the damage that his pretty head could do.

I'd seen a photo of that new haircut. I'd seen that it hadn't worked. Jimmy's beauty had just kept on streaming right out of that fine, square head in spite of the tufts and the bald patches and the pink nicks on the scalp. It may even have made him more appealing, in an exposed and blooded kind of way. The young Jimmy must have seen this too, must have realized that women would always love him as that poor girl had loved him: madly, dangerously, messily. He must have decided right then and there that he'd better get used to it, and that he might as well start using it.

He'd even tried to use it against me once, I remembered now; at the end of last year, when Eddie and I had gone down to visit Jimmy and Fay in Brighton. There'd been an early Christmas party. There'd been lots of drinking. A bit of dancing. Some flirting. And then there'd been Jimmy, grabbing me suddenly and roughly as I'd come out of the bathroom; making me jump, making me stumble and then fall clumsily into his arms. He'd been waiting for me outside the bathroom door, you see, and now he'd pulled me expertly and confidently into the fit of his body, quite sure that this was what I'd been waiting for too. There'd been a bit of pushing then, and some apologies and embarrassment. There was embarrassment again now, as I glanced over at the wretched Jimmy and blushed at the inappropriate memory. Why was I thinking about that? It hadn't meant anything. It was just a stupid, boozy encounter with no significance at all, except for the fact that it is the only time in my life that I have ever indignantly slapped a man's face, and I have to admit that this was probably more out of surprise than displeasure.

I pulled my eyes off Jimmy and went away to play some soothing music, to light some calming incense and to make some sweet tea, trying everything that I could think of to make him feel relaxed and comforted and safe, but none of this seemed to do any good. He just sat there, hanging his pretty head low and shaking it from time to time; slouching heavily on my settee, slowly sinking deeper and deeper into the cushions and gloom.

As the moments passed, I found myself trying to figure Jimmy out, to guess what he was thinking and what he might say next. It wasn't easy, though. That tangly hair and those complicated expressions kept getting in the way, rolling down over his face like a blind, making of his thoughts oddly moving silhouetted figures who could equally well be kissing or dancing or fighting.

'Like I said, it's about Fay,' he told me eventually.

'Fay. Yes. It's about Fay.'

'About the way I ended it with her.'

'Yeah. A-ha. Mmm.'

'I hurt her, you see.'

'Yeah.'

'I hurt her.'

'Yes. I see. Mmm. Well, you know, it happens. I mean, there probably aren't very many relationships which end without someone getting—'

'No, I mean I really hurt her,' Jimmy interrupted. 'I put her in the hospital.'

Over the next half an hour, Jimmy told me all about it. He told me calmly, clearly; relating the details with a dramatic succinctness that suggested he'd already told them to himself many times before; over and over again in his head, jiggling and cutting and reordering, as if firm narrative control might in itself help to explain or contain the horrors.

Some of the violence that he described was so rough that the mere telling of it hurt the ears. Had they come at me through my TV, I would probably have turned away from the scenes that I now found projected into the air of my living-room. But I did not turn away from Jimmy. I did not ask him to stop or to tone it down. Instead, I leaned forward, nodding the story along, wanting it to be every bit as bad as it was.

'Listen, Angela, you won't tell Eddie any of this, will you?'

'No.'

'I don't know if you will or not. I'll just have to trust you, won't I?'

'I won't tell him. I won't tell anybody. I can keep a secret, Jimmy.'

He looked over at me, glared hard to see if this was true. Yes, it was. It really was. I had a special safe place in my head for the misdemeanours of myself and my loved ones; a deep cell of a place where I could lock them all up tight and prevent them from doing any more harm in the world than they already had. This place I'd made in my head, this was memory jail; the place where the bad memories go.

'I just couldn't stand it, you see,' Jimmy went on. 'Eddie . . . all of them . . . they don't approve of me as it is.'

'I understand.'

'Do you? No, do you though?' Jimmy squinted over at me hopefully, as if I were a sudden bit of sunshine.

'Yes. I think so.'

'Do you know what it's like to be that angry? Do you know what it's like to feel real fury, the sort that makes you go all freezing cold and out of control?'

Anger, I thought. Anger like a black snowball gathering in your head.

'And depression. Do you know what that's like? Do you?'

Depression, I thought. Depression like a fat dwarf hanging on your back, making it hard to breathe and talk and walk.

'Well . . .' I said.

Jimmy's eyes clouded over. He went back to staring at his black shoes.

'No you don't. And it's good that you don't. I'm an awful person and you're not. You don't know what it's like to have done some of the terrible things that I've done, and I'm pleased for you. I mean it. Honestly. I am.'

I don't know why what happened next happened. Maybe I wanted to help Jimmy. Maybe I wanted to impress him. Perhaps it is just that being an awful person is such an awfully lonely business and that I was suddenly overwhelmed with relief to find myself in the company of someone who was just as bad as me. I have met an equal, I thought to myself. Jimmy and I were equal, you see, although I couldn't figure out exactly why or even exactly how we were equal. It is always more difficult to calculate in negatives, and this is where our similarity lay; in our negative emotions, our non-emotions, the emotions whose number was preceded by a minus. Now I leaned forward slowly, smiled calmly and then quietly told Jimmy about some of the terrible things that I had done.

Once started, we went on for hours.

It was like finding yourself in a hospital waiting-room, seated next to a person with the same disease that you have. It's not that you're proud of your illness. It isn't as if you don't spend hours of every day trying to conceal its scabs and scars and scents. You know how unpleasant it would seem to an outsider. Only now, here beside you, is someone who won't quail at even your most putrid parts, your most distasteful symptoms; someone who knows what it's like from the inside, you see, and suddenly you just can't stop talking.

'I broke her jaw. I heard it break, I heard it break.'

'I've had all sorts of men. Any men. Teenage boys and old fellas. All that.'

'Bruises. She had a black eye. One black eye and a lot of bruises.'

'It doesn't seem to bother me if they're ugly, or even smelly.'

'She couldn't even cry because it hurt so much.'

'I have to do it. I don't really want to. They just sort of look at me and I just sort of have to do it.'

'She was jealous, you see. I was after someone else; you know me, I'm always after someone else. But she couldn't handle it. Turned into a real nag. On and on and on, driving me mad.'

'A couple of times, I didn't even have the chance to wash between one man and Eddie. You know. That wasn't very nice. I do love Eddie, you know.'

'In the hospital when they undressed her, I saw this towel thing. Period thing. She had her period. Blood all over her, at each end. You never saw so much blood.'

'God. It's terrible. Jimmy. It's terrible, really.'

'Yeah. I know. We're terrible, us.'

We might have gone on all night if Jimmy hadn't carelessly mentioned the only disease in the world that I can't talk about; the one with the small name that swells in my throat whenever I try to say it. The conversation dried up suddenly at that point. I put out my cigarette and realized how drained I was. Well, it was late and it was hot and this gush of confession and empathy had almost emptied me, and it was time now for my defences to start to clot and seal over once again.

Jimmy, though, did not seem ready to stop yet. He just went on and on, like picking at scabs; asking me about my past, about my family, about my hometown, wondering aloud about how I might have come to be the way that I was. Well, I got rid of him pretty quickly after that. He shouldn't have asked that. I did not want to think or to talk about those things. Why would I want to talk about those things; I was a quiet and secretive person who had already said far too much.

After Jimmy had gone, I started cleaning my flat. The conversation had left my room feeling soiled, stained, and now here I was, getting busy with the cloths and fluids, as if my words were spilled drinks that could be blotted, sponged and then wiped away without trace.

Well, it helped for a little while. I felt OK for a little while, as I crouched on my knees, scouring and purging and dripping with good, honest sweat. But you know, even industrial-strength cleaning fluids in the hands of a professional have their biological and existential limitations, and at midnight I put my bucket tidily away under the sink, washed my hands and then sank down into a grubby chair and a whole mess of memories.

The town where I grew up has a cosy claustrophobia which I sometimes still miss.

I suppose it is a city. Quite a big city, in fact. I suppose that's how other people think of it, but my memories of the place are too few and intimate for me to think of it as anything other than a town; my home town,

It nestles snugly in the warm lap of a deep valley and is surrounded on all sides by great Yorkshire hills, which rear up benignly around the settlement, encircling like arms, gathering relatives and friends and strangers alike together into one giant, green, cuddle. You can see those hills from almost any point in the town. Beyond those factories, there is a hill. Behind this college and that cathedral, there is a hill. And those houses on that sprawling estate over there, well, they may look as if they're scrambling up and away, but don't worry, they won't get far; there is a hill behind them too, with a bony cliff on top, watching and waiting to elbow them gently back down to the centre. Only the very highest of the high-rise blocks manages to break that rolling line of horizon and peek over that kind wall, but even they have to stand tiptoed on the shoulders of a hill to do it.

The hills protect you. They hide and shield you. And they mark the outer perimeter of home for all to see, so that none might accidentally wander off and get lost for ever in the outside world.

I wandered off when I was twelve. I went to live with a quiet aunt, in a cold coastal town. Exposed myself in a bare, flat, open part of the country where you could see for miles but there was nothing much to see, where there was all the sky you wanted but it was never blue, where the air was fresh but blasted in so wildly and foully through the mouth of the nearby estuary that you would spend whole days in stale, central-heated rooms just to escape its abuse.

That violent wind took my breath away and almost knocked me clean off my feet as I stepped down from the coach on my first morning there. I looked around, feeling utterly lost. I said not a single word to the aunt who had come to meet me. I think I cried quite a bit. Quite a lot. I'm embarrassed by that. No, there's no need to be embarrassed; after all, I was only young then. What was I doing away from home so young? I don't know really. My parents had asked me to leave, I suppose.

My dad was still out of work at this time, you see, and still struggling to pay off that large fine, so financially things were very, very tight. That was the reason why I had to leave; pack a little bag and go to stay with my well-off Aunt Molly fifty miles away. They'd told me that was the reason; had managed to make it sound really quite reasonable somehow.

'It'll just be for a bit, love,' they'd said. 'Just until we get ourselves sorted out. You know. Maybe a couple of months, eh? That'll be OK, won't it, that'll be OK.'

'Yeah,' I'd said. 'I suppose so. I suppose that'll be OK.'

Well, the few months had passed. Then some more months had passed. And then some more and some more.

You'd have thought that an absent me might have left a yawning emptiness in that family, a big only-daughter-shaped hole, but if it did, well, they must have managed to fill it somehow. It was, after all, only a hole in space, in air, that I'd made and by the time I went back for my first visit, it was clear that the family had already begun to expand into it. My brothers' bodies and possessions and need for privacy had all grown startlingly and now, even if I had wanted to, I couldn't fit back in. There was quite simply no room; my parents had given mine away to my brother Mark.

In letters, they all made the effort to give the impression that I was gone but not forgotten and I appreciated that, but after a while, the letters dropped off a bit and then a bit more and then my mum and brothers didn't write at all and then I couldn't help thinking, Missing but not missed, that's more like it.

I was OK. I was All right. Fine. OK. Not too bad.

After all, I could see that it was a good arrangement really, that my family were much better off without me. My dad started to get bits of work again and they were able to refurnish their home with the money that they weren't spending on me. The place was looking great. The family seemed fine. They'd apparently managed to replace their sweet daughter with a peachy bathroom set, rosy new living-room wallpaper and darling velvet curtains, and if anyone ever did take to wandering the house top to bottom in search of their lost girl, well, at least they'd have the comfort of fitted carpets in every room.

Don't get me wrong. I did love my Aunt Molly. And I loved that attic room and the big house and its open fires and the cat and the books. I loved all of these things. It's just that I never felt completely at ease with any of them. I knew I really had no legitimate claim on my aunt or her belongings, and felt, as I've heard that some adopted children often do, that nothing was really *mine*. Not my house, not my parent, not my *things*. It was my home for six years, but until the day I left, I would still ask my aunt's permission if I wanted a glass of milk or a piece of toast and would still dread breaking ornaments or spilling drinks. I remained throughout my whole stay there as polite and careful as any other careful, polite guest would be.

A lot of friends would have helped. Hundreds of friends would have *really* helped me then, but I only made one or two, and I didn't even like them very much. They had their own personality problems; their own reasons for having to hang around with the shy, withdrawn new girl. I didn't talk. I didn't laugh or smile, and on the outside, I suppose that I must have seemed quite strange to the other kids. But then, I seemed strange to me as well, odd and uneven and unbalanced on the inside too, so I didn't argue with them much; well, not until I really had to.

The school bully came over to me one day at break-time; sauntered over to tease and humiliate and break me.

There was a moment of disbelief as I realized what she was up to, and then a peculiar smilingness as I realized her mistake. She'd thought that the fact that

116

I had no words meant that I also had no arms, legs, fists or guts. Silly girl. My voice might have been weak, but my muscles and fury were really quite well developed for my age.

She put up a bit of a struggle at first. Punched my head so hard that my neck said Oh! Calmly, I watched her reach out and grab my hair and pull my head down to the ground. My cheek grazed the tarmac, but I felt no pain. I felt no nothing. But then, suddenly, a chant started up around us; voices, girls' voices all around us, and all shouting her name, and then suddenly I felt lots of things.

I punched that big girl in the belly. Soft belly, hard, hard punch. The impact made her gasp and bow her head into my hands, offering up a breathless prayer for mercy. I considered this. I had the power to grant this; could easily have pinned her down to a full apology, and it would have all been over quickly, with no real harm done. Instead, I went for her eyes. I wanted her green eyes; wanted to pull those eyeballs out and roll them in my palms and then squeeze them and squeeze them until the colour and the fear dripped out and splashed onto the cold ground at my feet. She saw this. She saw what I wanted. She realized suddenly that I was more mad than angry, and after that, she just sort of caved in.

I had another fight, a few weeks later. There was a girl teasing me. There was a bit of pushing. Shouting. Snarling. Smiling. And then, suddenly, there was this big bit of red brick in my hand, and then, suddenly, there wasn't.

'What's been going on, then?' the headmaster said.

I shrugged.

'I want to get to the bottom of this right now. We're very surprised. You're a nice girl, Angela. A clever girl. What's all this fighting, then? You're not that

117

type. What's it all about? Would you like to tell me about it?'

I'd have liked to very much. He was a nice head-master. He seemed nice. But I wouldn't have known where or how to start, so I said nothing instead.

'Well. Let's see. You're in Melanie Hudson's class, aren't you? She's a good girl. Do you get on with her? And Annette and Marie Clarke. Are they your friends? Are they?'

No, they weren't. Certainly weren't. But the nice headmaster was making such an effort to make things all right, that I didn't like to say so.

'Or have you fallen in with a bad crowd? Is that it? Is it?'

No, it's not that either, I thought. I'd have liked to have fallen in with a bad crowd, but they didn't seem to want me any more than the good crowds did.

The Headmaster tutted and muttered and then waved me away. My chair scraped on the wooden floor as I stood up, producing the only decent sound I'd made since entering the room.

'You can go,' he said. 'We'll forget about it this once,' he said. 'Be a good girl,' he said.

He sighed. We both nodded. I went quietly back to my classroom and life, and then nothing more was said.

Oddly, winning these fights won me few new friends. I was strong now, but I was also still strange, and although no-one would mess with me any more, they remained equally reluctant to sit with me, eat with me, talk to me. At home-time I'd walk back to my aunt's house alone. I'd go up to my room alone. I'd lay my school blazer and skirt out gently on the bed, smooth folds, stroke lapels, and then fall into the great pockets of emptiness which were always waiting for me at the end of every day.

I felt vulnerable. All of the time. Open. Exposed. I

118

didn't have any family or any hills around me any more and the roughest elements could get to me quite easily now.

Looking back, I can see that if a drug-dealer had come along at the right moment and offered a bit of companionship and, here, a little something to make you feel better, then I would probably have accepted; would have become a twelve-year-old junkie and had quite a different story to tell. As it turned out though, it was teenage boys who started hanging around the school gates, smiling at me and saying, 'Hello, little girl, look what I've got for you.'

To his credit, my dad did write to me very often while I was away. He sent me many, many beautiful letters; four pages, five pages long sometimes, and always lovingly crafted in that eloquent script which inexplicably flowed from his thick fist.

I would read and reread them avidly in the stillness of my attic room, squeezing out every last drop of news and affection, but I never wrote back, not even once. I'd sit at my desk bursting with things to say, sit there all ready and poised to speak, but then I'd pick up my pencil and find that my hand seemed to have no words in it at all. Where had they all gone? I couldn't write them and couldn't speak them. Why not? What was wrong with me these days? Where had all my words gone?

Instead of writing with my pencil, I started drawing with it.

I was good at drawing. I had always been good at it, and as night after night of nothing else to do came and went, I got better and better. The faces and bodies that my pencil made were right. Eyes knew how far away from each other they should be if they were to follow you around the room. Torsos knew where they had to bend to avoid breaking. Fingers had jointed bones

instead of bananas inside them. I knew, without showing them to a soul, that these things were right. But, to
me, they weren't yet right enough.

After a while, it bored me, this drawing. The pictures
were too flat and obedient. It was like having a one-way
conversation, like I was doing all the talking, with the
paper and pencil just listening and responding meekly
to my requests.

At one point, I started to draw faces with their mouths
wide open, in an effort to make the pictures talk back,
speak up, tell me something. Wide, wide, these mouths
were; so wide that you had to give the exposed gums
fifty teeth each, so wide that you could almost hear the
crunching of jawbones beneath the hiss of soft lead on
hard paper. But this wasn't right either. Despite their
strained efforts, these faces stayed wordless and leaden;
muffled by their grey limits, by the dull grey of nothing
much to say.

So I stole some colour. From school, one afternoon.

I didn't really know why I was doing it. I just saw
that I was. Here's a brand-new set of poster paints. In
the stock cupboard. In my hands. In my bag.

I did not feel bad as I sneaked them away. I knew
what their fate would be if I left them to this teacher
and class. They would be forced into hard, heartless,
ruler-drawn shapes. They would be splashed and
wasted on the floor by insensitive boys. They'd be
prodded and sullied by rough, dirty, poking, brushes
until, in the end, each pot of pure colour would be
reduced to the sludgy level of the rough, dirty, poking
children who used them.

I did not feel bad, and the paints did not seem
unhappy, as they sloshed upstairs to my attic room.
They did not feel stolen, but liberated; I think they had
guessed that I would give them their chance to shine
and speak.

I wanted to get straight to the heart of the matter, so I started that night with a red.

Earlier in the week, some geography teacher had said, The Red Sea; and the phrase had been rippling in my head ever since. Red Sea, I thought now, with my paper spread out on the floor in front of me, and anticipation lapping up all around.

A thick brush dived in, then came out, gasping and bubbling and dripping with scarlet water. I leaned forward. Felt the stretched paper brace itself, and hold its breath as I drowned its bottom half in red. Red Sea. Red Sea. Now I sat back on my heels and watched, fascinated, as my little pot of liquid multiplied itself a million times and became an ocean miles and miles wide.

I liked that. My mouth was dry. I liked this.

You should put some blue sky on now, a voice in my head said. It was my art teacher; she who was happy if she could get us to make a bit of papier mâché and not too much mess. No. Shut up. I don't want a blue sky. I didn't want a blue sky, see. I didn't care if a sky was not blue. I was not in school now; I was not anywhere and I could do what I wanted. I could risk a green if I felt like it. No-one had spoken to me all day and I would speak to no-one all evening and I just had nothing much at all to lose from risking a green.

I picked up a new brush and watched it aim for emerald green, then saw it come up sparkling like rubies instead. At the last moment, it had swerved off in search of red again; had enjoyed it so much the first time that it just wanted more and more.

OK. If that's what you want.

A deeper red this time. Heavier, more boyish. Onto the paper it went, onto the top half of the picture, running, splodging, tumbling, then settling stoutly next to the first shade. The colours sat together well. There was some jostling, but no fight. Red and red on white, comfortable, familiar, the same but different, like a brother and sister playing on snow.

When it was done, I propped the red picture up on my dressing-table, in front of the mirror, in place of my reflection. It was finished, I was finished; sat on my bed for half an hour, staring and sighing, as drained as if I'd used my own blood.

I liked it, this feeling and this picture. It was right, in a way that not many things were right. The pencil had listened and mimicked me, but these drools and gobs of colour, they had a loud, surprising language all of their own, I could see and hear that now. I did not understand all the noises they were making as I looked over the open-mouthed pots on my floor, shouting at me with their Red! Red! Orange! Turquoise! Blue! Green! Green! Yellow! but no matter. I was not worried. There was time to learn, and much to say.

Soon the paints were all gone. So I stole some more. And then some more. From school cupboards, toy shops, department stores, wherever I could get my hands on them. I'd browse, then pinch, then slink back to my aunt's house and, furtive as a secret drinker, sneak upstairs to my attic room, where I could sit unseen in the corner and consume my new amber, orange, rosé.

I don't suppose that I really needed to steal. My aunt might have approved, if she'd known what I was doing, might well have wanted to encourage my habit; might even have been prepared to keep me topped up with a regular supply of quite legal colours. Only, I didn't want her to know or approve, did I, because then she'd show an interest, perhaps she'd even want me to introduce her to my pictures, and I no more wanted to talk to her about hues and tones than I did about the other shady things that I was getting up to of an evening.

See, even this wasn't quite enough.

When I'd first started the hobby, I'd been so happy that I was sure it was all I needed. But I had over-estimated the colours, or underestimated the need.

Some nights, the paints would get into a sulk and then they would not talk to me at all. Come on, pink, purple, I'd whisper, trying to stir up some conversation on the white paper silence. Orange and blue, come on, come on. Mix. Mingle. Chat. Let's hear what you have to say.

Brown, the paints would reply, shuffling lethargically round on the surface. Brown, brown, brown, and this meant leave us alone, go away and find someone else to talk to.

So I had no choice, you see. Two or three nights a week, those moody paints would have to go back to the cupboard and I would be back in the frustration, back on the streets, back to the boys.

The first boyfriend I had lasted for a good six months or so and the next one for almost that, but then they started to come and go more and more quickly. I didn't mind. They were a fairly interchangeable bunch; they liked the same things, talked about the same things and wanted the same thing.

The other characteristic that they all had in common was a complete lack of concern for my worrying in-ability to utter opinions, ideas, sentences. They didn't mind the fact that I was so shy and speechless, in fact many of them preferred it that way. Boys apparently had an essentially more visual and physical relationship with the world, and consequently they loved me for the way that I looked, for the way that I felt and also, to my delight, for the way that I could draw and paint. Well, once I had realized this, my sexual and my artistic talents developed at an astonishing rate, while my unneeded social skills remained as stunted as before. Well, I just had nothing to say, did I? With my gentle, deaf aunt, I seemed to have nothing to say. With my overworked schoolteachers, who themselves wanted only a quiet life, I seemed to have nothing to say. With the boys who just required me to shut up and keep still, I seemed to have nothing to say. With my loving father, who wasn't there to hear me anyway, I seemed to have nothing to say.

8

August. It was August. The air was heavy with heat. The city was buckling under the pressure. I was being followed; there was no doubt about it now. I had been feeling it for weeks and weeks, and had just had my suspicions confirmed by August's letter.

In his latest piece of correspondence, my pen-friend had ranted on as usual about how he was getting nearer and nearer, moving in for the kill, but this time he had backed himself up by mentioning the kind of details about my work, home and sex life which could clearly only have been recorded by a very attentive and very close pair of eyes.

I'd felt those eyes on me on the street, when every light breeze or sudden ray of sunshine would feel like a tap on the shoulder. I'd felt them on me in a tube station one night when I'd become disorientated in one of those empty corridor mazes which put a dizzy woman quite at the mercy of a fellow traveller with a bad intention and a better sense of direction. I could feel them on me now too, as I half-heartedly cuddled with a lovely man that I vaguely knew, in some woods by the graveyard of a disused Willesden church. Shadows fell heavy as stares over the skinny bush where we undressed. As we kissed, the light autumn breeze made a thousand leaves twitch like net curtains.

'Stop it. Get off me, please. I don't feel right. Stop!'

I pushed the man away suddenly and looked around

impatiently. This was annoying now. I'd expected this to be a good location and an enjoyable afternoon. I had a discreet, handsome man for pleasure, and condoms and a knife for safety, and I'd really thought that I'd feel quite happy and secure in this private moment and place. Only, now I found that I couldn't relax and enjoy myself at all. I just wasn't able to switch off and turn myself on the way that I'd once used to do. This wasn't entirely the fault of those eyes, but they really weren't helping.

Someone is definitely watching me, I thought, squinting around from tree to tree and gravestone to gravestone and then up at every disapproving window in the turned back of the church. Someone is *definitely* watching me, and I don't just mean dead people or God.

'I'm being followed,' I told Jimmy one evening.

I was at Eddie's flat. I'd come round to see Eddie. I'd been longing to see him and talk to him all day, but when I'd got there I'd discovered, to my horror, that I really had nothing much to say; suffocated by secrets, I'd found myself practically holding my breath, waiting for my lover to leave the room so that I could breathe and speak freely with his brother instead.

'What?' said Jimmy. 'What do you mean? Do you mean that Martin guy? Fuck! I've told you, let me find him. I know people who can find people. Come on. Let's put a stop to it. I can do this for you.'

'No.'

'But he sounds like a nutter.'

'He's probably harmless.'

'He says he wants to kill you.'

'He probably won't.'

'But you can't mess with people like that. Let me do this for you, Angela. Let me take care of you.'

'No. I shouldn't have mentioned it. I don't need looking after, you know. I'm not some . . . *little woman*!'

Jimmy laughed hard at that. He looked down at the dainty hands that I'd clenched into feminine fists and pointed out, 'Actually, you are.'

'You know what I mean.'

'Oh, tough, are you?'

'Tough enough.'

I punched him firmly but affectionately on the arm. He roared with delight and started hitting me softly with a cushion. Soon we were fighting like crazy; like brother and sister, I told myself, as he tugged my plait and wrestled me to the floor. We tickled and tugged. We pushed and teased. We rolled and nipped and giggled like kids, Jimmy and I, but then, all at once, it occurred to me that this innocent fun was a little too much fun to be entirely innocent.

Burroughs bounded in from the kitchen and started yapping and panicking around us, not sure if all this commotion meant trouble or a game; but then, I wasn't so certain myself.

'Calm down,' I said, as things began to look as if they might get wild. 'Calm down, boy, calm down.'

I struggled out of Jimmy's arms, straightened my clothes and hair and was all settled and tidy again by the time Eddie came back into the room.

'What was all the noise about?' he asked.

'Oh, we were just laughing at your mad dog. There's something wrong with that mutt, mate. He's just attacked me for no reason.'

I looked over in wonder as Jimmy relaxed in his chair, calmly breathing out cigarette smoke and chit-chat. He was good at this.

'Jim's right, Ed. He's loopy. Loony. Paranoid or schizoid or something.'

So was I.

We sat and chatted as if nothing at all had happened. Well, nothing had happened; there were two expert liars and no witnesses, so just try and prove otherwise.

'Woof, woof, woof!' said Burroughs. He was taking a while to settle back down again. Kept barking and jumping up to grab Eddie's attention; even snapped at me as I tried to pat him quiet.

'Shut up. Shut up, lad,' Eddie told the dog, but he just wouldn't, and in the end had to be sent to the kitchen for his disobedience. Once again, he was leaving the room in a state of disgrace. Once again, it was because of me. As he padded away that evening, the pet looked so hurt and frustrated that I was sure he was about to cry, and for a moment I was quite touched to see an animal so disgusted by the limitations of his own species; by the insufficiencies of his thought processes and by his inability to speak.

August droned on. There was some more weather. There was nothing on TV. There were some good exhibitions in town and a fire in Eddie's flat.

'In my bedroom, while I was out,' Eddie told me on the telephone.

'No.'

'It's a mess,' he said. 'The neighbours heard Burroughs barking in time, otherwise the whole place could have gone up.'

'No.'

'Bed's wrecked. Carpets. One of my good lenses and some of my work.'

'No! Oh no!'

Oh yes, yes. And he had even worse news for me than that. He said that it looked as if the fire might have been my fault; smoking in bed, in that bedroom that morning.

This time, I did not say No! I did not say anything; I

just put the phone down with a soft, sorry click, too shaken and ashamed to speak.

When I saw the room the next day, I was ashamed all over again. Soot walls. Scorched carpet. Dark cloud on the ceiling over the bed. Big black hole in the middle of the mattress that I just wanted to disappear into.

I sent Eddie and Jimmy off out shopping and then I started work on the room. Started cleaning the room. Carried on all day and well into the night and wouldn't let anyone help. Insisted that they didn't help.

Behind the locked door, I scrubbed and scraped, I washed and rubbed, I mopped and disinfected and sprayed and buffed and then, at midnight, exhausted and sick, I started with the painting. By the time I had finished, it was morning again and my hands were glowing with pink soreness and shiny blisters. My face itched beneath a smattering of emulsion spots. My back groaned along with the floorboards as I rolled out the new rugs, but that was all right, that was fine. As the sun rose, I fell into a chair, feeling ill and good, having done everything I could to put things right, to erase my mistake from Eddie's walls, air, memory.

'You've stopped?' Jimmy said. 'No! What, you've stopped, just like that? No. I don't believe it.'

It was an early evening. I was speaking to Jimmy on the telephone. He was gasping and screeching down the line at me, his words craning forward incredulously as I told him about my new decision to put an end to all of my disgusting old habits and destructive old ways.

'You've stopped smoking? Really?'

'Yeah.'

'No!'

'Yeah! And that's not all.'

'What, you mean the other thing? The sex thing?'

'Yeah. The sex thing. I promised Eddie I'd quit smoking and I've promised myself to stop doing that. I can't carry on like that. It's not healthy, you know! Listen, Jimmy, is Eddie there?'

'What? Oh, yeah. Well, no. He's in the darkroom. Working. Said not to disturb him. Looks like he'll be at it all night. You on your own? Hey, you shouldn't be on your own at night, you know. Just because you've decided to be good doesn't mean that your nutter has. I'll come over.'

'Still want to look after me, do you?'

'Yeah. Something like that. Listen, I'll come over and you can tell me all about the new you, all right? God. You've really stopped? How does it feel? How do you feel?'

I laughed and carried the telephone across the room so that I could stand in a patch of peach sunlight by the window. My best white dress wafted behind me as I moved forward. Expensive, wispy underwear fluttered around my breasts and waist and bottom and the soft, air-filled soles of my new shoes added further to the sensation of walking on clouds. How did I feel? I felt wonderful. I just felt wonderful.

Well, it had been a wonderful day. That morning, I'd floated in a hazy daze around the fluorescent aisles of the local supermarket, glowing with peace and purity in my new mood and my white dress, just like the angel that Eddie had always thought I was. I'd swung my basket gaily. I'd hummed softly. I'd selected only happy, good foods from the shelves, making salad bowls and orange lentils and fat yoghurt pots into the icons of this wholesome new religion of mine. At one point, a pretty young man by the peaches had tried to catch my eye, but don't worry, there was no need to worry, I would not smile or look at him. Safe and smug behind a row of amusing bananas, I had smiled at myself instead, and then moved softly away to caress the vegetables, to bless the dead fish.

The journey home had been a similarly uplifting experience, the pavements seeming to bear me along as easily as conveyor belts, requiring me to do nothing but relax and smile and go with the flow. I'd said Hello to some people I didn't know; to a nice old lady with a nice dog, and then to a poor old lady who couldn't afford a pet and had to make do with a tartan trolley-bag instead. Hello, hello! At some point, I'd almost stood in some dog shit, but that had been OK. I'd liked the dog shit today and the mischievous way it had hidden behind a clump of litter on the pathway, its smiley turds bending over themselves with mirth at the prospect of their practical joke. That was cute. That was good. Everything was suddenly good. If someone had been watching me right then, they'd have seen me smiling benignly at every stranger who passed by, then chuckling brightly at the warm sky, as if imagining that the filthy breeze in my face was the very breath of heaven itself.

As I'd turned onto the top of my street, I had glanced happily over at the church notice-board for some orange words of wisdom and encouragement. I'd expected it to say SAVE YOURSELF, as it had for the past few weeks. I had badly wanted it to say that, so that I could cheerfully reply, Thanks, that's just what I intend to do! Only, someone had gone and changed that poster, hadn't they? Now there was just some message about Armageddon, printed small, black on white, not very cheerful at all. Never mind, I'd told myself brightly, defiantly. It's just a poster. It's nothing. It's all right.

'Hello,' said Jimmy when I opened the door. He was standing on my outside mat, pretty as a present, waiting to be taken in.

'Tea? Flowers?' I said in the kitchen, lifting the kettle

with one hand and pointing at the blooms under his arm with the other.

'Yeah. Ta. Tea. Yes. Flowers.'

'Passed the cemetery on the way, did we?'

'What? Ha. Funny. No. I bought them. Great, aren't they? Look.'

I turned and I looked and I saw that they were red. Really red. Really, really red-red. So red that you could smell the red. Poppy-red, I thought, breathing in the heady pigment as Jimmy brought the vivid bunch closer to my face. No, actually they were carnations, but they were the exact colour of poppies and right then, as Jimmy stepped closer and whispered, For you, I got them for you, I discovered that they were quite capable of the same, intoxicating effect.

The kettle whistled and the shrill sound was like smelling salts, bringing me sharply to my senses. I said a polite Thank you. I said, You shouldn't have. I said, You go through while I put these in water, and then I shoved Jimmy's druggy flowers into a dirty vase, a dark corner.

When I went into the living-room, I was relieved to find Jimmy sprawling comfortably in the chair, with no sign of the nervous tension that I'd felt a moment ago. He made a joke. I made a joke. We chuckled and chatted and opened some wine and then the evening started to fly by.

Since our confession session a few months earlier, Jimmy and I always seemed to find plenty to talk about. There were fewer issues to dodge. Less subjects to steer away from. Knowing what we already knew about each other meant that we could ease off those controls that usually stalled our conversations with people, and let the words just flow and flow. We talked about Fay. About Martin. About violence and love and hate and about this, that and the other. The hours passed like ignored motorway signs. The words and the wine just flowed and flowed and flowed.

'Do you think I'm handsome?' he asked at some point.

'What?'

'Am I handsome? Me. Am I handsome?'

'Well, yeah. Of course you are. Yes. Everybody thinks so.'

'I know. But do you?'

'Yes. Don't be daft. Yes.'

'I got the looks, didn't I?'

'What?'

'Out of Eddie and me, I got the looks.'

'Yes.'

'Do you think he's jealous of that?'

'I don't know. I suppose so.'

'No. You're wrong. He isn't. Do you know why not? Because he got everything else.'

Jimmy sighed deeply and then rested his head back against the chair and closed his eyes. Ha! He knows he's handsome, I thought suddenly, watching the perfect angles of his tilted features. Of course he knows he's handsome. Of course he does. Of course he is. Look, look; he really is.

The lamp was tumbling a wash of yellow light down the left side of his face. I wondered if he could feel it, splashing over the fine cheek-bone, dripping into the hollow beneath and then running out along the strong chin. Light can touch you. A gaze can touch you. I wondered if he could feel me as my attention slid over him like a finger.

'Ouch! Ow! My finger!'

My finger. I'd burned my finger. My finger was burned. I'd been stubbing out a cigarette, but hadn't been concentrating properly. What was I doing? What was I doing with a cigarette? How had that happened?

'You've burned your finger,' Jimmy said.

133

'Yes,' I said.

'Give it here.'

He leaned over and blew softly on the hot spot; let out a cool, cool breath that made my whole hand, arm, body tingle.

'OK?'

'Yeah.'

'Shall I get some ice?'

'No.'

'OK?'

'Yes. Thanks.'

He kissed my hand softly, laid it gently onto my knee, then went back to his chair. I froze in my seat, feeling strange, feeling drunk and dizzy and quite weak as I looked miserably down at the place where the cigarette had stamped its small red 'O' onto my white skin, as if to clearly brand me a smoker and a breaker of promises.

After that, I couldn't seem to keep my eyes away from Jimmy. I'd call them off him, bring them obediently to heel, only to find them bounding like puppies across the room towards him again a few moments later. Well, he wanted me to stare at him, I know he did; sitting there like that, pulling at me without even looking at me, breathing and sighing enchantingly, surrounded in blue cigarette smoke that swirled into a fattening mass above his head, like a genie with wishes to grant. He was just so good at being looked at, that was the thing. He didn't pose. He didn't have to pose, I realized now; every casual movement of his face and body just made its own new beautiful picture. My artist's gaze swept thick brushes over his rich black hair. I traced his sharp profile with my soft blue pencil eyes. Now Jimmy looked across at me suddenly and looked suddenly delighted as he caught me sizing up the full figure of him, marking key lines in vital places, as if preparing for a nude.

'I'm terrible,' I said miserably, lighting another cigarette.

'Me too.'

'No. I'm more terrible.'

'No. You're all right. Fine. Everybody thinks so. Everybody loves you.'

'Ha. I don't think so. Not really. Not much.'

'Even I do.'

'Ha. Oh yeah? But how much?'

Now Jimmy turned to me slowly, carefully. His perfect lip-bow braced, then stretched, then sent over to me a gliding smile that pierced my dress, vest, skin, bones, heart.

'More than I love Eddie,' he said.

Well, I asked him to go. I gave Jimmy back his cigarettes and his flowers and I asked him to go. I'm still not sure how I managed it. It wasn't easy. I trembled with emptiness the moment he'd left and, several times in several seconds, I felt myself right on the verge of yanking my front door open and running down the road after him shouting, Come back, I didn't mean it, you can have me, you can have me! No. I mustn't do that. I knew that I mustn't do that. I'd done so many bad things thoughtlessly, and needed time to consider this one.

Over the next few days, I avoided Jimmy. It was my only plan: to not answer the phone, to shop in shops where he never shopped, to stay indoors as much as I could, hoping that his powerful pull might not find its grip so easily if I were a mile away, with my windows closed and several layers of silence wrapped around me.

I'd thought that I would be all right, alone in my flat like that. But I was not alone in my flat; my feelings had not left with him. They were still here and they were growing; growing fast, growing big, growing out of my body and into the world, claiming rooms as they went. At night, I would sweat my dilemma into the sheets, and soon my bed belonged to him. I gazed once into the bathroom mirror and said, Do you love him? and after that, every time I glanced at it, I felt the glass tighten and brace, awaiting a reply. In the living-room I sat and tried to suck mellow advice from a hundred cigarettes, but all I got was smelly and sore and even more woozy-headed than before.

Jimmy, Jimmy. I missed Jimmy. My chair, cushions, walls, doorstep missed Jimmy. Soon, I began to dread him calling round unexpectedly, for fear that he would walk in and immediately see what had happened here; sure that, at the first sight of him, my home would open like arms or legs, to welcome him warmly into the hole that he had made.

Around me, the weather and the city drooped. It was still early August, but the month was already tiring of itself, its limp white sky draping low overhead, saggy as an old sheet. Every now and then, there'd be a break in the tough fabric, a flash of silky sea-blue, but this was only a tease; a reminder that someone somewhere was having a wonderful summer. Well, it's not her or him, I thought, looking around at the people who looked like me, parading along the dry roads, dressed in pollution, as if we thought that it was smart, as if we liked it that way. I stayed indoors as much as I could, away from that fogged, clogged street air. I wished it was winter. I needed clarity now, and a cool, cool head, but that heat just kept pressing in closer and closer around me, as if trying to listen in on my thoughts.

One night, when I knew that Jimmy would be alone in the flat, I had a powerful urge to telephone him, to call him to me. I'd had a fairly good day up until then, had managed to think of him only a dozen or so times since breakfast, and now I'd settled into the evening with a drink and a magazine and the feeling that everything would be all right. I felt fine. My mood was friendly and tame; but my moods are not to be trusted. Half an hour later, I became suddenly desolate. My personality had turned on me like a dog, and there I was suddenly, with the telephone receiver growling in my hand and numbers and possibilities yapping wildly around in my head.

Stop it. Stop that. Stop, stop, stop.

I paced the room. Made coffee. Switched the TV off, then on, then off. Did what I could, see, but nothing seemed to work; I'd lose concentration for a moment, then turn around to find my arm reaching out once again for the telephone. Well, I hated that arm. I cursed that arm. And then I did the only thing that was left for me to do; I took a small penknife from the desk and I bled that arm until it was weakened and I was strengthened and I could be sure that neither of us would be telephoning anyone that night.

I tried to paint.

Yes, I thought one day, as I settled in the coolest corner of my bedroom, surveying my tidy painting equipment. Yes. This is what I'll do now, this is how I will explain it to myself. My heart rose. I felt, as I always did in the moment before I began, that there were no problems here, only solutions. Everything that I could ever need to see or say was here before me, fragmented into twenty-odd tubes, like so many brightly coloured puzzle pieces, and I was sure that if only I could assemble them correctly, then everything would make sense, everything would fit.

The point at which my paintings went wrong differed each time. Today it took just over five hours. As the afternoon ended, I sighed over my picture. Yellow. This time the mess was a yellow mess; the colour of old bruises, of nicotine stains, of jealousy, cowardice and sickness.

Tidying my paints, I felt each silvery tube like a dead weight in my hands, as I laid them out on the table, overlapping here and there like market fish. Slowly, I scraped and mopped the dirty paint from the glass. Sadly, I set about dismantling the wasted canvas, peeling the material like infected skin from the stretcher's wooden bones.

'How's my painter?' Eddie asked brightly that evening, wiping a smudge of oil from my forehead.

'I'm not a painter,' I replied.

'Oh, OK.'

'Well, I'm not.'

'OK. OK.'

Well, I wasn't, and this was why not: because I had no paintings. None. I painted every week, but I didn't have a single picture to show for it, other than the one that I was working on or destroying at the time.

Days passed and the weather did not improve.

Indoors, the air was stale and bored, but showed no interest in the windows that I opened for it; just sat around my room in lumps, as if waiting to be carried out. On the streets, the air was more active, but only in a desperate, thirsting sort of a way; rushing up like a crowd of beggars the moment it saw you, taking your sweat whether you could spare it or not.

Caroline came up to my flat one evening and we lounged around the warm lounge.

'We should go out, I suppose,' I said, but I didn't really mean it.

'Too hot.'

'Yes.'

'We could find a cool pub.'

'Too tired.'

'Yes.'

'Maybe I'll make some coffee,' I suggested, and this time Caroline was too hot and tired to argue.

I brought the drinks and some more silence into the room.

'I don't see David any more,' Caroline said loudly, abruptly.

'David? Oh, David, yeah. I don't see Jimmy.'

'Jimmy!' she muttered, squashing her features then sipping heavily on her drink, as if to take a bad taste away. 'Jimmy. I never liked Jimmy.'

'You liked David, though.'

'Yes. He was very bright.'

'Bright.'

'Yes. And nice. Courteous.'

'And?'

'And friendly. Warm. Attentive.'

'*And?*'

Caroline sipped some more on her coffee, pulled another face.

'And this is a bit strong. And he's homosexual.'

I leaned back in surprise. But I shouldn't have been surprised. I should have known that this attentive young man of Caroline's would, on some important level, be deeply disinterested in her. It was always that way with Caroline. It was the way she seemed to like it.

'Oh,' I said quietly. 'I'm sorry.'

'It's all right,' she told me calmly. 'It's drinkable.'

We laughed, and then we stopped laughing; fell listlessly back into the heat and our oppressive thoughts.

'It's probably for the best,' one of us said at one point.

'Yes. It's probably for the best,' the other agreed, and then we did not speak again for a long time. There was nothing to say. Nothing to do but sigh and droop and

139

sweatily contemplate the things we couldn't have, the things that we wanted quite in spite of ourselves.

I saw Jimmy by accident one day.

He was strolling handsomely up the morning high street and the sudden sight of him was like a kick to the head, bringing me to my senses, or knocking the last of them out of me.

I stood shock-still in the middle of the pavement, staring after him. This is how I felt: my heart pummelled my ribs; clenched breath made hard fists in my lungs; my teeth wanted to bite and my lips wanted to suck until they tasted blood. You'd have thought that a person with such feelings would have been thinking of murder rather than love, and perhaps it is so; whatever it takes to stop that violence in the body once and for all.

That night, I was not well. I did not feel well and I did not look well.

Eddie sat beside me and drew me very close, petting and caressing me, trying with whispering words and fingers to reach the heart of my unease. He didn't know what the problem was, but he believed that he could help; really thought that his huge, stroking hands had within them all the healing that I could ever need.

Well, he was wrong. And I was wrong too. I'd thought that any amount of trouble and secrets could be contained for any amount of time in the dark recesses of the mind, but now I knew that this wasn't true. Slowly, they leak out. Slowly, they drip into the bloodstream and get swept around to every part. Trouble gathering, vibrating, in trembling hands. Trouble rippling up in nervous rashes, or clumping like stinging nettles in the chest. Trouble in the system, trouble in the body. My heart hurt. It just hurt.

'We're going away,' said Eddie suddenly.

'What?'

140

'You and me. We're going away for a little holiday.'

'What?

'You can pick where, I don't care. I just think we should go. I think it'll help.'

'Help what?'

'Oh yeah. I forgot. You're fine.'

'Well, I am fine.'

'Well, I'm not. I need a break. We could go to the countryside. Or to the seaside. Come on. You're so funny and moody at the moment. It's terrible here, but it'll be better there. It will. Come on. Come on. What do you say?'

I got up silently and moved away; went over to clutch at the sturdy whiskey bottle in my cabinet, upset by the mention of mood swings, disorientated by this talk of here and there, when all I really felt was nothing and nowhere. Lost. Amongst my own familiar things and life, I just felt suddenly lost. That compass in my heart which always led me back to Eddie could not seem to settle any more; was caught between two opposite points, spinning, spinning.

'I don't know,' I said. 'I don't know.'

'I do,' Eddie said, standing up too, standing across the room from me, beaming and solid as a lighthouse. 'We're going, and that's that.'

'But what—'

'We'll go tomorrow.'

'But there's—'

'We'll go for three days and three nights. Just say yes.'

'I know, but there's so—'

'Yes. YES.'

I scowled at him and poured another drink. It was a small word, but a big thing to ask. I didn't want to go away. I had stuff to do. You know. Stuff. People and things to think about. You know. I felt the whiskey as cool and smooth as lies in my throat, watched a row of excuses line themselves up in my head for inspection.

'Well,' said Eddie as I paused. 'That's that, then.'

His face fell. His shoulders fell. His voice fell too; fell down and down until it was as deep and hollow as a cave.

'That's that. I've done all I can do. Look at me. What else can I do?'

I looked at Eddie. Then I looked again. He looked weary and changed.

It was the end of the week. It had been a long, rough week and now I could see that it had left its mark. Three deep frown scars on his forehead, two more dark cuts slitting down from each corner of his tight mouth and one pair of painful black eye shadows; these were the marks that those seven days had left on him.

'I suppose we could go for a day or two,' I said quietly.

'Three.'

'Can we go to the seaside?'

'Yes.'

'Can we go by coach?'

'Yes.'

'And we don't have to take Burroughs?'

'No.'

'OK then. OK. We'll go.'

'OK,' said Eddie firmly. 'Good. That's good.'

As we headed northwards the next morning, Eddie and I both began to feel happier, lighter. I don't know how it happened, but there it was; every mile, lighter and lighter, just as if gravity or some other helpful force were holding all our troubles back down there in the south of the country, behind us, beneath us.

We'd told no-one where we were going. Just think, not even the best of friends or enemies will be able to find us this weekend, I told myself. I liked that thought very much, and told it to myself again. No-one would contact me and I would contact no-one. Because I would have nothing to say. I wasn't here to worry or to wonder or to make impossible decisions. All that uncertainty; that was what we'd left behind us that morning. I'd waved it goodbye myself, from the back of the coach, as we'd begun pulling out of London's grey; spluttering through the bleary smog, heading for a place where everything would be blacker and whiter and bluer and yellower and clearer. We were just here for a little break, that's all. Lives on hold as we took a little week-end break from ourselves, with our lover along just for company, because after all, we had always liked each other.

Eddie felt the same way. He didn't mention our troubles once. Commented on the fat cows in a passing field or the colour of the sky, but not the previous week's shapeless silences or my pink eyes from another sleepless night.

By Leicester, we were properly talking again. Remembering past holidays and happy times; reliving ourselves, bringing ourselves back to life. By Grantham, we were holding hands. By Lincoln, we were kissing, and by the time we arrived at our destination all I could think about was Eddie and the weekend ahead and that magnificent sea, opening out in front of us like possibilities.

We decided not to stay out late on our first night there, because I was scared of our friendly seaside landlady.

She didn't like us much. When we first called in to enquire after a room, she gave us a terrible, filthy look. I don't know why. Perhaps she thinks I'm underage, I wondered, as her matronly eyes tutted over my loose pinafore dress and my two girlish plaits. I suppose I did not look my age. Sea spray and Eddie's lips had removed the last of my tired, adult expression and make-up. The sunshine had drawn out more freckles. *Everything* seemed to make me giggle and now I was suddenly aware that I really did not look or feel my age.

'I'll see what we have,' the landlady said, through lips squinty from years of disapproval. 'One room, was it?'

'Yes,' replied my shameless lover/teacher/Uncle Eddie, with me standing shyly behind him, scuffing my seaside sandal against the shag pile.

'Double bed, was it?'

'Yes.'

'And just for the weekend?'

'That's right.'

I blushed childishly. Eddie grinned. The landlady glowered. I had never seen a person glower before, but she did; she just glowered and glowered like a real pro. This impressed me so much that I wanted to be on her side, and I suddenly wished she would come out and ask me my age so that I could say, No, silly, I'm much, much, more old and worn than I look.

'Double bed,' she repeated next. 'Double bed. Well, I'll check, but I'm not sure what we have left.'

This obsession with the bed. Maybe it wasn't my age that bothered her after all, I considered now. Maybe it was young, unmarried, uninhibited couples in general that upset her. That would explain the dirty looks; she was thinking of foul midnight noises, impure intentions, sullied standards and soiled sheets. Sex. Sex! You're going to have sex, aren't you? she seemed to be accusing us as she studied her book one more time, but again she didn't say anything out loud, which was good, because this I couldn't really deny.

'Business that good, then?' Eddie asked innocently, craftily.

'Mmmm,' the landlady replied unhappily. 'Well, we might have something.'

I giggled. Eddie paid our money and took our keys.

We left our hostess standing there at the Formica hallway table, opening and closing her books and furiously, rhythmically, jangling her own bunch of keys, as if performing some magic, landlady ritual for warding off passing carnal criminalities.

The next day, the early sunshine leapt through the window and straight into bed beside us. Crawled gently over our bare shoulders. Stroked our sleepy eyelids until they opened.

We got up. We went down to breakfast. We jogged across to the beach. We began to have a wonderful time.

A local DJ on a beach radio did his best to spoil things later that morning, by announcing that a small incendiary device had been found in the town, but we didn't let him. We went for a swim, let the water in our ears rush out his tinny voice and mean news. We didn't need to hear it, I decided, as the hot light poured down on us like good fortune. Nothing will go wrong, not this weekend; nothing is going wrong, despite what the radios and the TVs and the papers say. What do they know? Nothing, so we will ignore them, we'll simply ignore their bad news, that's what we'll do; let it gather for us back home if it must, like letters in the hallway.

'This holiday was a good idea,' I said, as we strolled through the town that afternoon.

And this place had been a perfect choice.

I love it here, I thought. I love this cheap hats and sunglasses stuff. That salty smell of suntan oil and public lavatories and fast food and hot dog shit. The pink kids always at it with the whooping or whining, stuffed full of pleasures, and already greedy for more. I loved the fat Fish 'n' Chips man by the beach. I loved the way he winked and said, There you go then, can't get that abroad then, eh? to every customer he served; as if imagining that it was only his bits of fried food that had kept these holiday-makers away from the

Seychelles this year. I loved the voices, muffled in sunshine. I loved the cotton clothes and the ripped nylon clouds. I loved the plumpness of people; the shorts and the vests and the bellies and the unself-consciousness. And the laughter. I loved the laughter. There was so much laughter here, loads and loads and loads of it, as if the coaches in the car parks had been specially hired to bus it in for the week.

There was laughter and laughter and fatty, delicious food and a grandad taking photos of grandma's elbow and someone else's wife and water polo in the sea with a fluorescent football and rounders on the beach with everyone welcome. And through it all, uplifting it all, was that spirit of determined cheerfulness that is exuded by people who only have the one holiday per year and can't afford to let the weather or the terrorists or the sulks spoil it. The mood of these people, like the town itself, ran on an utterly self-generated gaiety. Look, see? Look at the indoor pool, with its wave machine and its golden sand and blue-sky wall mural. Look at the bright electric evening lights which run all along the promenade and will follow you up and down through wind and rain and starless nights, keeping your spirits strung high and twinkling.

This was my kind of seaside. My dad's kind of seaside, too, I realized suddenly. He used to like it here. I could see him now, dodging into that next betting-shop to waste his holiday spending money on a horse called Sandcastle or Seashore or Sunburn. He could be here. I felt close to him here. My dad; now that's something that you couldn't get abroad.

I spotted my dad on the street one day, while I was on the way to meet Eddie in a town-centre café.

I had been strolling quite happily up a pretty side road at the time, admiring the long rows of pastel houses that lined it: sweet, sweet houses, with frosted doors and cake-icing fronts. The day and the street and my mood were lemon and pink and soft. And then I saw him: my dad; big, muscular and black-haired and appearing in the sugared scene like a spider dropping into a nursery rhyme.

Oh, I knew it wasn't really him. I even said these words quietly to myself, but the message didn't circulate to the rest of my body quite quickly enough to stop it turning and following him out to the sea front and across to the pier.

The resemblance was uncanny. It's just uncanny, I thought, as the dark man in the white shirt whistled brightly and led his little family and me along the prom. One of his children laughed as he affectionately took their neck in the crook of his tattooed arm. Another tugged jealously at his other rolled-up sleeve, and was rewarded by a high swing that left her wobblingly proud up on the father's brawny shoulders. Me, well, I just watched, feeling hypnotized, feeling good, feeling that nothing in the world could stop me from following these people for ever; and maybe nothing could, except for the one thing that finally did.

The man looked around. The man looked at me. He looked at and past and through me without a single flicker of recognition or love, and then what could my heart do but stop? I pulled up on the spot and didn't move again for some time; just stood there, frozen in all that heat, watching the family walk away and disappear into a crowd without even noticing that they'd lost me.

I turned back when I couldn't see or imagine them clearly any more. I said, Silly! What are you doing? Silly! and then I headed up towards the high street and drifted dreamily off in search of Eddie, or someone.

'All right?' said Eddie now.

'What?'

'Are you all right?'

I'd been strange when he'd found me, loitering outside the café, pale but not at all hungry. What was wrong? Was I all right?

'Yes. I'm fine. Fine. This is nice.'

I turned onto my tummy and wriggled a little more tightly into the perfect fit of the sand. The sand was nice. I loved the sand. It had the texture of Eddie's stubble as it pressed against my cheek. It smelled of good sex.

'You do look better. You look nice. Peaceful.'

'Yeah. Yeah,' I said, closing my eyes and listening to the sea. Yes. This is what the sea did for me. It made me peaceful. It allowed me peace. It fretted, so I didn't have to. Waves, like thoughts of mine, one sweeping over the other, rushing forward like a good idea and then faltering back into a mass of frothy-headedness. Well, there's no point in both of us doing that, I decided, as I listened to the water fretting and turning and churning, working noisily away at some insoluble problem, while the sturdy rocks sat watching by its side, patient as a patient boyfriend. Eddie leaned over and whispered like water in my ear. I sighed deeply and fell deeply asleep.

One day. Two days.

I had a bit of a funny turn on a big wheel on a swooningly hot afternoon. Eddie had to shout for the attendant so that I could get off as the ride was starting and everyone stared and a few people booed.

Eddie took me back down to the sea front and I flopped heavily to the beach, feeling cowardly and unpopular.

'You!' he said, throwing grins and sand in my direction. 'You've got to cause trouble wherever you go, haven't you?'

'I'm sorry. I thought I'd be OK with you there.'

148

'I never realized you were that scared of heights.'

'Oh, I'm scared of lots of things, me. You'd be surprised.'

'It's not good to be so scared.'

'No, I know it's not good. I never said it was *good*. It's just the way I am.' My face wrinkled in frustration. My insides ached. I felt suddenly old again. 'Too old to change now,' I said sadly.

Eddie considered this for a moment, then he tugged me roughly to my feet.

'Come on,' he said. 'let's go up to the cliffs.'

As we climbed, I told Eddie quietly and confidentially, 'I thought I saw my dad yesterday.'

Silence, said Eddie silently, because he wasn't there; he'd left my side to rush up to the blustery edge of the high cliff.

'Be careful!' I called out. 'Come back! Come back over here, please!'

'No!' he laughed, waving wildly in the devilish wind. 'You come here.'

'No!'

Eddie laughed some more and turned to look out to sea and I thought that the lack of oxygen must be going to his head, because then he waved again and took another step closer to the edge.

'PLEASE COME BACK!'

'No. Come and get me. Come on!'

He was swaying in the wind. I'm sure he was swaying in the wind. I was very frightened, and would have cried if I'd thought it would help, but he wouldn't have been able to distinguish the real tears from the salt-wind ones from this distance, and anyway, he seemed quite merciless now in his determination to cure this fear.

'PLEASE!'

'NO!'

'PLEASE!'

149

'NO!'

I held my breath as he moved further and further forward, wondering how far he'd go to make his point.

His strong arm came around my shoulder as I shuffled towards the edge and him.

'Look down.'

'Nope. No way.'

'Go on. Look down.'

I lowered my head, but that didn't fool Eddie.

'Open your eyes. We're not moving until you do.'

'OK, OK.'

'There,' he said. 'See? That's all right, isn't it?'

'I suppose so,' I replied, gazing in horror at the rabid surf that frothed out from the jagged, dog-tooth rocks below.

'It's not as bad as you imagine, is it?'

'No. I suppose not,' I said, imagining myself splashed on the bit of beach beneath. Me. Down there, being licked at, mopped up by the sea. Me: a pink and white mess oozing out from a green gingham dress, like a dropped picnic.

'It's beautiful,' Eddie sighed, enjoying himself now, savouring the height and the clouds, loving every minute of floating in the sky with his Angel by his side. 'Just watch the sea. That's it.'

I watched the sea, watched the tide sucking hard on those rock-teeth, working away at the gaps as if to dislodge some piece of seaweed or driftwood or person that had caught there. Suck, suck, drag, drag, pull, pull, it went, and now I began to feel that pull extending up towards me; felt it take my balance as it climbed the rock-face and then my ankles, legs, torso.

I tried to back away from the panic now, but Eddie gripped me firmly and held me at its edge. Now his embrace made me want to bite and scream. Now I wasn't in a boyfriend's arms but an enemy's clutches;

not flying hand in hand across the sky with a lover, but being dangled by a madman from a tower-block window.

'It's all right,' said Eddie quietly, his voice very still as the shudders of panic shook me.

'Let me go! Get off. Get off!'

'Everything's all right. Trust me.'

'Stop it! No. Get off! Please! Get off!'

'I won't let anything happen to you. Don't you know that? Don't be scared, Angel. Listen to me. Don't be scared.'

He held me a little tighter as he whispered this.

When we'd settled on a grass bank a safe distance from the blustery edge and I had finally begun to get my breath back, I turned to Eddie and suddenly said, 'So it was quite a shock. You know. Yesterday. Seeing my dad on the prom like that. It shook me up, I can tell you. It was just so uncanny.'

'You mean, you saw a man who looked like your dad.'

'What? Yeah. That's what I said.'

'That's not what you said.'

'That's what I meant. You know what I meant!' I spat, sending Eddie a look of intense irritation and indignation. 'What, so you think I'm going barmy now, do you? You think I'm seeing ghosts now?'

My dad had never appeared to me as a ghost. Not a real one. I knew that it was just my imagination which kept summoning him and that, these days, he existed only in my head. Still, during the last few months, even his imaginary presence had been very strong. Strong enough that I could almost see the dent in the settee cushions as he sat beside me for a ciggie and a chat. Strong enough that, when considering my actions and excuses in the world, I had frequently to remind myself to think in terms of I, and not the more comforting We.

My dad had an affair.

He was fifty at the time and the girl he became involved with was nineteen. Looking back, I can see that he had probably had dozens of flings during his thirty-year marriage, but the affairs and the numbers had meant nothing until now, until this girl, who he thought was *the one*. He loved her, you see. He thought that he loved her, that was the thing, that's what caused all the trouble.

Love and guilt and indecision made him sick all that summer. He looked tired, old, slow and his spirits seemed sluggish and low, which was strange because his regular visits to the doctor showed that his blood pressure was at an all-time high. Finally, he collapsed after a bit of pale lawnmowing and then confessed it all as he came round on the settee afterwards, with our mum by his side, gently mopping his head and softly assuring him that everything would be all right.

The next thing she said was, Get out of this house! Said it loudly and sincerely. To her surprise, he went, and quietly too. To no-one's surprise, the young girl soon decided that she did not really want someone else's old man, and went back to her own husband, and then my father found himself nowhere and with nothing.

He slept in his car for a while, and then in a scruffy Bed and Breakfast, and then on the floor at his sister's flat. And then, finally, he found himself a home again. His new home was an old council-flat. A damp and dirty council-flat. On the unpopular side of a sprawling high-rise estate. At the rough end of town.

I went up to visit.

I called on my mum first. She was changeable and talkative, swinging wildly from, Sod him, sod him, sod him! to Why oh why oh why did he do it? and then the whole story all over again, to herself and anyone else who would listen. Extraordinary things make extraordinary shapes, and I suppose that repetition helps to wear down some of the corners that must be worn down if these things are ever to fit into an ordinary life. What did the iron and the cooker have to do with the fact that her entire being had been dismantled, rearranged? Nothing, absolutely nothing, and so she told her story while she was ironing and while she was cooking, in the hope that this might bring the two worlds together.

She also took the tale all over the house, into every room.

'I can't believe it, I just can't believe it, not after everything I've been through with him!' she said in the bathroom, hallway, bedroom, telling the walls all about it, as if it were very important that not a corner of her home should remain as ignorant and stupid as she had been.

The next day, it rained heavily as I got on a bus and headed towards the bleak side of town, towards my dad.

What did I find when I got there? What can I tell you about his flat? Well, I can tell you that there was a flowery purple sofa, a striped green armchair, a brown Paisley carpet and swirling orange curtains; a noisy assortment of second-hand colours and boggling patterns that hurt my eyes and my heart. I saw thin, sickly cushions. A feeble table with a poorly leg. An unlovable landscape picture in a damaged plastic frame. I saw my father standing in the middle of all this, smoking, fidgeting, and not looking too well himself.

'So what do you think of it, lass?'

I thought that it was unbearably sad. The place had the jostling, desperate feel of a home put together in a terrible hurry, and by someone in no position to be choosy, and seemed to so vividly illustrate the vulgar and shabby tale behind itself that I had to light a cigarette to cover a wince.

'What do you think?'

My dad smoothed a curtain fold nervously.

'C'mon. It's all right, isn't it?' he added, more quietly, starting to look around his home again and to re-evaluate the familiar in the new light from my sad eyes.

I turned away to an ashtray, took a deep breath and then I looked again. This time I saw things differently. Now I noticed the gleam that had been rubbed up on every ugly surface and how the carpet was just as spotless as a stained, spotted carpet could be. I noticed in the air the scent of furniture polish and cheap scouring powder and of working hard to make the best of things. I noticed how fresh the daffodils were, and realized that he must have gone out to buy them especially that morning. I imagined him carrying them carefully home in his big fist, then rolling up his sleeves and cleaning, cleaning, cleaning for hours and hours and hours, before finally sitting down to have a ciggie and wait for me to arrive; maybe jumping up every now and then to remove some small smear or to adjust some ornament, so that he would make a good impression, so that I would come in and say,

'It's lovely, Dad.'

'Aye?' He looked shy, pleased. 'Aye, it's not bad, is it? I'm doing all right, see?'

It seemed very still and quiet in that strange flat that evening, despite the two of us doing our best to chat cheerfully, and despite the grazing sounds of scrapping kids and drunks and dogs outside. There was some mad laughter. Bottles being smashed. Anger, singing, echoes. Beyond the window, the air was synthetic orange from the many street lights that stayed on all night, as if the people around here could not be trusted with proper darkness.

'Is it always like this?' I asked, flinching at a scream that seemed to bother no-one and mean nothing.

'Aye. You get to see it all around here. Prostitution. Drugs. All that. Gangsters. Jumpers. Oh aye. Someone went off this row just last month.'

'No!' I said, and meant it, but my dad insisted on telling me all about it anyway.

A middle-aged man had been waiting for the lift at the end of the landing. There were two lifts situated here, but neither came, and soon a small group of people had gathered around the first man. Now he pressed the button and swore very hard. Still the lift didn't come, so he stepped forward and pressed and swore again. Again nothing happened, and now the group began to notice the man becoming extremely agitated. A few moments after this, he turned towards the stairs and, with one short yell of frustration, hurdled a railing and flew down the outside of the flats, speeding through a few hundred feet of space, wheeling his arms and legs madly in mid-air, as if to make himself go faster.

The lift still did not come, but an ambulance did.

Witnesses reported that the man had landed face down, his body embedded into the patch of grassy earth below, his arms stretched wide, hugging the ground very tight.

He was always a funny bloke, his neighbours would later tell the local newspaper and each other. He was from the country, they said. Welsh or Irish, they said. Told us he were a farmer; always going on about trees and fields and potatoes and that. Wanted a garden, but the council wouldn't move him, no way, see, no way. Aye, it's a sad business, it is, but you know he always were a funny fella, always complaining and that.

I listened to this story very quietly and wondered to myself if the man had really wanted to die, or if he'd just got sick of waiting for those lifts that wouldn't come. I suppose it didn't matter either way. It had all come down to the same thing in the end. An overwhelming desire is an overwhelming desire and his, poor man, was to be reunited with the grass and the earth; to get out of these flats.

I was a little pale and chilled by this point, but my dad was warming to his theme now and started telling me how the previous tenants of his flat had been driven out by racist attacks. There was graffiti on the back of his bathroom door, from where the place had been trashed during one such break-in. It had been painted over a few times, but the white gloss was cheap and you could still make out most of the words; like its authors, that hard, cellulose spray-writing just seemed to keep on coming back no matter what you did. I sat on the toilet and read, Nigger bastards, don't sleep, black cunts, die, die, we are coming for you.

I was not surprised by any of this. This was a bad area, notorious. When I was a kid, I'd had dreams about this place, nightmares after we'd driven past here once, close enough to see the pale faces at the windows, the ten-foot-high swear-words on the community-centre wall, the gangs of youths kicking about in the play-ground.

Rough. It was rough. In a city full of high-rise, complex mistakes, this one towered grimly above them all, scaled entirely new heights of disastrous social planning. Those bleak blocks loomed over that friendly city like a warning; stood shoulder to shoulder on a high hill, where everyone could see them and the dark shadow that they cast. You could see them when you took your kids to the park. You could see them when you went shopping in the town centre with your partner. You couldn't help but notice that grey, grim structure and its grey, grim reminder of where you could end up if the system or your loved ones failed you, or if you failed them.

I broke off from my remembering at this point. I let

go of Eddie's hand, wrapped my arms around myself and shivered.

'The wind's getting up,' I said.

'Carry on with your story,' Eddie said.

'No. Let's go back. Come on, you've done what you wanted. I'm not scared of cliff-heights any more. See?'

I stood up and peered over the edge without fainting or vomiting or falling or jumping.

'Sit down. Talk to me for a few more minutes, eh?' Eddie asked. 'I like it when you talk like this.'

'No,' I told him firmly. 'We'll go. Let's go. Come on. I've done well for today.'

Another day and night passed. Another morning came. We woke up horny and hungry; had sex and then breakfast.

In the dining-room, the landlady frowned at our lateness and our untidy clothes and hair. She herself had dressed as if to attend an evening function as guest of honour, rather than to waitress bacon and eggs to a dozen dishevelled holiday-makers.

Her dress was starched, her hair was stiff and her make-up was so thick that it seemed to make a girdle around her features; a way of holding in the face's real feelings and form. Only occasionally, as she stood in the corner waiting for her guests to finish feeding, did a genuine expression manage to bulge out through those layers of tightly polite beige. I saw a sag of deep distaste around her cheeks as she watched a sausage disappear into a mouth, and then a creasing roll of nausea about her forehead and eyes as tissue-thin bread mopped a mess of tomato on a nearby plate. Eating. She didn't seem to like to see people eating, seemed to find the whole business quite unsavoury. It was a bodily function, and perhaps reminded her of other bodily functions; sex or maybe shitting. For their part, many of the guests waved napkins or hands or chatter

157

in front of their faces as they ate; deferring to her sensitivity and attempting to cover themselves as they did what they had to do.

'You've finished?' the landlady said to Eddie and me, appearing suddenly at our side just as we were beginning to digest our food and mull over our plans for the day ahead.

'You've finished!' she replied impatiently. Her tone was brusque, her words like two strong hands, gripping our collars and marching us out of the room.

'Pardon?'

'Breakfast is over. Nine o'clock. Breakfast is *over*!'

'Oh.'

I stared up at her blankly. It was too early for fury, and I had no other response to rudeness.

Someone coughed messily at the other side of the room and the landlady turned away to loathe them briefly, to squirt distaste towards them like air freshener.

'Well?' she said when she turned back, surprised to find us still sitting there. 'You've eaten, haven't you? You've had enough?'

'Yes,' said Eddie. 'I've had enough.'

He looked up at her slowly. His smile was gone, and I feared that his patience had too. I wasn't used to other people making a scene, and now I folded my hands nervously in my lap and waited for him to tell her off. I waited and waited but then, instead, he told her, 'You look nice today.'

'I beg your pardon?' she said.

I beg your pardon? I thought.

'I was just thinking that you look nice today,' Eddie repeated pleasantly. 'I hope you don't mind me mentioning it. It's your dress, I think. It suits you. It's a lovely pink. Or is it peach?'

'It's pink,' she said suspiciously.

'Yes. Pink. A soft pink. Very nice, don't you think, Angel?'

I looked at her, and then at him, and then back at her. 'Yes.'

He was right. I had to admit it. The colour did suit her. I hadn't noticed it before, but she really looked quite pretty in that colour. I glanced at them both again. Eddie was almost totally sincere. The landlady was unsettled. I was delighted.

This is what Eddie did sometimes. He liked to surprise people. It was the same instinct that made him swear in genteel company, or become ridiculously polite to some profane drunk that he might stumble across on the street. He could really surprise people, unbalance them; or perhaps he was re-balancing them, I considered, as I watched him hanging these soft compliments onto the neglected side of the brassy landlady's personality.

'Not many people can wear it. You've got good skin.'

I thought the mention of flesh was too much myself, but he seemed to get away with it. The landlady was charmed and disarmed; you could see it in the way she lowered her eyes flirtatiously and stumbled submissively away from our table. His silly flattery had penetrated her façade in a way that no ram of smart insults could do. This was Eddie's way. When I wanted to get in somewhere, I rushed up shouting and banging on front doors. Eddie just waited and watched and then climbed in through side windows, smiling.

We had a wonderful morning. A lovely afternoon. In the evening, our last evening, we had a drink, a salty supper and then sex in a bushy sand-dune.

We lay together for a long time afterwards, wearing nothing but beach. The moonlight made silver lamé of the sand, dressing us in night-time glamour. The gulls squeaked all around us, high and low, like an orchestra

159

tuning up. From here, we could see the full curve of the beach, and the tall, grand hotels that stood around it, like a smart audience awaiting the evening show.

'I'm lonely,' I said suddenly.

'What?'

'I'm lonely.'

'Are you?'

'No. I just wanted to see how it sounded. How it felt. I was lonely once. But not now. Not here, with you. If I'd known you then, I wonder what . . .'

'I'd have loved you.'

'Would you? Yes. No, you'd have probably just fucked me like everybody else did. You were just a boy.'

'I'd have loved you if I'd been there,' Eddie repeated. 'I should have been there.'

He turned away from me now, as if ashamed; ran his eyes searchingly over the sea, the sky and horizon, as if looking for a way into my past.

'I'd have saved you,' he said sadly.

'Yeah. Maybe you would. You're an extraordinary man, Eddie.'

Now I reached my arms over and pulled him back to the present.

'Hey, listen. I want to tell you something.'

'What?'

'I just wanted to say . . . I'm glad we came.'

'Yes. Me too.'

'It's good to be here.'

'Yeah.'

'With you.'

'Yeah.'

'It wouldn't be the same with anyone else, you know. I wouldn't want to be here with anyone else, no-one but you.'

I watched Eddie twinkle becomingly, flattered by the soft light and words. I saw the sea rolling in to lay soft

160

little kisses at our feet. I whispered something kind and true into my lovely lover's ear and then I rested my head on his shoulder and gazed up at the black sky and the gold stars it had produced, like rewards for my good behaviour.

That night we slept heavy as anchors in our deep seaside bed. The next morning, we awoke early and carried our bags quietly into the hotel hallway. At the last moment, I suggested that we sign out in the visitors' book, so that if she wanted it the landlady would have written proof that we'd really gone. Now Eddie got a gleam in his eye and wrote something about beds and coming again in the comments column, and then we ran away, giggling like children all the way to the station.

There had been no bombs on the beach that weekend, no trouble of any kind; just me and Eddie making our own mischief. I'd known that we'd be all right, that this town wouldn't hurt us. This town liked us, and looked pleased with its weekend's work as it waved us goodbye; beach curving like a wide, wise smile, sea applauding itself at the edges. Eddie and I returned to London that day intact and in love.

Jimmy took it quite well, really.

There was only one moment when I thought that he might try to kill me or himself. It was when I thanked him for helping me to see how much I loved Eddie, for showing me how to distinguish between what was good and what was bad for me, for being such a perfect metaphor for all the many mistakes that I had made in my life.

'I'm not a metaphor,' he said.

'No. Sorry. Stupid.'

'I don't only exist in relation to you.'

'No.'

'I'm not a fucking *metaphor*.'

Jimmy paced the room, scratched at his hair, wondered what to do next. I wondered too.

I expected him to pull away from me. I expected him to say that it wasn't such a big deal, that he'd already decided it wouldn't work out; to lie and swagger and make out that he didn't care. That's what I expected. That was his style, and I hoped he wouldn't start acting all out of character on me now, just as I was finally starting to get a grip on this story and turn it my way.

9

The summer and my good mood lingered for quite a while. The door to another month opened and this time I stepped into it confidently, finding the dark unknown suddenly lit by the beams of optimism and self-esteem which I somehow now seemed to be projecting several feet in front of me.

I was not available to any man any more, and they all seemed to notice the change. Strangers did not ask me to sleep with them because they did not expect me to sleep with them. Now my white dresses and pale skin appeared to represent to the man in the street an innocence to be smiled at rather than snow to be trampled over. Even the ones who did still insist on pressing their hard eyes hard up against mine soon gave up and shuffled away to try elsewhere, like casual customers approaching an interesting shop and finding it inexplicably closed.

So it was that, when the next hate letter arrived, I received it with serenity and surprise.

'A letter? For me? How nice.'

I opened the envelope slowly, delicately. I wondered whether to have cornflakes for my breakfast, or muesli instead. When I was good and ready, I sipped tea and smiled sweetly and read:

UGLY FILTHY WHORE BITCH DIRTY SCRUBBER
COVERED IN SHIT I AM HERE ARE YOU SCARED

NOW ARE YOU THINKING I'M SORRY PLEASE DON'T DO IT, WELL I WILL DO IT I CAN PICK MY TIME, PICK YOU OFF WHO DO YOU THINK YOU ARE? ARE YOU A STRONG PERSON WELL WE WILL FIND OUT I'VE BEEN MAKING MY PLANS AND THE FAT MAN WON'T HELP YOU NOW. I'M SO CLOSE I CAN SMELL YOU CUNT BITCH AND IT IS A FOUL THING I DON'T KNOW IF I CAN WAIT MUCH LONGER EVEN THOUGH I AM STRONG WELL IT WON'T BE LONG. HAVE YOU HAD A GOOD SUMMER I HOPE SO IT WAS YOUR LAST CHANCE TO HAVE A GOOD SUMMER I WILL TELL YOU SOMETHING NOW I HATE YOU BUT I THINK I WILL MISS YOU I AM SENTIMENTAL YOU ARE GOING TO DIE YOU KNOW IT'S TRUE AND YOU KNOW IT'S RIGHT AND YOU ARE GOING TO DIE.

When I'd finished reading, I sipped some more tea and said, 'Boring. Boring. You're just getting boring now.'

I yawned elaborately, sneered sarcastically and slowly repeated myself, then watched the insults blink uncomprehendingly up from the page. The weedy paper seemed to cringe a little beneath my sudden indifference. The closing line shouted again, YOU ARE GOING TO DIE, YOU ARE GOING TO DIE, as if I must not have heard it properly the first time.

Ha ha. I liked that. I liked that desperation and this disinterest. They had come out well, my yawns and my sneers and I had cheered myself right up; only then I went and let myself right down. On my lap, my fingers were twitching of their own accord. Hidden in the shadow of the letter, they hadn't seen how confident and brave I was and they were going twitch, twitch, twitch, twitch, twitch, and when I looked down at them,

I found that they were counting. Counting months, you see; a quick check to see how long I had left. This was September.

Well, I did not die in September, but Burroughs did. We came home out of a warm day to find him laid out cold as tiles on the kitchen floor.

Oh.

'Burroughs.'

Oh.

'Burroughs!'

On no.

'Burroughs? Burroughs?'

People put a lot of faith in words at times like that; dropping words like anchors in the real world, as shock carries them off to somewhere distant and silent.

'Burroughs! Burroughs? BURROUGHS!'

Eddie let his jacket, bag, keys and newspaper fall to the floor and then he joined them; sank on to all fours beside the dead animal. He petted a lolling head. Squeezed and rubbed and pushed at a limp body. Rifled urgently through the static, dry fur, as if he might yet find some spark of life trapped in its thickness.

'Burroughs. Come on,' Eddie said, stroking the expressionless face.

'Burroughs!' he shouted sternly, pulling the animal into a sitting position, trying to raise some last bit of obedience from his faithful old pet.

'Burroughs,' he said once more as the body crumpled away from him and settled into a strange, untidy heap, and now the word was no longer a request, but a sad address to something so changed that it needed naming all over again.

Eddie pushed me away when I tried to embrace him. I tried harder, but he just pushed harder. I made a third

165

attempt, and this time Eddie did not have to push; he raised his lips to a snarl and let out a long, low sound that was so much like a growl that I immediately backed away from him, tucking my interfering hands behind my back for fear that they might be bitten clean off.

After a while, watching his pain made my eyes hurt and I had to turn away.

I saw an aeroplane appear on the patch of sky beyond the window. From this distance, it looked tiny and dinky, like a toy. It looked as if some kid somewhere had launched it just for fun, just aimed and chucked it across the sky towards some other big kid at the other end of the city; down there, South-West, where the Heathrow gang hang out. The metal body flashed brilliantly in the clear light, twinkling like a pretty silver pendant against the cotton-dress blue. Some plane-cleaner did that, I thought, and silently congratulated them on their work. Now the plane disappeared and the day started to end. The sun was sinking hotly, hand-somely, going out in a blaze. Satisfied yellow flowers on the ledge arched around to say thank you and goodbye. A wasp swooned.

When I turned back, I felt OK again. My sadness for the dead dog was pink and orange and hung around the room in wide, dispersing strips of softness. I still felt emotion but, like the sky, there was no real heat in it any more.

There was a dead animal in the middle of the kitchen, but apart from that, everything seemed normal. The table was no more happy or unhappy than it had been before. The fridge hummed and sighed in the corner, but not out of sympathy, and the cooker, cupboards, jugs and rugs were all exactly as and where they had been when we'd left them that morning; showed them-selves to be utterly unmoved by the tragedy in their midst.

Well, it's just death, I thought simply. It all seemed so simple now, so much clearer when dressed in animal terms and form. Dog gone. Skin empty. Coat discarded. Bodies like clothes, I thought, as I watched Eddie fussing over the bundle, unfolding its creases, smoothing its lines. Bodies like clothes, growing tatty and old-fashioned in the face of Nature's fickle seasons. Souls like sensibilities; just moving with the times.

I knelt down and tried once more to bring some comfort to the mess of pain before me, but my face and calves soon started to ache from the strain of my sympathetic pose. Not that Eddie wanted me there anyway. He pushed suddenly at me again, trying to elbow me away from this private moment. Trying to keep me away from Burroughs, I realized suddenly, as if he'd imagined this to be the pet's last request as he'd lain listening, head to head, with the animal on the floor.

'I think we should make a move,' I said next, with the last heat and flies of the day settling around us. 'I've left a note for Jimmy. There's nothing we can do here. We'll take Burroughs to the vets, that's what we'll do. Come on, let's go, eh, Eddie? Eddie? Let's go.'

He raised his head slowly and looked at me furiously, as if I'd interrupted an important conversation. There was a prickly dullness in his eyes. There was a stiff sigh. There was a last whisper into the dog's fur, the sentence curling up and then down at the end like a solemn question. When Eddie finally picked Burroughs up, I saw the animal's long, pink tongue loll loosely out from the side of his slack mouth, becoming animated again for a second or two as they jogged out to the car.

Summer ended quietly. The sunshine petered out and Burroughs' death slipped peacefully from our conversations. Eddie was OK. He seemed to be OK, although his temper had shortened with the days.

'You, you, you,' he sneered at me one evening when I was in the middle of a long monologue about my hard day and thirsty work and dry hands. 'That's all you've talked about since you got here. That's all you think about. Why don't you ask me how I am for once? You! You're obsessed with you!'

I lowered my head in genuine shame. My cheeks turned as sore-pink as my palms, and something about the colour must have suddenly warmed Eddie's heart, because then he said, with sadness, but no anger, 'Unfortunately, so am I. Come here.'

The only other change was in the amount of food that Eddie was eating. A lot. He was eating a lot.

A hearty, three-course breakfast took the place of his morning dog walk. At teatimes, he would produce huge and elaborate meals which took over an hour and a half to prepare and consume; about the same amount of time that he'd have formerly spent on the evening park visit. There were many bright, light-hearted snacks at various points during the day where Burroughs might have wanted to play, and then, as night-time approached, Eddie would retire to the sofa with no dog but a heavy supper tray sprawled across his lap.

Several times, very late at night, I would peep around the kitchen door to find him eating again. He'd be sitting at the table, gazing at the space in the corner, whilst mechanically pushing cakes and biscuits and bread into his mouth and belly. Each time, I would creep back to bed and never mention that I'd witnessed his manic midnight stuffings. Food was Eddie's particular, chosen method of filling holes, and who was I to argue with that?

*   *   *

As September came to an end, the weather changed abruptly. Grim October nudged up impatiently, industriously, startling the unusually frivolous month into a late rush of gales and storms and serious skies. It was autumn. It was definitely autumn, and soon it would be winter and soon after that, it would be the end of the year. Well, I tried not to let any of this get to me. I tried to stay sunny and to look forward to next summer, but there was really no escaping the fact that things would have to get much worse before they got better.

A bleak Wednesday. A stormy evening. A gloomy me on my way to work, getting caught in the dark, in Camden Town.

I'd taken a short cut down a long, narrow street that the houses had turned their backs on, leaving it to the pooing dogs and the pissing drunks. I was heading to the office, heading for another evening of smeared desks and scarred toilet bowls and rotting apple cores, and now I shuddered suddenly as I hurried through that dirty-beyond-repair side street, scowling hard at the shabby futility of it all.

There was a scraggy mongrel chewing on some rubbish. An ash-blonde woman with a cigarette sheltering and yawning in a back doorway. The pavement was scattered with hundreds of black puddles, flat and glassy, as if some great mirror had been broken over the head of the city during the afternoon's flashing, splintering storm, and now I stepped carefully around each cold and jagged piece in my path, keen to avoid whatever pain or bad luck they might have to pass on.

A car came hissing and peeping suddenly up from behind, making me jump and making the dog hop back onto the pavement out of its way, just in time. I swore and the animal glanced upwards with big, wet eyes and then fell amicably into step by my side. He was such a puny, drenched little thing that I wasn't scared. I suspect that he thought the same about me, and now we pit-a-patted along the street together with a truce and some understanding between us.

'Where would you rather be then, dog?' I said as we stomped on, heads down, fed up. 'Not here, eh? Me neither. I want to go home. I might go home, or to my Eddie's. I might even take you with me, eh? Eddie loves me and he likes stray doggies, and he might give the both of us a good feed and a fine petting. You'd clean up well, you. I bet you'd come up lovely once you'd had your past brushed out of you, eh? Come on, boy. Come on.'

At some point, I realized that I hadn't seen that car pass. I glanced back. There it still was, moving very slowly along the road, lurking ten or twelve feet behind. It peeped again. The smoking woman showed some interest, but I set my eyes straight ahead and strode on.

A few minutes later, the car came up almost level.

Shit. It was following me. Shit. Someone was following me. Shit, shit, shit. Don't you try nothing, I have a dog, you know, I thought, then watched dismally as the unfaithful creature turned left and headed off up another alley on some urgent bin-sniffing mission. Peep again. I didn't look. I practised Piss off in my head, and then the car door sprang open.

'Piss off,' I said.

'Hello,' Martin said.

I turned my head to find him leaning across the passenger seat, grinning up at me through the open window.

'Hey, Angie! Get in!' he called, but I didn't slow my pace and now, with the woman in the doorway watching enviously, Martin started to follow me crawlingly along the kerb.

'Come on. Please?'

'What do you want?'

'I want you to get in. Come on, eh? You're wet.'

'I'm all right.'

Getting into someone's car out of a rainy night is an intimate thing to do at the best of times, like letting someone wrap their overcoat around you while they are still wearing it.

'It's nice and warm in here. Angie? Angie!'

He raised his voice, and now I darted my eyes around, taking my bearings. It was a good five minutes run back to the street I'd just come from, and the main road with its strong lights was still some way out of sight. Before that, all turnings left and right led only on to darker, smaller alley-ways, full of scary shadows and threats of dead ends.

'Angela!'

I clutched at my bag. It felt light. Damn. Damn. I did not have my knife with me. I had stopped carrying it around because I was tired of always expecting trouble and of often getting it and because you have to start somewhere, don't you? Only, now I was here, *here*, on a dark street with a dangerous man and no knife. I suppose that's just the risk you take when you give up your defences before you give up your enemies. I should have known that. I did know that. Damn. Damn!

'What do you want?' I repeated weakly.

Martin smiled. He had taken his bearings too, and had realized that he had lots of space, lots of time.

'Fancy running into you here,' he said slowly. 'My friend Angie. I'm glad to see you, my friend Angie.'

And he did look glad. Of course he looked glad.

'I mean, after all this time. You do remember, don't you? You do remember me?'

171

Yes, I remembered him. Of course I remembered him.

'Aye, it's quite a coincidence, meeting up on this deserted old street tonight, just you and I. Quite a coincidence, eh? Oh aye.'

Only, of course, it wasn't.

I prepared to run. Martin clicked open his passenger door. The car stalked on, its engine growling low, ready to pounce.

'I should say we've got some old times to talk about, eh? What do you say? Why don't you get in?'

'No.'

'Hey, Angie, I just want to talk, you know. Come on now. Just get in.'

'No.'

'What's the matter with you? I'll not ask again. Get in!'

'No!'

And then he swore. And then he pushed open the passenger door. And then I was very frightened.

And then, and then, out of the black of a side alley, a bright young couple emerged, kissing beautifully and laughing prettily and strolling handsomely towards me. They looked wonderful, and I waved in delight at the wonderful sight.

'Go away, Martin.'

I smiled up ahead and waved again. The boy and girl exchanged glances, checked behind them and then half-smiled back. Martin paused. He looked at me. At them. Back at me. And then he said, 'Fine. All right.'

'Goodbye, Martin.'

'Aye then. I see. I see how you want it.'

'Bye-bye.'

'Right. Right. Bitch!'

There was a violent slam of a door, a screech of tyres, and then he was gone.

*　　*　　*

172

'But he didn't touch you?' Jimmy asked kindly when I told him about the evening in Camden Town. 'God! Fuck! I've told you! Let me see what I can do. Let me go and see him. I'll sort everything out. I'll sort him out. Let me help you.'

'No, Jimmy. It wouldn't help. More and more trouble, that's not the way.'

'Well, what are you going to do? You can't have someone walking around in the world hating you this much. It must feel terrible.'

'It feels . . . uncomfortable.'

'You must never sleep properly.'

'No.'

'Scared all the time.'

'Yeah. I'm a bit scared now, I admit it. I think he's mad. And I think I've got to tell the police now.'

'What do you mean? I mean, you can't, can you? I mean, wouldn't that mean that Eddie might find out?'

'Yes. I know. That's why I'm going to have to tell Eddie too.'

With my decision came a deep sense of cleanness, a feeling of corners being swept, of crannies being dusted, and of complex cobweb-traps being destroyed; the fragility of their structures revealed by a single, simple swipe.

I went to the black cupboard late one night and brought out Martin's letters. I fetched the metal bin from the bathroom. I took off all my clothes and then, closing the doors so that the smoke would not reach and wake Eddie in the bedroom, I started a fire.

It was a small fire, but a good one.

I laid aside one letter for the police, and another for Eddie, and the rest I lowered slowly into the small, good fire. The smell that would still be lingering in the

173

air tomorrow morning would, I realized, take some explaining, but that didn't seem to matter any more. Everything would be explained soon enough.

It was fascinating, watching those letters crumble under the flames and then disappear. They went so quickly, that was the thing. I couldn't believe how quickly they went. Terrorism, as flimsy as flimsy paper; black words and cold threats wiped out in a second by even this modest amount of heat and light.

I smiled over the sight. The flames chuckled and slapped each other on the back. The letters cackled in the pit of the fire like souls in hell.

No, not hell. This is not hell. It's a litter-bin.

I don't believe in heaven or hell, I reminded myself, my warm excitement cooling a little now. I don't. I can't. If I did, then I'd have to fret over at least one family member who, under the rules as I understand them, must surely have qualified for a place in the latter.

I will not think of my dad down there sizzling alone in some underworld, I resolved, as I brought the box of his letters out of the cupboard and over to the fire. I will not do that. I worried quite enough about him when he was here.

No-one dropped in to see my dad while I was there at his flat on the night of my visit.

Nor, apparently, did anyone ever, except for his big sister Mary who still loved him, and two big, angry men who didn't; who'd turned up outside his home a few days earlier and tried to beat his door down with their fists, leaving a deep scar in the plywood, like an illiterate note to say that they had called, and would be back.

There were weapons hidden around my dad's flat that night. He showed them to me keenly, as if they were part of the decor that he'd so wanted me to approve of. A hammer tucked behind the front door. An ornate brass poker in the corner of the living-room, leaning in towards the electric fire. Another hammer pushed down the side of the settee where my dad would sleep or not sleep that night.

'What's going on, Dad?'

He kept his eyes on his steel-toed boots as he hunched over in his easy chair and told me about the visitors he was expecting; kept a fist in his hand as he spoke.

'I've had word that someone's after me,' he said calmly.

'What do you mean? Who?'

'Don't know. I weren't in when they came. Old Roy next door came out when he heard 'em banging. Two big lads, he said. All got up in black hats and scarves and all that. Asking for me. Two big lads. Could be anybody.'

'But who do you think they were? What did they want?'

'Trouble, by the sound of it.'

'But who?'

'Could be anybody. Me past catching up with me, eh?'

'It could be her husband, couldn't it?'

'Aye, I suppose.'

'It could, couldn't it?'

'Aye, it could be him.'

'Aren't you bothered?'

'Well, it don't make no difference. I'll find out soon enough, eh?'

'What about the police, Dad?'

He thought about this for a moment.

'No. I don't think it was them.'

'No, I mean what about calling the police?'

My dad looked at me as if I were mad, then started

telling me that he could get hold of a gun if he needed it.

The mood went a bit funny after that, and so did time. Long evening. Long, long, evening. The clock was a meter suddenly, ticking; the room a waiting-room now. We played Scrabble with our boots on. At one point I put K.N.I.F.E. up against my dad's B.E.L.L.Y. for which I got thirteen points and unnerved.

Waiting.

We tried to chat, but the conversations were strained and empty. I could think of nothing to say. No trivia, no amusing stories, no jokes; all I could think about now was hammers, and they weren't funny at all. And anyway, when we did talk, I had the sensation that we were only pretending. I could hear us not listening to each other, knew that as soon as we stopped speaking, and many times in between, our ears would fly to the door, press against the front door, keening for any sound beyond which might herald the arrival of unwanted guests, dressed for the occasion and maybe bringing household tools of their own.

Waiting, waiting.

When a sound did come, I would feel my dad's heartbeat starting up, like war drums, over the sound of my own. They beat together, loud as boots on concrete. Loud, louder, as the boots reached our door; so loud that in the end maybe we wouldn't even have heard the long-awaited knock or ring or kick. Loud, louder, LOUD! And then, finally, less loud; two heartbeats quietening, slowing, as the danger passed, fading, fading, like two footsteps walking away.

We sat together looking nervous, handsome, alike. Same head held erect on strong neck; proud, or bluffing. Same blood flush, high on same cheeks. Same denim eyes, only his pair too blue and young tonight for a man at his time of life, in his state. My dad, I was thinking. My daughter, he was thinking. I stroked my arm to soothe him and he drew in a deep cigarette breath to relax me, or maybe these things happened the other way around, I don't know.

'Are you scared, Dad?' I asked at some point.

'Eh?' he replied.

'Are you? Are you scared?'

'Eh? What?'

My father blinked and gave me a complicated and baffled look; the look of a person who has so much to say that they can't say anything at all. He chuckled. He breathed. Finally, he mumbled, 'What kind of a question's that?'

It was a daft question, that's what. An impossible question. I couldn't tell, he couldn't tell, what the words meant any more. I couldn't tell, he couldn't tell, what to worry about first or most; what the visitors might do to him, or what he might do to them. He shrugged and told me that he thought he might lose control and throw them over the landing or verandah. I didn't doubt that this was a possibility, and did not ask again if he was scared. It was a ridiculous question. By now the man's fear was utterly indistinguishable from his rage.

More and more waiting.

I balanced a slab of concrete time on my head. My dad had one on his head too; rubbed his neck from the strain of it.

He was in pain. He was in pain and I wanted to cry for him, only in the end it was he who took pity on me. He started to roll his great, tight shoulders and make out that everything would be all right. He sighed. He yawned. He twiddled his thumbs, wove his fingers like a clever lie, then rubbed his eyes and said that none of this was as bad as it looked.

'But it does look pretty bad.'

'Nah. They probably won't be back. Probably came

round in the heat of the moment. These hammers and stuff, that's just me being daft. You know what I'm like. I won't need them; should put 'em away. Don't worry, all right?'

'Yeah.'

'All right?'

'Yeah.'

'All right, lass?'

'Yeah. We're just being daft, aren't we?'

'Aye, we are.'

'Will you be putting the hammers away, then?'

'Aye. I won't need 'em.'

Cleaning up after supper, I found a large knife on top of the tall fridge. I put it tidily back into the drawer where it belonged, then came in again an hour later to find it back on the fridge, under a tea towel, its blade aimed pointedly at the door.

Around midnight, my dad lay down on the settee to watch TV. Nodded off with his boots on, with me keeping watch over him and the doorways. Beneath his closed lids, the raised dome of each cornea moved slowly from side to side, sweeping like two spotlights, scanning the borders of sleep.

He drove me to the station the next morning.

'I don't like leaving you like this,' I said.

'Don't be daft.'

'Why don't you go and stay at Mary's for a bit until things calm down?'

'Aye, I might do, I suppose I might.'

'Or come down and visit me? What do you think? Come and visit me.'

'Aye, that'd be nice.'

'Will you then? Will you? When will you?'

'Stop fretting, lass.'

'I'm not fretting.'

'Go on. I'm all right.'

178

'Yeah. OK.'

'Yeah.'

I turned away, and then back.

He waited for me to speak, wanted me to say something, only I didn't know what it was, and neither did he. We filled the space with a clumsy hug.

'Stop worrying about your old dad,' he said, feeling like a boy in my arms.

Time all funny again. Whistles blowing away our last moments, his last words.

My dad looked small and pale and strange as he waved me off from the platform, as he turned away, turned back to his own new, odd, shrunken life. The next time I'd see him, he would be paler and stranger still; dead, in fact.

It was late autumn then. My dad in his big coat, shivering at a train station, steaming a goodbye out into the cold air. Autumn again now, the night drawing in around me as I stoked my memories, threw letters on the fire.

September then, September now, with everywhere the sense of time running out.

Night-time. Me and Eddie, in bed together again. My bed, my bedroom on a cold night; autumn ending and winter coming faster than I'd have liked.

Eddie put his arms around me. I didn't look at him, but I could tell that he wanted to make love. I also wasn't looking at the room and its things, but I knew what they were doing too. Grey sheets, drying in front of a cold radiator. Discarded jeans on top of the chest of drawers, laid out like half a dead body. Curtains hanging, and the four walls of my bedroom, smooth with their one door closed, running around and around me, encircling us in their little square, pacing out the limits of how much space and air we would have tonight; this much, and no more.

If I wasn't already lying down, I might have collapsed with misery.

I'd planned to tell him tonight. I'd known for over a week that I had to, and now the time had come. I'd planned it. This night, this bed, this bedtime; now, now, NOW.

I heard Eddie murmur soft, disarming sounds. I felt him sighing and stretching and snuggling beside me, moving freely in his loose pyjama top, his day-cares untied like boots, left beside the bed. He hadn't had a good day, and tomorrow might be even worse, but for him, this time in between, this was soft and easy and safe; this was bedtime, and nothing bad would happen now. I suppose you have to believe this, otherwise how would you ever sleep well? I do not believe it, and I do not sleep well. And I am not the only one. I have heard of people who can only sleep when their partner is wide awake in the same room, watching over them. Thousands of others need pills to put them out, to induce the blissful ignorance which is the first stage of sleep. And many, many, children and crime victims simply have to keep a light on all the way through the dark hours; they know about the monsters that the night can bring. I'd heard about my dad in the darkness, in a late telephone call just after midnight; just after I'd dropped my clothes and eyelids and defences.

Tell him.

What, now?

Tell him.

I don't know.

Tell him.

Wait, wait, I'm not sure any more.

'What's up, Angel?' Eddie said suddenly. 'You all right? What is it? Tell me. Come on. Tell me.'

It was a cliff-edge moment. One step, a sentence or two away from ending it all.

'Tell me,' Eddie said again.

'OK, tell him,' Jimmy had said.

'You've got to tell him,' Caroline would have said if she'd known about all this; and then, of course, there was Martin, whispering from the black cupboard next door with the most persuasive argument of all. Only my dad stood down below me, by the rocks and the suicide messes, looking up sadly and calling out, No, don't do it, love, don't do it; I did, and look what happened to me.

'No. Nothing to tell. I'm fine. Just tired. Really tired. Come on. Ssshh, let's sleep now, eh? Good night, lovey. Good night.'

I shuffled my body into his and gave it up. Listened to Eddie's slow, rhythmic breathing. Felt the moment of truth ebb away as waves of sleepiness lapped up over me from the bottom of the deep, warm bed.

I hadn't told him. I couldn't. My head had been prepared to do it, but my head was all talk; and anyway, I was in heartland now. Come on, heart, do the right thing, show us what you're made of. I'm sorry, I can't. I just can't. I'm too wobbly-scared. My heart was made of soft stuff; soft, yellow stuff.

10

Next morning. Another morning. It was just another ordinary morning, and I awoke early, feeling heavy in the bones from another light sleep.

I opened my eyes to have a look around the room, then I opened the curtains to see how things were outside. A bit dull, a bit grey, and very ordinary, that's the way the world and I seemed that October Saturday. A yawn and a stretch and a bit of drizzle and nothing special.

The day the world ends will begin like this. With whistling milkmen and postmen on the streets. With sleepy drivers on the roads. With mist and dog-walking around the edges of the parks. With buses starting to bus, with a familiar radio station and some stale pollution on the air, and with other stuff like this; other ordinary stuff.

How a day can turn on you.

I slipped back under the covers, and looked over at Eddie. Across the arm-stretching width and along the eye-straining length of him; from where he began, on the pillow beside me, right down to where he ended, a long, long way off. His head looked uncomfortable, butting my headboard like that. His feet hung out into space at the other end. In between, he wore my duvet like a flowery horse blanket. He looked funny. He looked too big. It's not me that's too big, it's the world that's too small. I remembered this and smiled.

You shrink when you're dead, I thought. People who are dead or old or very ill, they shrink. It is the stuff of life in them contracting and compacting and withdrawing. You can see it happening; the poor spirit deserting the sinking body, or does it happen the other way round, I don't know. Eddie is not dead or dying, I thought. Look at the great, lumpy size of him. Here is a man absolutely full of the stuff or the stuffing of life.

I giggled, and wiggled beside him. Sighed.

Cotton sheets. Furry boyfriend. October's cool linen mornings. I snuggled happily into these things, but then, as soon as I settled, I became unsettled. Nine o'clock. It was past nine o'clock. The post should be here by now, I realized, and scurried downstairs to check. It was the first Saturday in the month and there was I, running untidily down to the hallway to scoop papers from the mat; to tuck and hide them neatly away before Eddie had a chance to see my letters, my letter, and the mess that I had made of things.

There was no letter.

There were two envelopes with my name on. A lucky draw offering me two weeks away from it all. A promise from a finance company that they could insure me against the unexpected. But no letter. The first Saturday of the tenth month had arrived, but October's letter hadn't. I crept back upstairs and started breakfast and fretting.

What are you up to? I thought, as I broke and churned eggs, burned some bread. Where's my letter? What have you done? It's not fair. You can't stop or start yet; it's not the end of the year or me just yet. I don't like this. Where's my letter?

The butter-knife grated on the toast and on my nerves. I left the scrambled food to seethe under the grill and went over to the window.

OK. So maybe he's forgotten to send it on time.

Simply forgotten. That could be it. It could be that simple. Or there could have been a delay in the post; my letter could arrive on Monday morning, just two days late, with no real harm done. It could even have got lost. It could have been dropped, stolen or scrunched and hidden at the bottom of a sack; misplaced, mislaid or mishandled, you see. After all, I'd seen for myself how clumsy postmen could be.

I watched my postman come back down my road. He looked handsome and capable in his uniform. He swaggered confidently as he passed my house; his bag satisfyingly empty and his job well done.

My letter could have been lost, but it wasn't. Not lost, not forgotten, not delayed. It wasn't that. It was something else, I could feel it. Something else was wrong.

'Something wrong?'

Eddie came into the kitchen, came to sit and calmly eat the frazzled breakfast that I'd rustled up for him.

'Don't go,' I said, when it was time for him to go.

'Eh? Don't be silly. I have to meet some people at ten.'

'But you don't have to. You don't really *have* to. We shouldn't have to work on Saturday. Why should we? Why don't we just stay here together? We could do that. We could, couldn't we?'

'Yes,' said Eddie, and then he smiled happily and put his jacket on.

'I'll lock the door. Then you'll have to stay.'

'Come round to mine later, eh?'

'Tie you to a chair.'

'We'll have some tea, then I'll drive you to your evening job.'

'Break your legs.'

'I'll be back about six.'

'Don't go.'

He turned around and squeezed me hard. His hair brushed my face and set it tingling. The buttons of his coat pushed through my thin pyjamas and made dents in my breasts and belly.

'See you later, Angel.'

He squeezed again, grazing my lips with his stubble.

'Take care,' I said into the silence that followed him, then I wrapped my arms tight around myself and winced deeply. My whole body hurt from where he'd left me.

Just after Eddie had gone, Jimmy rang. He said not to call the police yet. He said that he thought he might know where Martin was living and that he was going to go and see him, to have a chat, or something.

This confirmed my sense of foreboding, but did not entirely satisfy it.

At lunchtime, I set off for an afternoon clean. The house I was heading for belonged to an old lady, a nice old lady who was ill in hospital at present, and wanted the place hygienic and well-behaved for her return. I wasn't feeling at all well myself by this point, but I didn't want to let the old woman down. She had cancer, but didn't like to talk about it, and this was the least I could do for her; do my best to remove from her home any tactless whispers of upset and decay.

I took the Hoover and the cloths and the creams and the brushes to the top of the stairs and looked down. The pretty house sat quietly before me, waiting to be fixed, like a nice child with tangly hair. This afternoon, though, I just didn't have the patience to enjoy the task. There was something about this day which would not be soothed and smoothed and beautified; a curly unruliness of mood that flicked up like a cat-lick every time deep breathing and reasoning seemed to have pinned it tidily into place.

I started with the cleaning, eager to bag the hours ahead, to get them finished and packed up and chucked away, but it was heavy and uncomfortable work. Even the minutes seemed to drag like feet through litter. Almost every room had a clock and as I moved through the noise they made, I felt the ticking little seconds fidgeting against my skin, itchy as dust mites.

In the bathroom, I impatiently flicked up the nozzle of my window-cleaning gun and sprayed the bathroom cabinet with a thousand tiny, toxic bullets. I paused for a moment to consider how my face would look under acid, and then I selected another bottle and splashed more chemicals over the sink and bath-tub, dousing them as rigorously as if I intended putting a match to the room.

Reaching the main bedroom, I flung the door open wide and watched dust-balls scurry away across the floor. Of course, it was only the draught that carried them off, but right then it seemed ever so much as if they were fleeing in terror, as if they had just been warned about this bad-tempered killer that the sick old lady had hired; as if they'd heard for themselves the bleached germs screaming in the toilet next door.

In the living-room, the vacuum cleaner broke down, and so did the last of my patience. Well, that's all you can expect from vacuum cleaners, I thought as I stroked the carpet-fluff into submission with my little hand brush and watched the pale balls gather in my dustpan like the heads of a captured army. Vacuum cleaners! I hate vacuum cleaners! All wind and whining and no guts, I said aloud, kicking out at the little body and remembering why I must not have babies.

At three o'clock, I went back to my own house.

Caroline spotted me lurching palely up the steps and invited me in; made a headache solution and a space for me to be silent and pained.

'What's wrong?' she asked finally.

Shrug.

'It can't be that bad.'

'Mmm.'

'What's the problem? Are you just fed up?'

'S'pose.'

'Come on, things could be worse.'

'Yeah. Things could get much worse. That's the problem.'

'Well, I think you'd better tell me.'

'Mmm? No. I think I'd better go. Thanks. Sorry. Bye.'

My secrets swelled in me uncomfortably today, but I had to resist the urge to confide in Caroline. My troubles were not like boils that could be cleanly lanced with a single, swift confession; they were more like an infection, and best left untouched. I thought of Jimmy, driving around London in search of Martin and violence. Sometimes a trouble shared is a trouble doubled, I decided. Doubled and trebled and spread like a plague.

Around five o'clock, I telephoned my cleaning supervisor and told her that I was too poorly to come into work that evening. I put on my red coat. I swallowed another headache tablet. I wrapped up warm and went round to see Eddie, to see if he could make me feel better.

Hooray, I said when I saw Eddie's car outside the house. I let myself in the front door and hurried upstairs. Hooray. He was here. He was already here. The door with the pretty glass butterfly panel was unlocked and flapping slightly in a draught, waving me in. On the hallway table were Eddie's keys and crumply newspaper. Over there, his big overcoat hung fat-body-shaped on the wall. He was definitely here.

Only, where was he? There was no answer when I called his name. The doors to all the rooms were slightly open, but showed only squints of darkness within. Kitchen? Bedroom? Living-room? Eddie?

He wasn't here. No, wait. One of his boots was here; there, in the lounge, in front of his armchair. And one of his legs was here too. A hand. The cuff of a jumper. A prickle of unmistakable rough hair, bristling up just over the high back of the animal-coloured furniture. Oh. He was here after all, see; only sitting so quiet and still that I'd quite overlooked him the first time.

I walked slowly into the room until I could see Eddie's profile. His eyes were open and, although fixed forward, must surely have noticed me and my red coat circling their range, stalking their attention, but still he didn't move, seemed determined to stay for a little while longer just as he was, drawn into the pattern of the room and its shadows. Hidden. Hiding.

Things were not as they should be.

There was no music in the room and Eddie was rarely without music. No smell of coffee or food, and he was never without these things. The lights were still off, despite the busy teatime gloom which chattered up against the windows. The air was chilled, dead, and so was Eddie. He blinked. No, he was not dead. That wasn't it, and yet, it was something very like that, something mysterious that put him suddenly beyond my reach.

I braced myself.

I'd had some experience of sensing when an end was coming, and I could feel one now, as strong as if he'd already told me what was wrong, what disaster had happened, who had died. I felt it as a twitch of the reflexes, an involuntary opening of the body, a part unfolding to accept the new way of things. And then this: a terrible lurching of the guts, like flesh swelling and closing around the new, raw end, already starting to seal the wound.

I was good at it, see.

'What's wrong?'

I could deal with this.

'Eddie?'

It wasn't so clever, I'd just had a bit of practice, that's all.

'Tell me.'

In recent months, I had even begun to come to terms with the idea of my own end and I knew that if he would just tell me what was wrong, then I could easily deal with this.

A street lamp came on outside, stirring some orange life into the grey-greys by the far window, but it did not brighten the scene. The ash-flavoured orange made me feel sick. The remaining shadows lengthened, sharpened; became more like deep scars than decorative tattoos on the surfaces around me, and now the dimness gathered in a dense fuzz around the chair where Eddie sat, as if all the gloom of the room were emanating from there.

I did not move. He did not move. I unmoved some more, and so didn't he.

Twilight. Everything seemed to have got stuck in twilight, and the unnatural pause unnerved me. Out of the corner of my eye, I was aware of the dimness of my reflection in the mirror. I didn't like that. That dimness. Already, you had to squint to see that it was me. Soon, I might not be there at all. I really didn't like this sneaky way in which the evening was sapping my solidity, making a ghost or a memory of me.

I strode briskly into the middle of the room, but the room continued to have no reaction to me. I watched the short hand of the mantelpiece clock squeezing against the six like a trigger, but still the air didn't flinch.

'Come on! What's up?' I shouted finally, desperately. 'Eddie? Eddie? What's wrong? What is it? WHAT IS IT?'

Eddie turned and stared at me.

I should have been afraid. It was just plain cocky of me to stand there looking at him when he looked like that, and to feel unafraid. He had bad news in his eyes. Something shocking, something big. Something powerful enough to knock the giant man's feet right out from under him, forcing him to collapse into a chair and sit there meekly, turning as grey as the evening furniture.

What could be so bad? Eddie was alive. We had no children to fret over. My mother wasn't the type to die suddenly and my dad couldn't do it twice. I ticked these things off in my head like checking limbs after an accident and felt that, with these items intact, nothing could be so very bad.

Eddie breathed in very slowly. Eddie leaned forward very slowly. Slowly, slowly, Eddie said, 'I got this today.'

'What? Got what?'

His first breath left him; he pushed it out to its very end, then hauled another huge one in, his chest heaving from the effort. Next, there was a pause, a thought, and then a long hesitation, as if he only had the strength for a certain number of words, and did not dare waste them.

'This. This . . . thing.'

He unfolded his arms.

He showed me the thing in his hand.

I recognized it immediately, and now my heart sank low and made a sunset in my belly.

It was a letter.

It was my letter.

I recognized that tatty file paper with the damaged edge. That plump writing: a series of supple circles which sprawled over the lines like an emotional child. Those two folds in the thin sheet, which made the letter cave in under its own weight, then flap open, flimsy as the doors of a weak mind, spilling its filthy thoughts out and into the world. It was my letter.

That's my letter! I thought, and almost snatched it clean out of his hand. That's the letter I should have had. The letter that was mine, that should have come to my door today and said to me Watch out slag I know you look for me slag bitch whore. Eddie drew the thing back to his chest possessively. I clutched a breath and held it tight as I realized that it was *his* letter, as I stood back in silence and horror and wondered what it had said to him.

I felt reality tilt. I felt the spin of the earth in me. I felt a small man in my head standing straight and still, with his arms out to the side; trying to keep from falling over. And now, I could not easily deal with this. I had been wrong. This could not easily be dealt with. Now I felt the kind of feeling that makes you scared to turn on the evening news. The kind of feeling that makes you want to sit in the dark and feel nothing, at least for a few more minutes. Time was suddenly diamonds; too cold for comfort, too clear to hide in. Please. Just a few more minutes. As precious as the very last moment of a life. *Please, please, just a few more minutes.*

'It says that you've had sex with a lot of men, while you've been with me,' said Eddie quietly, and then the end began.

'At least a hundred, it says. Look. That's what it says.' He held the letter out for me to see, but would not let me take it, rip it up, swallow the remains. 'At least a hundred. At least.'

I never did like numbers.

'It says you often picked them up in that Camden pub you go to after work.'

Or details.

'It says that you couldn't say no to anyone.'

191

Or truths. I glared at the letter in his hand. Especially hard, black-and-white truths such as these that sat in lines like tough jurors on a bench; squat and stiff and beyond your reach and corruption.

Eddie folded the accusation back into his lap, without asking me to deny it. The possibility of a denial just did not seem to occur to him. It did occur to me. It was, after all, my first instinct in most situations: to deny, to stall, to distract the attention with wide blue eyes, while I gathered up the known facts and shuffled them swiftly in my deft hands. It's what I did. It's what I was good at. Only now, just when I needed my skill most, it deserted me. Beneath the glare of Eddie's suddenly intelligent eyes, I was all fingers and thumbs.

'Look . . . I . . .'

'What?'

'Well . . . I . . . see . . .'

'Say it. Why can't you say it?'

'Well, I just . . . sort of . . .'

'You used to be honest with me once. When I first met you. You were straight with me then. Remember?'

I thought about this. I remembered this.

When I'd first started getting to know him, Eddie had thought me an earthy and artless girl. What do you like about me, Eddie? I like your heart and your face and your energy and your honesty. It had been an easy mistake to make. Just out of hospital, I was suddenly young again. I'd been peeled and scrubbed, turned inside out and rebuilt and now I moved around in the world like a new thing. My senses were open, like a child's. My nerves were raw as fresh meat. I must have seemed too thin-skinned to have anything to hide, or anywhere to hide it.

Eddie thought that I had been honest back then. He wanted to believe that I'd been honest then and that I could be honest again now; needed to use these small

192

blocks of truth like book-ends, to mark and hold all the dubious time in between.

'Say it,' he said.

I drew a breath and myself in. Clutched my confession so tight that a policeman with a gun would not have got it from me.

'Say it,' he said.

Blackmail would have been useless. Pain would have been nothing.

'Angela.'

Eddie turned his soft face slowly towards me. It was a small gesture, with no threat.

'Yes,' I said. 'It's true.'

'Slag,' Eddie whispered next, and now I flinched away from him.

'That's what it says.'

'Yes.'

'Slag, bitch, whore. That's what it says about you.'

'Yes.'

'Couldn't say no to anyone.'

'Yes. No. I mean, I couldn't, but then I did. I mean, I did that, but then I stopped.'

'When?'

'When I realized that I had to.'

'When?'

'When I realized that I *could* stop.'

'When did you stop?'

'I haven't been with anyone for a long time.'

'How long?'

'I just haven't felt the need.'

'How long?'

'Well, for quite a while.'

'Angela.'

'Oh, I don't know. I don't know. I suppose it's . . . about . . . six weeks.'

My explanation flagged and floundered and gave up.

Heavy sarcasm came down like a boot to finish it off.

'Oh, well, that's something then, eh?'

'No. I don't suppose it is.'

'No. I don't suppose it is.'

I needed to sit down. But I couldn't sit down. I hadn't been invited to sit down. I didn't deserve to sit and be cushioned and comfortable and comforted. Eddie and all that was Eddie's was against me now, I could feel it. The blue armchair seemed a long way off, as if it had scampered back in disgust. The clock tutted and tutted over and over and over. If Burroughs had been here, he would have bitten me now, and maybe this time Eddie wouldn't have stopped him; and, maybe, neither would I.

'You'll go away and feel bad about this,' said Eddie quietly.

'I do feel bad. Do you think I don't?'

'Just listen for a minute.'

'Do you think that if—'

'Angela. Shut up. Just listen to me for a minute! I only have one thing to say, so just listen. OK? OK. You'll go away and feel bad about this. You'll sit down and you'll brood over your mistakes. You'll think: this is what I did wrong, that is what I did wrong, and I shouldn't have done this thing, and, if only I'd done that thing. You might spend days or weeks going over it in your head, trying to work out exactly the moment that led to all this, and, even then, you'll never be quite sure. So. I'll save you some time and trouble. OK? Are you listening? Your mistake was this: you didn't tell me.'

'I wanted to. Just last night—'

'No. Ssshh. No. Listen. You didn't tell me. That's the mistake.'

'But last night when I—'

'Didn't I give you the chance to tell me?'

'Yes. I know. I can see that now. But I was scared—'

'*You should've told me.*'

'But at the—'

'That's all I have to say. That's it. That's the mistake and that's that. You *should* have told me.'

'Yes.'

He crushed the letter in his hand. It did not make a sound as it dropped to the floor. It did not need to make a sound; its job was done.

'*You* should have told me.'

Silence. A silence like no other silence developed between us. Purple. The air congealed and it made purple; purple and black around our stiff bodies, like settling, dead blood. Silence and then more silence and then I suddenly wished that Burroughs *was* here. I wanted feelings to burst out like wild fur. I wanted bared gums and open flesh and weeping wounds. I wanted to suffer redly. I wanted a scar on me, a scar on my body, like a ring on a calendar; a mark in the world to say that this had happened and would not be forgotten.

Somebody should bite or shout or cry now, I thought, but then I looked at Eddie and I looked at me and I realized that neither had it in us. Something about this grey evening and that dirty letter and the small, pale shabbiness of it all had muted our passions, drained them out like colour from a face.

'I'm sorry,' I said weakly. 'That you had to find out like this. I should have known. The year's running out. I should've known that he had to make a move soon.'

'Who? Who do you think sent it?'

'I'm not sure.'

'But who do you think?'

'I don't know. The handwriting's obviously disguised.'

'But who do you *think*?'

'Well . . . there was this man—'

I shuffled my feet, stumbling over the word 'Martin'.

195

I did not want to say 'Martin'. Eddie had known him, almost; had met him a few times while picking me up from cleaning. Hadn't much liked the look of him, I remember. And now, it didn't seem right to say that word. The letter had estimated the amount of men I had slept with, so Eddie knew now about the numbers, but I wasn't at all sure what names, faces, would do to him.

'Just someone I met. A man. A married man. I slept with him. And then I stopped sleeping with him. And I think he—'

Eddie shook his head at me.

'I think he got—'

'No. Don't go on.'

'In January, he started sending—'

'It doesn't matter.'

'He started sending these—'

'Angela.'

'What?'

'It doesn't matter any more. It doesn't matter.'

'Oh. No. I suppose not.'

He was right. I shut my mouth and closed my eyes and saw that he was right. It didn't matter any more. I didn't matter any more. I could have said 'Martin' after all. I could have said anything, *everything*, and it would all have been the same, would all have come down to this. A whole life story reduced to sixty-odd filthy words on a crumpled sheet; one small, cheap piece of paper which could easily be crushed and thrown away and not missed.

'You'd better go now,' he said. 'Please don't get in touch and don't come back.'

'I'm sorry,' I said.

'Goodbye,' he said.

'Goodbye,' I said, and then it was all over.

This was the end. This was the end that I'd felt when I'd entered the room a few minutes earlier. The last word is said. A pair of electric blue eyes switch off with a dull click. A door closes gently in your face. Love ends.

'No. I don't know where he is. He's just gone. Not to our parents, no. I don't know where. I don't *know*!'

Jimmy was tiring of my endless questions.

'Where is he, Jimmy?'

'I've told you.'

'You must have some idea.'

'I don't.'

'Come on. Where is he? Where is he?'

I regarded Jimmy suspiciously, then cast my eyes around the quiet living-room, searching for clues.

'*I don't know!*'

'You're lying!' I said in frustration, and now Jimmy tired of me.

'Look. I've told you. He said he was going away, and then he went away, and that's that. That's it!'

'Oh well, that's great. This is great. This is getting me nowhere. This is getting me NOWHERE!'

I spun away in fury, went whirling around the tidy room, shouting at the brother who wouldn't help me, blasting insults at the chair where Eddie wasn't sitting, upsetting papers and delicate ornaments with the sheer force of my anger.

Jimmy stood by the doorway, letting me rage for some minutes, and then he said quietly, 'Go home, Angela. Just go home.'

Home. Home. Well, that stopped me right in my tracks. Home. The empty sound of the word, the very thought of my empty rooms just knocked all the wind out of me and now I trailed miserably back towards Jimmy and hung onto his arm as I gasped, 'Please, Jimmy. Please help me.'

I saw immediately that this was a mistake. I saw Jimmy's body stiffen and his lip curl away from me in distaste. He didn't like to see people beg. A begging woman brought out the worst in him.

'Get a grip, will you. For God's sake. Let go.'

'Not until you've helped me.'

'Get off. Fuck! What are you doing?'

'Just tell me something. *Any*thing!'

He looked down at me. His mouth squirmed as if it wanted to spit.

'All right, I'll tell you something,' he said. 'You've lost him. That's all. That's it. You might as well accept it. It's what you deserve, so the least you can do is show a bit of dignity now. He's gone. Understand? Gone. Lost. Accept it.'

'Yes,' I said. 'Yes.'

Well, I let him stay lost for one, two, three days, and then I started my search.

'He said he was thinking of leaving the city,' a nearby friend told me. 'No. I don't know where he might go.'

'Yes, he's left his job and the area,' a work colleague confided. 'No. I don't know where for.'

'I got the idea he was heading north,' speculated a fellow photographer in west London. 'Or was it south? It could have been south.'

Search, search, search. Have you seen Eddie? Have you seen my Eddie?

Grilling his acquaintances, I was persistent and pushy, cajoling this one, bullying another, unwelcomely occupying busy workplaces and whole lunch hours. Calling on his good friends, I was less confident. Eddie's good friends were good people and I was a little ashamed to face them. Had he told them about me, I'd wonder, shivering on a doorstep or dialling a number with trembling fingers, and when each answered the door or telephone to assure me that no, they knew nothing, nothing at all, well, I must admit that I was relieved as well as disappointed.

Of course, I was sure that some of them were lying.

Once, one of them sadly said, 'It's not like Ed to just disappear, is it, leaving his job and home and everything,' and I could tell that this meant, 'Look what you've forced him to do, you evil woman.' Another time, I moaned to his best friends, 'I can't find out anything, not a thing. I'll say this for Eddie, he certainly knows how to inspire loyalty in everybody!' and at that they'd both looked suddenly very pink and pained, as if biting back the words, yeah, everybody but you.

Even those friends who genuinely had nothing to tell me were still careful to keep their mouths shut. Eddie was gone and that was good enough for them and when I entered their homes, anxious and pleading, I would discover that Eddie's absence had already got there ahead of me and was hanging around the rooms like a dignified silence.

Soon I found it unbearable to be around our friends, his friends. No-one was blatantly unwelcoming or unpleasant, but now that I'd had Eddie's stamp of approval withdrawn, I felt them all subtly downgrade me in their affections. I left them with a thank you and a request that, if they heard anything at all, would they please, please, get in touch with me? They all said, Yes of course, but left me in no doubt that, if it came to a choice between him and me, then there would be no choice at all.

I'd planned to look for Eddie in places that we'd made our own, in places that were ours, but I soon realized that we had none, or too many. We'd loved the great London parks, but without favouritism. We'd messed around roughly in many playgrounds and trees, but none in particular had snagged our affections. The endless cafés and pubs that I'd visited with Eddie had all seemed extremely charming at the time, but in retrospect I could see that we ourselves had brought most of that charm with us, and that we'd always been careful to take it away with us again when we'd left. When Eddie and I were together and happy, it didn't matter where we were or who else was around; our attention would fall like a spotlight on each other, with everyone else rhubarbing around like dull extras in the background, and the surroundings rolling by like painted scenery on a scroll.

We'd made everywhere our own, and that was where I had to look for my lover now.

Search, search, search. Have you seen my Eddie? No. No. No.

I ran into so many brick walls that week that the black rings around my eyes began to feel more like bruises than tiredness, but still I searched. Thursday and Friday and Saturday and Sunday and Monday. Walk and ask and sigh and try and search, search, search. And in between searching, I waited. I sat in my flat, rigidly calm and carefully pretty, and I waited, waited, waited for an unexpected call.

The prettiness didn't last very long. It was a strange thing. As the days passed and my body and my optimism tired, I found that I had the energy to put on make-up, but not to remove it, to apply talcum powder and deodorant, but not to shower. I kept adding layers to my clothing, sometimes troubling to rifle through two suitcases for the right lucky cardigan, but I was having great difficulty in changing my underwear.

By the end of the week, my silhouette was plump with woollenness, but Caroline was not fooled.

'When did you last have a decent meal?' she asked.

'Don't know. Couple of days ago.'

It had been at least four.

'You look very gaunt.'

'Do I?'

'Yes.'

'Don't I look nice?'

'Not really, no.'

'Oh. No. I suppose not.'

'You have to eat.'

'Yes. I suppose so. Yeah. You're right.'

I relaxed a little in my chair now. Removed a jumper. Sighed. Felt a little of my weight returning as my taut muscles sagged into the soft armchair.

'You've got to eat! You've got to eat, Angela!'

Her words were nice. Her impatience was nice. It was nice to be told what to do.

'You sound like a mother,' I said fondly, grateful that she did, that she cared.

'I didn't mean to!' she replied roughly, frowning hard at my sudden softness, frightened to death by this small threat of vulnerability.

'Oh. OK. OK.'

Caroline stood up and edged backwards out of the room.

'I'd better go,' she said.

'OK,' I said.

'Work. You know. And I'm tired. And I'm expecting a phone call.'

'Yeah,' I said.

'Bye. Take care of yourself. Bye.'

'Yeah. See you,' I said, but I did not see much of Caroline at all after that.

Search, search, search.

I met a man in a West End pub near Eddie's workplace who said that he'd known him. That he used to go in for lunch every now and then. That they'd chatted sometimes. When I told this man that Eddie had gone missing, he shrugged and swigged his beer. When I said that I had to find him, he looked blank and swigged

201

again. When I said that I was *desperate*, the man put his glass aside and leaned forward.

'Well, yeah. We were mates, me and Ed. I told him my troubles and he told me his. Yeah. Mates, I'd say.'

'Do you know where he is?'

'Well,' he said, with an unhurried smile. 'I'm not sure I could tell you that. Don't know if I can trust you, do I? A person could only give that sort of information to a very close friend.'

'But I am a close friend. Honestly. I've known Eddie for years. A very, very close friend.'

'Yeah, yeah, yeah. But are you a close friend of mine?' he asked, taking my hand as if to seal a deal.

I walked away from him, of course. It was ridiculous, of course. Eddie would never confide in a man like that. Of course. It was obvious. Still, my heart had thudded all the same at the idea of success, at the scent of Eddie's nearness, and I can't honestly say whether it was good sense or only dirty underwear that had prevented me from dropping my knickers right then and there.

On Thursday night, I curled up in the darkness and watched the circles in my head. I looked over the clues that I had gathered so far and squinted against the picture that they were making. I tried not to see that, no matter where or how far I travelled each day, my journeys always and only led me back to this same quiet, dark place and fact: that I was here, and Eddie was not.

I tried Jimmy again. Went round to see him one night.

He sighed a hello and let me in as far as the hallway but, despite the black and fierce evening, insisted on keeping the front door open behind me.

'What are you doing here?' he asked, regarding with distaste the curled, soggy person and leaves that had just blown into his house.

202

I shrugged.

'What do you want?'

I shivered.

'I've got no new information about Eddie, if that's what you've come for.'

I shook hard with cold and hunger and confusion. Yes. That's what I'd come for, that's what I'd wanted, but now I suddenly realized that I would take anything else that was going. A drink of hot, sweet tea. A warm word. A gentle explanation for why my friend had turned on me so harshly. Jimmy stood with his hands in his pockets, avoiding my gaze, showing me that none of these things were on offer tonight.

I tried to get through to him. I gave him a smile. I said Please and Sorry and Do you remember . . . ? I even tried to be funny; tried everything that I could think of, see, but it was no use. His dull responses to my desperate attempts made it very clear that anything I did now would only increase his dislike of me, and nothing would reverse it.

I am on the outside of him, I realized suddenly. That was the feeling. I was on the outside of him, and even within the mess of pain I felt for Eddie, I was still able to experience this particular sadness very clearly. The warmth was gone. The bond was gone. I could still see his friendship somewhere inside him, but I just could not reach it any more.

I stayed for a few moments more, pressing myself against his glassy eyes like an urchin at a yellow window, and then I moved quietly along, back into the darkness.

Search, search, search. Eddie, Eddie, Eddie.

If someone was following me as I was following Eddie's trail during those strange, searching weeks, I was not aware of it, had not noticed them. My sight had just one purpose now as I pushed it around through the busy London streets. I was no longer afraid of the man who hated me. I did not worry any more about attacks and beatings and cuts. My Eddie was missing. He'd taken my Eddie away, and what else could he do that would hurt me more than that?

Every now and then, during my searching, I would think that I had found Eddie, and these would be the best and the worst moments of all.

Someone would say, Yeah, I think I saw him, yeah, and then my heart would fill with hope; until, when pressed, they went on to add that, No, actually, they couldn't say for sure when or where or even if it was really him, and then I'd start rattling and scraping like an empty water tank all over again.

At other times, I'd spot him in a park or a street; would glimpse from the corner of my eye a dark, magnificent shape, moving, waving at me, and then I'd raise my hand and wave back and then I'd miserably lower my arm and sink inside, because it always only turned out to be another stranger or tree.

But I knew he was around somewhere. I just knew it. I could feel it. How can somebody be everywhere and nowhere at the same time, I wondered as I wandered. I didn't know. It seemed impossible, but God could do it and so could my Eddie; look, look, there He goes, hanging around the city, floating about in people's hints and eyes, only to disappear without trace the moment you look too closely or try to get a straight answer.

By this time, I was quite thin and ill.

I wasn't intending to starve myself, it wasn't that. I didn't want not to look nice; it was just that my spirit could not work up any more interest in the raw red of a hungry stomach than it could for the orange canvas in my bedroom or the memory of blue skies. All of these things had become bleached of meaning.

When the cramps began to interfere with my walking

and searching, I did try to eat. I went to my cupboard one night and brought out golden syrup, speckled crackers, tinned peaches and tomato soup. Food. This is food, I told myself, surveying the table of tins and packets suspiciously. It's just food. Just eat it. But as soon as it stopped being food, it became vomit, and the colourful mush would start spouting violently from my mouth, as if it knew that it didn't belong in my unhealthy body and couldn't wait to get out.

I tried again a few days later, but this time it was even worse. Now the peaches and the crackers refused to enter me at all; just sat in lumps in my mouth, peering down a dark throat and saying, No, no, no. So in the end, I gave up. I rejected the food before it had a chance to reject me. I stopped visiting the fridge and the bread bin, then the last of my coffee ran out, and then I hardly needed to go into the kitchen at all. My body and my movements around the flat became a little bit smaller. Things closed in around me a little bit more.

After five or six more days of walking and searching and not eating, my body started to creak and moan. I became aware of the sensation of crumbling. My resolve was as strong as ever, but I felt my skin, belly and bones drying and wasting beneath me; felt that if I tugged even gently on an arm or a leg, it would come right away, with no fuss at all.

And then, one night, I accidentally slept. And while I slept, I accidentally dreamed. And in this dream, I found that I had accidentally murdered myself and was now trying to get rid of the incriminating remains. Patiently, I unhooked limbs, separated organs, rolled skin. Calmly, I hid these parts and parcels around my home; head beneath the floorboards, giblets in the fridge, heart down the toilet.

I had other dreams too, strange dreams, terrible dreams. This was no good. They were coming too often and taking too much. The morning after each visit would find me sweating, shivering and exhausted, as if the nightmares were vampires come to drain out the last of my energy and my positivity. Soon I began to fear that my strength would end before my search did, and then I had no choice but to stay up all night, in a chair, in a room hung with tobacco-smoke and bright lights, guarding myself against sleep.

There must be somewhere I haven't looked, I'd think to myself as I sat up night after night, reviewing the day's fruitless travels and planning tomorrow's. There must be somewhere that was ours, just ours. There must be, there must be, but the only place that came to mind was my bed, and he wasn't there; I'd looked and looked, and he definitely wasn't there.

Come on, think, think, I chanted desperately one desperate evening, wandering around the flat, looking for inspiration. Think, think, think! as I upturned tables, pulled open drawers, spilled the guts of my cupboards all over the floor. Think! Think! Think! Think! Think! as I punched my head over and over, as if to loosen a new idea.

The next day I put on my best frock, packed a small bag and went to the seaside.

Well, it was a mistake, that frock. That pretty, thin frock: it was a terrible mistake. I had dressed for the seaside, but the seaside had changed.

The coach tipped me out into the clutches of a coarse wind that felt me all over, lifted my skirt. The air whistled viciously all around as the jacket came off my shoulder to reveal a low neckline, and then the hard sky looked over and joined in too; spat with derision at my bared legs and my soft, girly sandals. I tried to hide in a hood, but the cotton coat I had chosen to wear that morning had no hood, and now my loose hair slapped me about the head for being so stupid.

What had I been thinking? What had I thought I'd find here? I must have expected gentle breezes, warm sands and friendly waves; must have expected the town to be as nice to me today as it had been once before.

Silly girl! the locals' eyes said as they stared at my pink face and pale legs. Go home! Go home! cried the seagulls. Thunderstorm! threatened the sky. There's nothing here for you! said the wide, empty beach and the closed shops, and then the salty wind laughed again in my face, brought tears to my eyes. No! No! I replied, gathering my dress and my resolve around me. I am here to find Eddie. I was here to find Eddie and I wasn't going to be scared off, no matter how bad the weather or the shakes got. I'm not scared! I shouted at the cliffs, and then the trembling ended and the searching began.

On the cold beach, I found deck-chairs hugging beneath tarpaulin. I saw the rough edge of the tough sea run towards a dog, bite it on the nose, and then run away again. I watched a few dark figures with steely features wielding metal detectors very grimly; scouring the sands for any last bits of money and happiness that the tourists might have left behind.

The fortune-teller's hut was padlocked and dusty. The wooden slats of its seaward side creaked and groaned in the howling breeze and the garish paintwork was paling quickly in the face of the attacking wind and salt and sand. The cruel weather had rolled in to poke icy fingers and fun at the eccentric old lady in the hut, and it was just as well that she had seen all this coming and had cleared off months ago.

Along the promenade, not much moved apart from the litter and myself. It was just me and a paper bag and some sweetie wrappers, blowing up and down that deserted stretch; up and down, up and down, only pausing when the wind or our thoughts changed direction suddenly.

I looked for the Fish 'n' Chip man. He'd been nice before. He'd help me now, I thought, rushing off back to the town centre and a bit of hope. Only, the Fish 'n' Chip man had gone. I couldn't believe it. I'd never have thought he'd have gone; couldn't imagine him anywhere but here. I must have thought that he'd lived in that tiny cabin; slept and ate and loved and lived in there, but now the mobile home stood silent and empty in front of me, shrugged off like a shell. I walked slowly away, following a trail of memories to the amusement halls we'd played in, but when I got there, I found that the flashy arcades were all empty too, their wide windows filled with darkness, like bright eyes with the life unplugged. Only one small souvenir shop remained open on that sea-front stretch, and this was a sad business, pushing its portraits of a pretty, summery seaside at you with the ridiculous, fading pride of an aged beauty.

Around the town, I saw local men standing and mumbling and smoking and frowning at the coming winter. I stopped a few times to tell them that I was looking for a big man, giving them a chance to make a joke and a bit of friendly contact, but today they just shook their heads with disinterest, couldn't be bothered. Only a few months ago, they'd been leering over seafood stalls or flirting in the fairground, but those long days were long gone and now they found themselves once again out of work, out of favour, out of season and out of sorts.

Some of the local girls, I noticed, still gathered in small groups and shelters around the pier, huddling together, heads down, as if planning an escape. Others sat in a line at the coffee bar of the local bingo hall, chatting loudly about nothing, thinking quietly about their summer lovers; waiting and fading like prizes won and never claimed.

I spoke to many, many, of the local people that day, showing them my desperation and Eddie's photo, but I didn't get a single kind word or a bit of help from any of them. They were all the same: the woman who short-changed me in the café, the old man outside the closed betting-shop, the teenager with no money and no friends in the corner of the snooker hall. They all had that same expression and mood about them, that same sense of having been used or deserted or cheated. Even the small children I passed that day seemed to have it, and mumbled grumpily in their anoraks and pushchairs, remembering sunshine and paddles and smiles and trying to work out how life could be so warm one minute and so cold the next.

Well, I could make it warm again. That's why I'd come here; I was searching for the one thing that could make everything everywhere all right again. I would find Eddie and talk to him and thaw out his heart before winter had a chance to set in good and proper.

I searched that seaside town for three, four, five hours, walking up and down and around' and around until I was quite dizzy and strange. Eddie will be here. Eddie will be here. The wind chopped me into little bits, but the bits went right on searching. Eddie will be here and we will talk and smile and turn this whole thing around, yeah, yeah, that's what will happen, that's it, yeah, yeah, yeah. Only, he wasn't. And we didn't. The day ended and everything stayed just as it was: sky thin and derelict and about to fall at any moment, waves blupping up like oil onto the shore, and the horizon line of the sea in front of me looking for all the world like the end of the world.

I had considered staying here for a night or two, but

as the light faded, so did the appeal of the idea. All around me, friendly hotels had closed like hearts. Their warm windows were shuttered now, their welcome mats withdrawn. The wealthy hoteliers were all in Spain, away for the winter, while the less well off had retreated to their parlours to wish the winter away. No-one was prepared for guests. No-one wanted guests. Only mad people would come here in this season and weather, and they didn't want that sort in their homes thank you very much.

No, I wouldn't stay, I decided as I wandered crazy-haired and wild-eyed once more along the sea front. There was nowhere to stay, and no reason to either. There was nothing here. I swept my stinging eyes one last time along the barren beach and finally realized that there was nothing and no-one here and that I might as well go home.

'Yes?' said the landlady.

'Hello,' I said.

'Yes?'

'My name's Angela.'

Pause.

'Yes?'

'I came to stay here in the summer.'

'Oh. And?'

She frowned. I felt foolish.

'I came to stay here. In the summer.'

'Yes. So you said. I don't understand. We're not open now, you know.'

'No.'

I shuffled my feet and frowned right back at her. I didn't really understand this either, now that I came to think about it. One minute I had been heading off back to the station, and the next I'd been here, on this sweet street, my legs retracing old footsteps with a will of their own, like dogs on a familiar scent.

'So!' I said brightly.

'Yes?'

'How are you?'

'Fine.'

'Right. Right.'

Pause.

'I'm fine,' the landlady repeated firmly, as if I'd failed to believe her properly the first time.

'Good. Good. I'm glad.'

Pause. And then another pause.

'The weather's horrible though, isn't it? The beach looked ever so sad just now. Everything seems so ugly here now, doesn't it?'

'Does it?' she said defensively, shrinking a little in her clothes and passing a hand over her face as if to wave away my critical gaze. I noticed suddenly that the lady looked just as fat, but somehow not so big, as when I'd seen her before. She had made some efforts with glittery eye-shadow and glinting jewellery, and yet she had definitely lost some of her sparkle. For all her make-up and cardigan sequins and hairspray, there was something undressed about the woman today, as if her personality had been taken off and stored in mothballs, in a wardrobe somewhere.

I forced myself to stop staring at her and she forced herself to stop glaring at me and we both stood in silence for some minutes. I was damp. I was freezing. Behind me, a strong wind and a powerful urge pushed at my back, edging me a little closer towards that warm, dry hallway. Behind the landlady, there was a muttering radio, a smell of weak, mid-week stew, a heap of laundry and a small, bobbing man, and now she pulled the door a little further closed, embarrassed by my glimpse of her little husband and life.

'I'm looking for someone,' I told her. 'I'm looking for someone.'

I showed her Eddie's picture. I recalled our room number and the dates of our visit. I related the conversation she'd had with Eddie during our last breakfast there, and now she turned a little pink, and then I was sure that she remembered him.

'Yes,' she said. 'But no. He hasn't been back.'

'Oh.'

'Why would he come back?'

'Well, I came. I'm here.'

'Well, he isn't.'

'No.'

'No. Definitely not. He isn't here. No.'

'No.'

I looked at the landlady steadily, saddened and satisfied by her reply. She wasn't kind, but she wasn't dishonest either. At least with her I didn't have that feeling that I'd had with all the others; that sense of Eddie standing just behind their doors with his back against the wall and a finger to his lips.

'No. Of course he isn't.' I muttered, 'I'm sorry. He's not here.'

'So where is he?'

'Disappeared.'

'Disappeared?'

I shouldn't have said disappeared. The word made her think of London and criminals and bodies in the Thames. This was a nice neighbourhood, a friendly community, and now she pulled away from me a little; didn't want to get involved.

'He's left me,' I explained.

'Oh.'

'He's left me. Gone away, and no-one will tell me where. I keep asking, but no-one will tell me, see.'

'I see.'

'I deserve it. I know that, don't get me wrong,' I spluttered now. 'He was right to leave me. I'd leave me if I could, only you can't do that, can you, no, you have to just stay in your body and live with yourself for ever, don't you, night and day, night and day.'

'Yes.'

I looked at the landlady. The landlady looked worried. My hair and hands were waving wildly now and my face was strange; even from the inside, I could tell that it looked strange. I thought to myself, Shut up now, Angela, just shut up, but I didn't shut up, I just went on and on; no longer able to stop the flood of hot words that rushed to my cold lips.

'I lied to him, you see, that's what did it. I lied to him all the time. You'd have thought it would have been one lie for each man I went with, wouldn't you, but oh no, that's not how it works. Numbers and lies, they have a way of adding up, don't they, they can't seem to help themselves, multiplying like rabbits or something, do you know what I mean? And then, suddenly, they're like all over the place, making this . . . mess, making this big mess that you can't clear up even if you wanted to because by then it's all one big mess, and if you took the lies away then you'd have nothing left, and that's what happened with Eddie and me, you see. He thought he loved me, but it was just a trick. I tricked him into it, and this is what happens next; the lies go and so does he, and that's all there is to it, that's it, that's that, that's what it's all about, you see, do you see though, do you though, do you see?'

My voice started to crack up. My legs started to buckle. I stopped talking and leaned against the doorway for a breath and a thought.

Why am I doing this? Why am I telling her all of this, I wondered as I shook my head, shook all over. I didn't know. I still don't. Perhaps it was that I thought I'd seen something in her once, just for a second or two, some ember of warmth beneath the cold manner and the frosted hair. She looked like she'd lived a life, and she looked like she'd had other lives too, that she'd very nearly lived. She'd been in love and she'd been disappointed, I was sure; the shuffling husband in the hallway seemed proof enough of that. I thought that she'd understand. She couldn't help. I wasn't even sure that she'd sympathize, but I felt sure that this big woman with the stiff hair and the brave bosom would at least have it in her power to understand.

Well, that's what I'd thought as I'd poured my story and my heart out onto that landlady's doorstep that evening. But I'd been wrong.

'I'm afraid I can't help you,' she said flatly. 'I have things to do. I'm sorry. Goodbye.'

I went back down to the beach, spat at the sea, came home.

Home again. London again. I searched again, only it was different this time. Now Eddie wasn't around the next corner or about to pull up outside my house. Now I looked for him in places he'd never been, questioned people that he'd never met.

A morning. October still, I suppose.

I was exhausted, as usual. I was cold, as usual. I set off, as usual, to begin another day of walking and questioning and disappointment. Everything was happening just as usual, you see, but then, as I approached the tube station, I began to notice something very different about the day.

The people on the streets. The people all around me. They were starting to smell.

At first I thought it was just another of those tricks that my mind was playing on me lately, but as the morning progressed, the odours intensified and by lunchtime there could be no mistake. These people smelled bad, and not just the man with the five coats or the woman with the streaky tights, but all of them: traffic wardens, secretaries, schoolchildren, business-men. Yes, yes, *all* of them.

Of course, I realized that I wasn't so clean myself any more and that the London air was also more foul than usual, trapped as it had been for days by the layer of smog that had closed on the old city like a coffin lid. But these people, well, their stink easily overruled these others. They smelled really bad. Really dead bad. So bad that soon I was having to hold my breath every single time a passer-by passed by.

That afternoon, I fainted in a busy Soho street. A kind café-bar assistant tried to help, tried to make me come in and have a drink of water and a little rest, and you know, I almost did. I almost stopped. But then he moved nearer and then I found that, despite his clean white uniform, this nice young man smelled bad too. And when I asked him my question, he just looked blank and said, Who's Eddie? and that soon sent me scuttling on my way.

The end of the week. The end of the day. The sun dropped as if shot and then there was darkness.

At ten o'clock I arrived back at my flat. Once inside, with the door locked and the lights off, I let my clothes fall away from me and my body crumple into bed.

Tired. The soles of my feet itched and burned. My eyes were as sore as if someone had come along and lined them with London road grit while I wasn't looking, and my body felt heavy enough to sink right through the mattress and the floorboards and the three flats beneath me; sinking, sinking, until it finally came to rest in the soft, brown earth below.

It was over, you see. It was all over.

Eddie was gone, really gone, as far as the eye could see or the legs walk or the mind imagine. I felt his absence filling the whole world. He was not here. He was not anywhere. He was gone, that's all, that's it and that's that. Finally, I accepted it.

It was very hard to get out of my bed the next day. It was a cold, hard morning and I had no plans and no immediate plans to make any plans.

Nine o'clock, ten o'clock, eleven o'clock and still I didn't get up. I did not want to get up. Why would I want to get up? The bed and the bedding were being soft with my body, moulding sympathetically around each aching curve, and I was sure that I had nothing more comfortable than this waiting to be slipped into; that this gentle moment right here was about as good as this October day would get.

Anyway, movement is overrated, I thought, as I watched a hand reach out of bed and then flop hopelessly back down onto the covers. I've done plenty of writhing and wriggling and moving in my life and where has it got me? Here, that's where. Right here, in this room on this day in this state. I may never move again, I decided. I may just stay here for ever. Stay here. Stay here. Let the trouble end as the trouble began: with me on my back in a bed.

I was cold all day. Nothing could stop the coldness. I wore thick trousers and two T-shirts and a jumper and a cardigan, and I turned my electric fire on full, but it was no use; my skinny bones and slack white skin seemed quite oblivious to outside heat, and it was like trying to warm the dead.

But of course, I was not dead. Not quite. Not yet. The rope circles of my internal systems still held all my vital organs in place, and the thick coils of my deepest secrets remained potent and undisturbed, like sleeping snakes in the pit of my stomach. I was definitely still alive, although actually living was a different matter; that was clearly going to be rather difficult from now on.

At some point during that day, my cleaning supervisor rang to say sympathetically that I had been sacked.

'It's not right,' she said. 'You're just ill, aren't you? You should complain!' she said.

'It's fine,' I replied, in no mood for a fight. 'Thank you. Goodbye.'

The other jobs soon followed, because it is difficult to clean other people's houses when you can't even leave your own. I understand, I said each time. Thank you and goodbye.

Days passed. Nights passed. Nothing happened. More days, more nights, more nothing. My clock had wound down and my TV had broken, and there just seemed to be nothing happening anywhere in my flat or anywhere beyond it; just nothing happening anywhere, see. I wondered once what might happen *after* this, but it was hard work, like imagining something outside the universe, and the thought itself soon drifted out into space and disappeared into nothingness.

My mind was like that these days. It couldn't stay focused on anything for very long. It would wander, and wander, and then wander some more, and then it would forget that it had wandered at all, and would just sit down where it was and hum softly like a contented child.

Every now and then, I would worry for my sanity and would send out a small search-party to bring it back. Each time, though, they seemed to take longer and longer to find it. My mind was white and the place it went to was white and it was like looking for a snowball in snow.

Caroline came up to see me one evening.

She walked in. She pulled back a curtain. She looked around her and looked disgusted. I glanced about me too and noticed, with no surprise or interest, that my flat had started up its own little cycle of deterioration and despair.

The clinging grey of road dirt had taken hold of my wide-eyed windows, and now they saw everything in a different, sadder light. Furniture, ornaments, surfaces had all dulled too, my dust settling on them like a layer of tiredness that they just couldn't seem to shake off. There was a small invasion of opportunistic insects in some of the corners. There was a terrible pair of lucky underpants lying on the coffee-table; discarded. The skin of my carpets was dry and flaky, the air everywhere was stiff and dead and the bins, well, they were the worst of all, quietly brooding and seething in their dark, unvisited corners; them and me both with nothing to do but stink and decompose.

Caroline brought out a handkerchief and held it up to her nose. She took a deep breath, and then she told me that she was leaving the country, and then we had a row.

I don't know how it got started. I hadn't asked for the red cheeks and the hot words and the flaming eyes that she'd brought with her. All I wanted was to be left alone, you see, left alone in my chair, in my flat, in the thick white silence that I'd packed around me like ice.

Caroline didn't care about that. Caroline leaned forward and shouted and snarled and spat, but still my anger stayed curled in my lap like a dozing cat. She provoked me, accused me, circled my sore spots like a wrestler trying to get a grip, but each time I just dribbled right through her fingers, weak as water.

'Come on! Say something!' she begged finally, but I could only gaze back at her, weary and confused. I didn't know what to say. I didn't understand this. It wouldn't be until much later that I'd realize why this argument had happened. It had happened because Caroline had made it happen. She was leaving, and now she was here to claim back her part of our friendship, to take it from me like a parting gift. She'd handed in her notice at work, she'd settled up with the electricity company and the newsagent and I was the only complication left. Caroline was going, she had to go, and now the last few sharp words at the door made for a clean break. I heard my best friend running away down the stairs, running off to prepare for her new life. I sighed, gently closed the door, and then went back to my armchair to prepare for mine.

I want to tell you about the next week now. But I can't. I can't remember anything about it, you see, not a thing.

Darkness and whiteness and silence. There was a lot of darkness and whiteness and silence, I'm sure, but when I try to think about any of these things in any detail, my eyes start to roll back in my head and my mind closes like a mouth.

As far as I can tell, I settled with my lemonade in my chair in my gloom that Sunday night, and I did not move from it again for seven days.

11

And then, suddenly, the silence ended. And then the noises began.

Banging, banging, banging. Coming at me. Coming for me. Down from the ceiling and up through the floorboards. Banging, banging, three or four times a day; what was all the banging?

BANG! BANG! early one morning, from the door this time. Caroline behind it, forcing her way in.

'I've been strange,' I confessed to her immediately. 'I keep hearing noises.'

'Angela.'

'Banging from nowhere.'

'Come on. Come on.'

'From in my head, I think.'

'It's all right, Angela. It's not in your head.'

'No?'

'No, no,' she said, reassuringly. 'It's just the neighbours, knocking to complain about the noise. You've been screaming.'

A sensation of floating came over me. A feeling of hovering on the edge of a decision. It was like when you wake up suddenly and find yourself suspended for a moment between two worlds, knowing that what you say now will make sense in one, but not the other.

In the end, I made the wrong choice. I made Caroline jump. I made a wide 'O' with my mouth and I shouted at the top of my voice, 'You think I'm fucking zig-zaggy!'

'What? What?'

I immediately saw my mistake reflected in Caroline's puzzled face, and tried to correct it.

'No. I'm fine,' I said pleasantly.

'What?'

'Thanks for coming, but there's no need to worry. I'm fine.'

'Angela—'

'Go away now, please, Caroline. Goodbye. Thank you. I'll show you to the door.'

I stood up. I fell down.

'Angela!'

'I'm fine!' I told her again, from the floor this time. And I *was* fine. I was fine down here, thank you, and I didn't understand Caroline's flapping concern. I had fallen, possibly broken, but I wasn't a valuable thing, no need to worry.

'You go home,' I said firmly, still face down on the carpet. 'Go on. I'm all right, honestly. Go away. You shouldn't even be here. What are you doing here? Leave me alone. Go away. Go on! Go! Just go!'

Caroline picked me up and put me in my chair and then she sighed and then she went. She went to the bank. She went shopping. And then she came back.

'You seem to have had a bit of a breakdown,' Caroline said that evening, her voice as practical as a repair man's as she stood before my chair, hands on hips, poking me gently and thoroughly with her eyes.

'What?'

'You've had a bit of a breakdown,' she repeated. 'But you're going to be all right.'

'What?'

'Don't worry. I'm here now. I'll take care of things. You're fine. You're fine.'

She waited for me to nod or smile or say thank you, but I didn't do any of that. Instead, I just stared up at her and ungratefully said, '*What?*'

Oh, I knew that she had probably saved my life, moving in like that, making me drink and breathe and eat, making me come back from the dangerous and wonderful nowhere place that I'd been. Already she had paid some bills and scrubbed the flat clean and herded my insects and their creeping diseases back into their holes. She'd undressed me and showered me and then wrapped me up in fresh, sturdy clothes, all the time whispering softly about how this might have happened and what would happen from now on; carefully, gently trying to piece things together, carefully, gently, rebuilding me. She had saved my life. She had saved my life. Without her, I might have stayed there in my chair for ever, starved and dead and slowly turning hard then soft then as soupy as the vegetable mush which she was now endlessly spooning into me.

Well, I knew all of this as I stared up at my smiling friend that night. But I knew something else as well. I knew that I wasn't right. She could stand there admiring her handiwork for as long as she liked, but each moment that passed only made me more and more certain of it: when Caroline had picked me up and put me back together that morning, she just had not done it *right*.

I felt that each of my vital organs was ever so slightly out of place. I felt that my internal systems were running backwards, if at all, and that every nerve was on the very verge of sparking into flames, as if they had been rewired all wrong. Worst of all, though, was the mess of my mind. That's what really worried me. Several essential components of my mind now seemed to be missing, you see. I don't know where they'd gone. I didn't even know what they were called; I'd always just thought of them as walls.

Where are my walls? I wondered, as Caroline told me again that I was fine. What kind of botched job was this that left me without walls? I'd always had a lot of walls. I had the kind of mind that needed a lot of walls; without them thoughts could just stroll around wherever and whenever they liked, strutting from room to room to room, causing total anarchy. Now Caroline mentioned a biscuit, and for no reason at all, I suddenly recalled a bespectacled girl whom I'd once smashed in the face, cracking several of her front teeth. There now. Do you see what I mean? I needed my walls. Imagining life without them was like imagining a jail without bars, a zoo without cages, and you can see how dangerous such a thing would be, with animals and memories growling and prowling and allowed to roam free.

'You should have left me as I was, I didn't want to come back, you should have just left me as I was,' I told Caroline quietly, calmly, rationally.

Caroline said nothing. Caroline just smiled kindly, because she was my best friend and because, at the last moment, my reasonable sentence had come out as a shriek.

The first memory caught up with me on the sixth day of Caroline's stay.

All week, I had stayed very silent and still in my chair, keeping my head down, hoping not to be noticed by the thing which I had felt creeping all around the quiet room night and day, night and day.

It was no use.

It was a morning. A November morning.

I knew that it was November because November's letter had just arrived. Caroline had carried it in half an hour earlier and propped it up on the mantelpiece for me to see, for me to open and read if and whenever I

223

liked. I had not touched it, though. I did not need to read it. The handwriting on the envelope had told me all that I needed to know, its dirty black scrawl leering across the room at me in an unusually large and gleeful way, its fat vowel shapes jiggling untidily on their lines as if chuckling with uncontrollable mirth, its upstrokes all seeming to slant slightly to the left, like a man leaning smugly back to survey and enjoy his work.

I'd pulled my greasy hair across my face and turned away to look at the day. It was a rainy day. The air inside and out was fuzzy and grey. Caroline was in the room, pottering and chatting and sprinkling out general cheerfulness, while I hunched in the chair by the window, letting silence blossom over my head like an umbrella. Everything was fine. Everything was quiet and all right for some time. And then, suddenly, it wasn't.

The rain slid down the windows and my fingers dripped absently along some old scar lines on my arms, and suddenly I was thinking of my brothers. My eyes widened slightly and my attention pricked up. Why would I be thinking of my brothers? I never ever thought of my brothers. We weren't close, that's all. We didn't live near each other, didn't speak regularly, didn't look alike, had no shared interests. Just not close, you see. It seems to happen quite often in families who've had their troubles; either they cling together like sinking sailors, or scatter like frightened rabbits at the first opportunity.

Somehow, we had all managed to leave that home town, that place which was supposed to be so hard to leave. One of my brothers was now in a Lancashire prison, another was keeping his head down in a mental hospital in Scotland, and the third was similarly remote from me in a secure, semi-detached, Suffolk marriage.

I thought of Mark. Mark with his marks. Mark with his tattoos: with the deep blue pain of an ex-girlfriend's

224

name, and a peeling heart, and skulls and demons with many faces pressed hard into his poor skin. I thought of Stephen. Stevie and his piercings. He'd started with the ears at fifteen and now he couldn't seem to stop. The last I'd heard he'd pierced his own eyebrow and nose and nipple and I didn't like to ask what else; it was too painful for me to think of my prettiest, babiest brother being all perforated like that, as if he'd considered his perfect body to be somehow incomplete without all those holes. And then I thought of Michael. Michael, who seemed fine, who had escaped to that quiet suburban wife and life. Michael who had done so well. To some extent, he was the one amongst us who really had escaped, although not entirely unscathed. Those who knew him when he was not doing so well could tell you why he always wears such a bulky great watch over his left wrist and such a thick, unfashionable gold bracelet over his right.

I softened suddenly. Now I worried for my younger brothers, and wanted them to come to me. Where were my brothers? Where were they? Scattered, that's where. Scattered and lost.

Maybe I should go and find them, I thought. Track them down, ferret them out into the open, herd them together and ask if they are all right and, if not, why not? My concern was so intense that it lifted me clean out of my seat. I must find them. My head spun from my sudden emotion and movement. I must find my little brothers. My legs wobbled and gave way. But not right now, I decided, trembling and breathing heavily. For now, I would stay here. For now, it was enough just to be thinking of brothers. It didn't matter that we seemed not to be close; today the noisy rain and the stroking of familiar, damaged skin brought them all back to me.

*　　*　　*

Some more days and nights passed. Mornings and afternoons and evenings came and went, but Caroline and I never saw much of any of them; I'd insisted that the curtains be redrawn and now, in this room, the passing of time only registered dimly, as slightly varying shades of gloom.

I never really thought to wonder what my friend was doing there with me. I was already far too strange within to find anything strange without. These days, I did not feel I had the right or the fight to question the world about any of its ways; I just accepted everything as it was the moment that my attention fell on it. The windows were rattling. There was an odour in the air. A spider crawling up the wall. Caroline was not abroad, she was here; off work, on my settee. That's just the way it was.

I don't know how it was outside. The outside world meant nothing any more. I had shut out as much of it as I could, although occasionally the November city would still somehow manage to push little bits of itself into my room and consciousness. There was the smell of moist, dead wood and roasting, dead animals from a party in a nearby backyard. There was the sound of fireworks or gunshots from the street. There were orange and yellow flashes that set my curtains briefly on fire and left a thick sense of wilful destructiveness hanging in the terrorized air. Well, all of this was all right with me. Those silly Londoners could riot all night and it wouldn't bother me. Eddie was not in this city, you see, and so this city could burn itself to the ground for all I cared.

One week passed. Nothing much happened. Caroline read tedious books all day. I sat, smoked, went to the toilet. Some dull food got made and a few basic words were exchanged.

Soon, two weeks had passed, and still nothing had

happened but more nothing. Caroline wound my clock and then we spent whole days just listening to the boring machine chattering monotonously on and on about time, its one and only subject. No-one wrote to me. No-one called around or telephoned. Overall, things were going pretty much as I wanted them to go; all I wanted was to be left alone.

And then, in the third week of November, the second memory came to me.

It was night-time. Caroline was in my bed. I was in my chair. Outside, the wind was beating up the street; kicking dustbins over, pummelling litter against walls, banging like wild baboons on the roofs and windows of passing cars.

It was very late and the room was totally silent, but for the rattling of the windows and the ticking of the enthusiastic clock. No. I'm mistaken. There was another sound too, a shuffling, fluttering sound that seemed to be coming from between my ears. This was nothing to worry about, though. This was just the noise of the trapped dreams; without deep sleep to release them, they stayed shut up in my head like birds in a box.

I had birds in my chest too, but these ones were not all right. These were bad. Tonight, they were very, very bad; worse than they'd ever been before.

All evening, I had carried a narrow corset of tension around my body and now, as I stretched out in my chair and tried to relax, its strings pulled in tight, squeezing the air from my lungs, crunching my sides inwards until the ribs closed like bony fingers around the soft organs. Well, there was pain. Pain as I bit down on a dry lip. Pain in tingling fingers, and in the white arms which lay like marble by my side. Pain in my flapping heart as I lay there drenched and simmering and very lonely, waiting for the final outburst to come.

It did not come.

227

The pain eased. It just eased. After having me exactly where it wanted me, it suddenly loosened its grip, retracted its claws and then retreated altogether, leaving only soreness and surprise. Well! I thought, as my body became soft and tame beneath me. Well! Well! as black crows turned to white doves and started cooing peacefully away in my chest.

Cautiously, I gathered my thoughts and my body into a ball. I did not move for a long time, but felt the darkness carry right on fidgeting all around me, as my prowling past circled the quiet room.

My dad was alone when he died, I thought now. Alone in his flat, safe behind strong locks when the attack from within began. There was nobody beside him, nobody to turn to for help, nobody to listen to his last words or his, Uh-uh, oh-oh, my heart, uh-uh! It can't have been very nice, that. Someone should be there to see you off, to hear you go. Maybe you have something to say before you die; not just noises, but something important.

I lied. I am sorry. I lied to you, and to myself.

My father wasn't just lovely. He was also extremely violent, and a little insane.

I remember there always being violence in my home, in the same way that others remember always being surrounded by books or pets.

Up until the age of six or so, it didn't really bother me though. I don't know why. Perhaps you are just more equipped to deal with madness at that age. Childhood doesn't care much about right or wrong, normal or abnormal. Fear and fun, these are the only things that really matter, and even these seem to get mixed together quite casually at times.

I pinned my biggest little brother to the floor, laughing and torturing his face with a plait of warm, wiry hair. He puffed and shrieked and pushed up pinkly with his belly, unbalancing me for a moment, but I quickly recovered and smothered his protests with my upper body. Next, I started blowing in his eyes. Then I drooled a spit-threat out from the centre of my lips. This seemed to give him new energy and now his little woolly shoulders flew up and jolted me backwards and he would have broken free right there and then if I hadn't grabbed and pulled the yellow jumper and the little brother firmly back under my control; ruthlessly wielding my extra year and strength against him. His legs kicked up desperately, but I knew that I was out of their range, and now I lifted my face to the ceiling and howled in triumph.

We must have looked a sight, an untidy squash of elbows and cheeks and shrieks in the middle of the living-room carpet. We must have looked wild, but we weren't, you know. We knew exactly what we were doing. We were playing.

The game was an easy one: to see how long it would take the other to submit. The point was even simpler: to win. The few rules were unspoken but clear. You must not bend bones into shapes they did not want to make. You must not use fingernails or teeth or weapons. And blood, you must never draw blood. Not ever, ever. And if one time you accidentally did, well, the flash of red would be like STOP! STOP! and you *would* stop, immediately; the game would instantly end and apologies and bandages and order begin.

My brother's tight body jerked beneath me once more, his skinny pelvis kicking out at the point where I sat, but it was no use, I had found my centre and would not be bucked off, and his movements soon became sad and weak, as I absorbed these last few death throes of his will.

'I submit. Submit. SUBMIT!' he shouted, and at that I grinned and then climbed off. It was over. It was over, and now we lay on the floor together, panting and giggling and equal again. My brother rubbed his itchy face, hauled his jumper back into place, and then started wondering aloud about what we could do next. He had already forgotten that he had lost. There was no real shame in it.

Another day, another fight.

'I'm sorry!' said our mum. 'I'm sorry!'

This was the adult version of I SUBMIT, and our dad should have stopped right there.

'No!' our mum called out as a lamp or a pot vase clubbed her on the back; the ornaments she'd fondly polished just that morning turning suddenly against her, turning to shiny weapons in our dad's hands.

Red! Red! Red! said her forehead or nose or leg. Stop! Stop! Stop! but he didn't.

That was the first time we'd ever seen our dad breaking the red rule, and it was the moment we realized that this was no game, or at least not one that we'd ever heard of or wanted to play. It had no proper beginning or end, it made no-one laugh, and our mother clearly never stood any chance of winning, so there was just no fun or sport in it at all that we could discern. He must beat her and then leave and then come back hours later, crying. We must heed the alarmingly red warning in our dad's eyes or on our mum's body, and stand back to silently wait for the finish, and she must sit there on the kitchen floor, with blood trickling onto her shoulder from one part and seeping through her skirt from another, splashing and pooling onto the spotless linoleum beneath her. That's what he and she and we must do. They were the rules. They would be the rules in our house from now on.

Beaten again, that's what we thought as we approached our mother after each fight, as we heard her embarrassing sobs, as we regarded the wet patches on her clothes with such distaste that you'd have thought she'd peed herself or something, and on purpose too; as if it were her own lack of self-control that had caused this whole mess in the first place. Beaten again. She had been beaten again, and it was each time a defeat so total and humiliating that, even as we tried to pick and patch our mother up, we could barely bear to look at her.

We kids only really got seriously hurt if we were particularly brave or slow that day, and got in the way. It was, though, surprisingly easy to get in the way, because our dad didn't think to give us much of a warning when he felt the storm in his head brewing. Sometimes you'd come home to find the hallway table upended submissively on the floor, and then you'd know that your dad was in the mood to be obeyed, but such obvious signs were rare. Mostly, the trouble seemed to come thundering out of nowhere, and all for no reason at all, except for the only one that mattered: that our dad was right and somebody else was wrong.

One night, my youngest brother's arm got broken; snapped like a soft fish bone as our dad waded through a carpet of children to get at our mum. Another time, another brother got badly squashed beneath a falling mother, and someone else almost lost an eye when a flying saucer crash-landed on their face. It's all right, though. It's not as bad as it sounds. A fist in the guts is not, in itself, enough to smash a spirit; not if you can keep yourself soft and learn to absorb it and fall gracefully.

Well, I learned all right. I learned in the same way that you learn about hands in fires: Ouch! That hurts! I'll try to avoid it next time. Michael was a bright boy and he learned quickly and well too, and young Stevie was soon dodging and yielding with the rest of us, but Mark, well, my Mark was different. He couldn't seem to get the hang of all that. He couldn't even pretend

231

to bend; just couldn't do that buckling thing that our dad needed all the people around him to do.

As ornaments and people flew and fell all about him, Mark would stand still and straight. In the middle of the whole mad mess, there he'd be, terribly still and horribly straight, and in the end I would have to run out and do his bending for him; grab him around the middle, fold his little body in two and then drag it away to safety. I worried a lot about Mark. It terrified me to see how stiff and hard that brother could be. I knew that that wasn't the way to survive this. To survive this, you had to be supple and crafty in your body and mind, that's what you had to be. Take a look around you. One glance at our home and our injured furniture was enough to show you that, around here, what did not bend got broke.

Caroline took me to the park the next morning. She insisted on it. She was adamant. I was terrified. It was my first trip out in over four weeks.

It was early. It was wet. I was strange. The night before, I had accidentally fallen into a strange, strange, sleep, one so dark and deep that coming out of it had felt like climbing from a grave. I'd opened my eyes to see Caroline beaming down at me. She was very pleased to find me snoozing because she knew that I hadn't slept properly in weeks, but I wasn't pleased, not at all; I'd had this bad dream, see.

'I don't want to go,' I said, nervously.

'I don't either, really,' said Caroline, crafty as ever. 'Let's just set off and see how far we get.'

'I'm not ready for this.'

'Come on.'

'I'm not getting better yet, you know.'

'I know. Come on.'

We reached the park. Sudden green. Laughing, glowing couples. Pink, puffing joggers and red-scarfed squealing or scrapping kids. My eyes smarted from all these bits of bright life going on around us. Caroline strolled along breathing it all in deeply, pointing out here and there the rust, bronze, grey, gold beauty of the day. I skulked behind, eyes to the ground, glad to have my thick, heavy, black overcoat between me and this colourful world, where sudden violence or pleasure could break out at any moment.

'I'm really not ready for this.'

'OK.'

'I want to go back now.'

'OK. In a minute.'

I stopped dead still in the middle of the busy path.

'I'm going back now.'

It was meant as a threat, but Caroline didn't take it too seriously. She knew that my storming off home alone would involve working out where I was, and then figuring where I wanted to be, and then plotting exactly how to get there; negotiating streets and roads and people and dogs and cars and trees and dreams, and oooh, just the thought of it made me tired. She knew that I was bluffing and said, 'Let's sit down.'

I lurched towards a park bench, collapsed onto it next to a pretty young boy; scowled at him until he went away.

We sat there for some time. I don't know how much time. Minutes and hours were still in the habit of dropping through holes and disappearing without trace.

I was aware of sighing on that bench. I was aware of Caroline sitting and sighing beside me. And then I wasn't aware of anything else again until I began to feel my fingers pulsing with dull pain. Oh. I am here, I remembered. I am here. In the world. In the park. In the middle of some weather. The sky had darkened somewhat. There was a chill in the breeze. The cold air had wrapped itself around my bare hands and tugged me roughly back into the real world, and now I looked around me and said or thought, 'I'm freezing!'

Caroline gave no response, so I repeated my announcement, pushing my concentration behind each word, so as to be sure of getting them out of my head this time.

'I am freezing!'

'No you're not,' said Caroline; said it so firmly that I believed her, and felt instantly warmer.

'It's starting to rain,' I said next. There were a few drops of wetness on my forehead and nose.

'No it isn't,' Caroline told me and, again, I was immediately convinced. I was in no position to argue. I didn't want to argue, to win, to prove her wrong. I wanted Caroline to be right; felt it was important that at least one of us had some idea of what was going on. I dropped my complaint, decided that it must have been some bird or something spitting or shitting on my head, and left it at that.

The little boy who'd been on the bench earlier came back. Came right up to us. Threw a spongy ball at my legs, then stood giggling nearby, waiting for me to return it. I looked back at him coolly.

He was very small. His eyes were very blue, his cheeks very fat. Pretty. If I saw him now, I'm sure I'd think he was pretty, but back then, he just seemed silly. What a silly creature a child is! I realized, as I watched this boy smiling and smiling and smiling at the world, at the unpredictable weather, at the deep lake, at the mad dogs and the dangerous strangers. There were hazards all around him. I saw hazards all around him, but the boy saw nothing but games, and carried right on standing there, waiting and grinning and *silly*.

234

'Play!' the boy said. Now he was toddling over, picking up the soft ball in his fat woollen mitt, placing it gently in my lap.

'Play!' he said.

Poor thing. He'd taken a liking to me.

'Hey, you! Play!' he grinned.

Poor thing, silly thing; he didn't know that I wasn't ready for all of this.

'Piss off! Go away! Stop staring at me. Go away! Go on! PISS OFF, WILL YOU?'

I might have lurched forward as I shouted this. I might have made a grab at him. I probably did; there was no-one else around who was close enough to have snatched his smile so suddenly away.

The boy looked at me blankly for some moments and then, all at once, his features rushed to the centre of his face and stayed there in a huddle, as if conferring on their next move. We'll cry, they decided eventually. That's what we'll do, we'll cry.

So he cried. Loudly, wildly, impressively; those mighty, wailing trees had nothing on this small boy. And yet, even within this unhappy noise I could hear the ring of an innocence that the trees had long since lost. He had faith in the world. You could tell. He had faith in its people, and in himself, and in his scream's ability to make someone rush over to scoop him up and hold him and save him.

Still, at least he seems to have learned something, I thought, as I watched him running away. He stumbled. He fell to his little knees. And then he got up again and carried right on running, as fast as he could, away from me. He'd learned something, then. I had taught him a little bit about friends and enemies, about trust and mistrust. He had learned a useful and unkind lesson about the world today and, clearly, it had come as a bit of a shock. He hurried over to his parents and told them all about it. They petted and cooed and pretended, as best they could, that it wasn't true.

I closed my eyes. Listened to the wind getting up, to some bad clouds jostling for position over my head, to birds fluttering and flapping. When I opened them again, I saw two parents storming over in my direction. The mother said something to us. She sounded upset. The father said something to us. Threatening. I heard Caroline say something soothing to them and then, walking away with their child in their arms, they shouted back that I should be locked up, and then I felt fury rushing into my ears and then I didn't hear anything else for some time.

Here is what happened next.

I froze. I sweated. I had the sensation of ears popping, only when I raised my hands to my head, I found that my ears were fine and that the popping was actually happening in my eyes. I felt them swell. I felt them strain. And then they flexed and gently burst and colour was suddenly very loud, louder than I'd ever known it to be.

What was happening to the colours? Why was that blue crying and that green shaking its fists at me? How can a yellow scarf squeal as if it is being strangled and what's all this about a swearing grey? I did not have much time to think these things over. I was just forming the words, That's ridiculous, when Caroline's red gloves came screaming towards me and I had to run for my life. Danger! Danger! There was danger here, I was sure of it. Black shadows turned into great birds as I ran and started flapping their wings in my face and peck-pecking at my head. The silver rain worsened, sharpened, and came down at me in long, nasty lines, like a shower of skewers. Danger! Danger! There was terrible danger here, I was sure of it, but then . . . in the end . . . everything was all right. It was all right. It must have been. We must have got home quite safely from the park because, the next thing I knew, I was back in my living-room, warm and all right, gazing at a magazine that I had not bought, sipping at a cup of tea that had also come from nowhere.

Caroline would later tell me that, as she led me home from the park that day, I'd suddenly started swearing and trying to spit at people. I do not remember this, but I do not disbelieve it.

'Oh, hello! You're back, then?'

I looked up. It was going dark. This concerned me.

'What time is it?' I asked.

'You've been in a daze for hours and hours.'

'What time is it?'

'Half-past seven.'

'Is it evening?'

'Yes. It's evening. How are you?'

'Yes.'

I am here, I told myself, leaning back to watch my awareness rematerialize in the yellow light of the dim room. I am here. These are my hands. These are my knees. This is my flat. Blue walls, orange curtains, brown smell, yes, this is definitely my flat, only there's something different. I glanced about suspiciously, sent my attention flying off around the room, looking for changes. It found none and curved back towards me like a boomerang. I know what it is. I know what's changed. It's me. The realization hit me smack between the eyes. That's what's different: me.

'You've been strange today, Angela.'

'Yes.'

'Even by our standards, you've been strange. Can you tell me about it?'

'No.'

'What happened in the park? What happened?'

'I don't know. I don't know.'

237

There was a sudden, fierce pain in one of my shoulders, and I became aware that I was slouching very awkwardly in my chair. I tried to straighten up, but soon found that this was not possible. I was too heavy. I was suddenly very, very heavy; as heavy as if my clothes were lined with concrete and each strand of my hair was a plumb-line bobbed with lead. You'd have thought this would have been an unpleasant sensation, but it wasn't, not entirely. I ached as if dropped from a great height, but there was some amount of comfort in the pain. I had reached rock-botton, you see. I seemed to have reached rock-bottom, and it wasn't so bad after all. There was no more falling to do, and that was something. Even the throb of bruised bone and spirit was better than that endless feeling of falling and falling and falling.

'Everything's OK,' Caroline said.

'Everything's OK,' I repeated, still wanting to believe her, but I knew that this time she was mistaken. Everything was not OK. Something was still frightening me. The darkness. That's what it was. I didn't like the darkness, didn't like the way it was knocking on our doors and windows like that, banging and banging and searching me out like a policeman or a debt-collector.

'What time is it?'

'Seven-fifty.'

'What time is it?'

'Almost eight.'

'What time is it?'

'Eight-fifteen, nearly.'

'What time is it? What time is it?'

At nine o'clock, Caroline got up and went to the window. She looked out of the window. And then, to my horror, she opened the window and let my cigarette smoke drift out and the darkness rush in. I began to wail. I didn't know why. I didn't know what it meant.

Was I going mad or getting better now, there seemed to be no way to tell, but then Caroline softly suggested an early night and another deep sleep and then I decided that, before bedtime came around, I would find out, one way or the other.

'I had this bad dream, see,' I told her.

So there's this girl. In my dream. There's this girl. A young girl. There's this young girl in a house, you see. The girl is eleven and the house is empty and it's late evening, and she's not happy about any of these things.

The house seems very big tonight. As the hours pass, it will seem to grow bigger and bigger.

The large window of darkness that stares at her from across the living-room makes the girl shudder and shrink. She's never liked the darkness, never. Even when surrounded by family, even with all the light-bulbs blazing, she's always been aware of it prowling about outside their bright group, like animals circling a fire. She gets up to pull a curtain across the black eye, then comes back to curl up in a corner, beside a powerful lamp. She stays here in this corner even when she wants some food, even when she wants to pee. The toilet and the kitchen at the back of the house suddenly seem a long way off, and she prefers the known borders of the empty stomach and stretched bladder right here to the shadowed expanses of over there.

At certain points during that long evening, the girl thinks that she sees things moving about in the room. Objects, chairs, *things*. They seem to be shuffling about just beyond her field of vision; rearranging themselves, edging a few inches to the left or the right, playing little furniture tricks on her. She spins around several times but, fast as she is, she never catches them at it, and in the end decides that it must be her mind that's playing the tricks. She has, after all, that kind of mind.

In the future, her mind will continue to be unreliable. Looking back, she will find her memory of that evening strange and patchy; she will be able to recall every colour in the dress that she was wearing, but she won't be able to tell you where her brothers or her mother were that night. They weren't there, that's all. That's all she knows and that's all that matters.

It gets to nine o'clock, and then ten, and then the girl begins to realize that there must have been some mistake. This can't be right. Something must be wrong. Alone and alone for hours and hours, with bedtime and everybody gone; that can't be right. She puts on the TV for light and normality, but every programme she watches is dark and unfamiliar. She's usually in bed by this time. She's not usually allowed to watch *this*, and now the adult dramas and the grim news features only confirm her feeling that she is wandering into a place that she should not be.

And then there is a noise. At some point, there is a noise: the sound of a car pulling up outside her house. Its engine rattles like bad lungs, and then dies.

When she hears the back door open, she drops her loneliness, picks herself up and dashes into the kitchen. And then she stops. Stops mid-dash. Mid-breath. Mid-air, it seems. A lightness comes over her, a sensation of floating that begins now and will last for a long time.

Her dad is standing in the doorway. He is covered in blood. He's covered in blood. He's just covered in blood.

No. That's not how it seems, not to begin with. There's too much blood for that. It's all she sees at first; not *him* but *it*, as if the blood had just walked in and brought bits of her father with it.

Slowly, the colours and the shapes come together to make sense and no sense of what she is seeing.

Her dad has a wash of pink over his face.

Her dad's thick, black hair is thicker and blacker than before.

Her dad has turquoise eyes.

Her dad's shirt was green, but now it isn't.

Her dad's hands are fisted.

Her dad has something clutched in his fisted hands. A jacket. It's his jacket. She recognizes the glint of its black buttons and recalls that, in a previous life, it was a fawn, cotton jacket. Now the fabric is choked and heavy and, when it falls to the floor, it lands with a dead thud and settles at her father's feet like conquered prey.

Her dad's boots have undergone a similar transformation. They had been brown the last time she'd seen them. A nice brown, a nice tan-brown, the colour of healthy cattle in sunshine. Now they are a new colour, or an old one; the suede splashed again with red, as if the animal had been slaughtered for a second time.

Her dad looks as if he's going to be sick.

The girl wants to be sick too, even more than she wants to pee.

Her dad has a smell. It is rich and moist and metallic, like raw liver on a fork.

Her dad is covered in blood. He is just *covered* in blood.

For a moment, no-one speaks, but the air seems filled with noise. A strip of fluorescent white light shrills overhead. The fridge shudders and whines. The tiled floors and surfaces ring audibly with the chill and the hard undertones of the smell that the man has brought in with him. He's made a butcher's shop of his own kitchen, and now he stands by the door, looking around as if he doesn't know where he is.

He takes a step towards her. She moves back. He takes

two steps forward and now he is close enough for her to see the streaks of blood that have run down his neck and dripped from his hair, as if he had been swimming in the stuff. There is a thick, viscous sound from his throat, almost a gurgle. He clears it and tries again.

'You've got to help me,' he says.

The girl doesn't scream, she doesn't rush to him, or to a neighbour, or to a telephone box. She can see that her father is in trouble, but it doesn't occur to her that he might be hurt. With a speed that will later make her trust and abhor her animal instincts, she has already realized that the blood is not his.

He comes closer.

It just doesn't suit him, you see; this colour, this gush of vulnerability.

Closer.

It does not smell like him, or her.

'We've got to wash it off. Wash everything. Get it off afore they get back.'

He removes his shirt and she sees that she was right; there's no wound on him, not a scratch. Her dad is all right. He is always all right. He is all right and someone else, somewhere else, is not.

'You've got to help me,' he says again, holding the stained shirt out to her. His hand is trembling, but his voice is very firm, and there's no way of telling if this is a plea or an order. It doesn't matter. He is her dad and the effect will be the same either way. She takes the shirt.

The bathroom is downstairs, next door to the kitchen, and for a while they work side by side, each taking detergent and a scrubbing brush and a deep breath with them into their respective rooms. They don't speak, but the girl hears her father grunting and swearing quietly every now and then as he grasps and grinds the jacket

242

between his two fists, as he scrapes the brush along a length of limp sleeve.

At some point, the girl's fingers start to cramp. There is a graze on her hand that she can see but not feel. She realizes suddenly that the water in her sink is very cold rather than very hot. Of course it is cold; they only put the water-heater on three times a week, and this is clearly an off-day. Well, that's good, she thinks as the numbness spreads. Cold water is good for removing blood.

Salt's good as well, she remembers, and says out loud, 'Dad! Salt's good!'

She doesn't have to explain what it is good for. They could be talking about nothing else. And besides, she likes the sentence as it is; it seems to imbue the grains with a deeper and wider cleansing ability than they actually have.

Her father rushes in from the bathroom, takes the salt cellar from the cupboard and brings it over to the sink, then stoops to watch how she uses it, bowing to her womanly knowledge of such things. It starts to work. The green shirt that's turned red turns brown then grey then green again. It's working, and now the girl swells with relief or pride. She is good at this. Well, after all, she has had some practice. She's been there many times to help clean up a battered mother and to quietly mop little brothers whom distress has messed at both ends. She has held a father in the sweaty throes of violence; tugging him away, clasping his hand as tightly as if she loved him *even now*. She knows about touching without feeling. About holding your breath until the headful of air begins to raise you above your own disgust. About not thinking what you are thinking in order to do what has to be done.

The socks that have been stuffed into the mouth of the boots come out as sodden and rolled as chewed meat. The girl picks them up with her fingertips and wraps them in neat newspaper shrouds. The boots themselves, though, are too expensive to be so easily thrown and explained away and so she sets to work on them with the salt and the scouring powder and the wire wool. She struggles with the shoes, and they struggle with her, small hands and matted suede bristling alike under this mad, rough treatment.

Now her dad comes back out of the bathroom, takes off his trousers and hands them to the girl. His near-nakedness makes her embarrassed. His trousers make her sick. She has never liked corduroy, and she will like it even less from now on. As she lifts it to the sink, she finds that the tufted material is twice as heavy as it should be, the surface plump, gorged on blood. In the fattest parts, she finds gobs of thick jelly, colourless as drool. These come away stringily, and easily enough, but there is hard work ahead. Elsewhere, the red has soaked very deeply into the grained fabric, settling into the furrows like slurry in a field. She concentrates hard on these lines. For a long time, she sees nothing but lines and lines and lines, going on forever, stretching out before her, then coming around her like a landscape.

Her dad goes off to tend to the car's insides, then returns to check on her progress. She has done her best. She's washed and washed and washed, and now it's time to wash again. Her dad pulls out the old washing-machine. She plugs in its various rubber tubes while he sets water to boil in kettles and pots and, when it's all ready, they solemnly lower in the laundry. No-one says, This has to work, but the sentence hangs over their heads like hot, damp air. She wipes the sweat from her face, crosses her fingers. He sprinkles detergent like magic powder over the load.

They soon see that their hand washing hadn't been as thorough as they'd hoped. The surface on the tubful of water quickly turns brown and scummy. Its steam smells like beef soup, heavily salted.

The girl switches on the machine and her dad pulls off his stiff vest and then motions to his daughter to remove her own clothes. She doesn't want to do this. She really doesn't want to do this, but then her father looks at her impatiently, furiously, and she realizes that, if she were going to defy him, she would have done it long before now.

Stripped to their underpants, they shove the last of their juicy clothes into the mouth of the washer, then the dad boils more water, empties the tub and then fills it again. The girl gets to work again too. She cleans the sink and the surfaces and the floor and then, to the sound of the machine chewing away in the background, she goes away to the bathroom to try and clean herself.

When the mother arrives home with a bunch of grubby brothers, she is amazed to find laundry flapping on the line in the dark backyard and the whole kitchen scoured to a gleam. The dad meets her at the door with a big, white smile, and brightly explains that he had got dirty that afternoon while fixing the car. Noticing the small dress blowing in the background, he calmly adds that the daughter had wanted to help him, and that she'd got dirty too.

'But I could have done it,' the mother says, surprised, suspicious.

'No need.'

'But I'm washing tomorrow anyway.'

'It were no trouble.'

'But you don't even know how to use the washer!' she accuses him roughly, and the dad squirms a bit at that.

'Aye, well,' the dad says next, motioning to the girl. 'She did it, didn't she?'

The mother smiles and nods smugly, as if she's discovered his secret.

'Well, she didn't mind, did you, love? Said we'd best get it out afore it dried. It's lucky she were here. It were her idea. She's a good lass.'

And now they all smile, and now the mother puts the kettle on, and ushers all her children upstairs to bed and now the girl leaves the room, taking with her more than her fair share of praise or blame.

At some point, it is over.

The girl is in bed. It is late. Her mother and brothers are next door sleeping, and she should be sleeping too, only the very thought of it makes her want to laugh. Ha ha ha ha ha ha ha. Silly! She won't sleep tonight. No chance! Not tomorrow night either, and not the one after that or the one after that. Maybe never again, she thinks as she stares red-eyed into the darkness, but she's wrong, of course. She will sleep. And when she sleeps, she will dream. And when she dreams, it will be in colour; mostly just the one.

There are hours of silence, and then a soft tapping on her door. Her dad opens it gently, and edges slowly into the room. He has come to tell her something. He's been thinking things over, and now he's come to tell her this:

'It were a dog.'

'What?'

'It were a dog.'

He moves into some yellow moonlight, rests lightly on the side of her bed.

'That. Earlier. It were a dog.'

'A dog?'

'Yeah.'

'A *dog*?'

'Yeah.'

They sit in silence for some minutes. They breathe. They swallow. A clock ticks. A car drives slowly by the

246

house, sending searchlights across her walls and ceiling. She thinks she sees her father duck slightly at that, and when he continues, it's in a whisper.

'It went for me. You know what they're like.'

'Yeah.'

'A big 'un, it was. I had no option, see.'

'No.'

'I had to do it.'

'What did you do?'

'I bashed it.'

'What with?'

'With a rock.'

'On its head?'

'Aye.'

'Did it die?'

'Aye. Aye.'

She sits up in bed and, for a moment, becomes very excited as she wonders if this could be true. A dog. A dog? Her mind sends out questions, like wading sticks, to test the depth of the statement. Then why didn't he say so before? And why is it such a secret? Why can't we even tell our mam? And why do we feel so bad? But he doesn't want the questions. Every time one forms he just flattens it out with his blank assertion.

'Look, it were just a dog.'

'Then—'

'It were a dog.'

'But—'

'It's true, love.'

'But—'

'It were. It *were*,' he insists, pushing the idea towards her, urging her to take it graciously, like the act of kindness that it is, and then her heart falls as she realizes that this is one of those truths that is meant to be accepted rather than believed.

'All right,' she says.

'All right?'

'Yeah.'

'All right, then. We'll say no more about it, eh?'

'No.'

'All right. Good lass.'

He wants to hug her, but then, at the last moment, he doesn't want to. It's OK. She feels the same way. The blood is between them now. It will always be between them; a conduit for electrifying emotions, a charge around their bodies that will make them ever after reluctant to touch. She has a flash of the future, of how difficult it will be to find a way of living, together, with what they have done.

Soon, the father will begin to find it difficult to look at the girl because of the pictures in her eyes. Soon, he will be unable to speak to her easily, for fear of what she might say. Shortly after this, he will ask her to leave, and to leave quietly, because although she's had her uses, he just can't afford her any more.

'Just a bloody *dog*!' her dad says once more, as he leaves the room that night, hanging the words in the air by the door, to jangle like wind chimes throughout the long hours ahead. And then, through the darkness, she thinks she sees him smile. He smiles. He can *smile*. He is clearly handling this better than her, she realizes; more accustomed, as he is, to reducing the human to animal.

'Photographs of me? Are you sure? All of them of me? I don't understand.'

It was December. I was on the telephone, speaking to Jimmy. Since I'd started getting better, I'd got into the habit of ringing him every now and then. He was no longer a friend. He was positively unfriendly these days, but I didn't care about that. As my health had returned, I'd found myself hungry again for information about Eddie and if I was lucky and did not appear too greedy or needy, Jimmy would sometimes toss a scrap or two into the thin conversation.

Today Jimmy had told me that Eddie was looking well, that he'd been offered a show in a London gallery, and that the exhibition was to be made up entirely of photographs of me.

'But why? I mean, why? He never planned to show the pictures he took of me. Why now?'

'I don't know.'

'Which ones is he using?'

'I don't *know.*'

Jimmy was holding his telephone receiver very close, like a microphone, and now the amplified sound of his impatience rasped in my ears.

'But, I mean, those pictures are private. I just don't understand. They were always meant to be private.'

'Well, clearly, he wants to go public now.'

'What do you mean?'

'Think about it. He's going to show you to the world. Think about it!'

Jimmy laughed unpleasantly as he thought about it, but I just carried on listening and not understanding; the meaning of his words slopping around my head like water, refusing to go in.

'He's going to *reveal* you to the world!'

Jimmy laughed again and I was about to slam down the phone when a terrible idea made a grab at my stomach.

'Jimmy. Wait. No. Listen. Eddie's got a lot of, like, nude photographs of me. You know. Naked. Explicit. You don't mean . . . you don't think . . . he wouldn't do that, would he? No. Jimmy, you don't think that he would show *them*, do you?'

I was sick in the heart and the sink after that telephone call. Yes. Jimmy thought that he probably would.

Well, of course Eddie had photos of me naked. He took me as he saw me: in all states, in all moods and from all angles. I hadn't ever thought of these images as sexual, as such, not even the ones with the wide eyes and legs. The sensuality of the gaze which swept over these things had seemed no different from the one that watched me washing my hair or ironing a dress of a morning. These nude pictures, they were not something to be ashamed of. When Eddie had taken them, I had not been something to be ashamed of, and so they had come out looking like love photos, just like all the rest.

But love can be used against you. I knew this. I had done this, and shouldn't be so surprised that Eddie was capable of it too. It was, after all, his turn to do it, and this was how he planned to do it; by pinning me naked to the walls of a public place, like a spiteful teenager scrawling obscene graffiti on a toilet door.

'But that's terrible.' Caroline was bewildered, angry.

'No, he wouldn't do that. Not Eddie. Can he do that? I mean, legally? I'll find out for you.'

'No. Don't.'

'But you can't just stand by and watch him humiliate you.'

'I'm not going to watch it. I'm going to go away. I don't know where to. Just away.'

'But—'

'Eddie can show me up if he wants to. Jimmy can carry on goading him into it. Martin can kill me if he can find me. It doesn't matter. That's that. End of story.'

I went off to brush my teeth, to show that the conversation was over.

I did plan to leave. I planned and needed and wanted to leave, but somehow, something tripped me up every time I tried to actually do it. Plans fell through. My last bit of money dried up. There were delays and confusions and complications and, a week later, I found myself sitting in the kitchen, nursing a coffee and a frown and saying over and over, 'I am going. I really am. I mean it.'

'So am I,' Caroline said.

'What?'

'My Spanish cousin and job won't wait any longer. I'm leaving tomorrow.'

'Tomorrow?'

'Yes. At nine o'clock.'

'Nine o'clock.'

'In the morning.'

'A-ha.'

'I should've mentioned it before.'

She offered me a biscuit, gently, like an apology. I took a custard cream, graciously.

That evening, I helped Caroline pack her things. It didn't take long; about an hour, which was a little over my original estimate, but not by much. When we'd finished, Caroline perched herself up high on a packing crate and waggled those large feet that she never could seem to keep still. Hooray, I'm going, she was thinking. Oh no, she's going, I was thinking, and had a sudden urge to hold on to her slender, slippery limbs. She noticed the urge and looked frightened, but I did it anyway. I knew that we wouldn't stay in touch. I knew that the friendship was over. The rules that we'd carefully built between us just didn't seem to matter any more, and now I strode straight through them, like a child sweeping pieces from a gameboard.

'Why don't you go and see Eddie?' Caroline said when I released her.

'What? No.'

'Go on. Go to the gallery. Go and see him and talk to him and sort it out. Go on. Go on.'

'No. No way! No.'

'OK,' she said after a pause. 'Then come with me.'

I caught my breath. Another rule broken. I knew that Caroline never took anyone with her when she went away. That was the whole point of going. She took no people and very few things. I suspected that, if there were a way to arrange it, she would not even take herself.

'It'd be a new start,' she was saying now. 'New country, faces, people, new everything. I'd look after you. You could paint there. It's a lovely country.'

She made me repeat a few Spanish phrases, made me try on the words to see how they'd fit, like a mother selecting holiday outfits for her daughter. I did my best. I tried to like them and to squeeze my accent into them, but they just weren't right.

'That's not bad,' Caroline said as I stumbled over the simplest statements and struggled even to say clearly who I was and where I was from.

'Really. It's not bad,' she lied.

'It's not good,' I said.

'No.'

We were quiet for a while. We were both a little sad. We had realized together that I would not be going with her, although I was pleased for us both that she had asked. In my heart, you see, I just didn't want to start from scratch, to sit in a room somewhere, unable to speak a word; no, I'd done far too much of that. I wouldn't go. Thank you, but no. Goodbye, goodbye, thank you and goodbye. Caroline had been right the first time, after all. I still had things to say in this language, in this city.

Heading towards the gallery the next day, I was terrified, but OK. I found the right street. I found the right number of the right street. And then I stood outside for several minutes, gathering up the courage to do the right thing.

The art-gallery atmosphere met me at the door and ushered me in, its fluorescent lights hissing gently, like a finger to the lips, its stealthy quietness insisting on taking my street mood from me. As I stepped through the doorway, I felt the same rush of warm fear and longing that I always felt when I entered a church or a doctor's surgery. Art, medicine, theology: the rooms that contain these things have much in common. Each has this same charged calmness in the air, as if a revelation were expected at any moment; that same sense of gathering there to get at some truth or other, no matter how unpleasant it might be.

The gallery assistant glanced up from behind her counter, then stared hard as I crossed the room. Yes, yes, I am the girl in the pictures, I thought as the strong lights beamed down on me hotly and the wooden floor tapped like a stage beneath my feet. For a moment,

I felt famous and swelled into this new, expanded presence, until I suddenly remembered that I had not looked at any of the pictures yet and, as yet, had no idea what I was famous for.

I tried not to see anything at first. My eyes skimmed and blurred as I sent them off ahead to take our bearings and the measure of the task ahead. Black and white. That's all that registered to begin with. The pictures were all black and white. Well, that's good, I thought. That should make things easier.

A little calmed, my gaze went round again, only this time, shapes started to shout like colours from the walls. I saw an ovoid mouth, a triangle of shoulders and the plump semicircle of a bare breast. A bare breast. I suddenly had a bare breast staring right at me and demanding to be stared at, the way that bare breasts do.

Well, perhaps I can't do this after all, I thought now. You can't do everything. Not everyone can do everything. I can draw, paint, sing, juggle a bit, maybe that's enough. Maybe no-one will mind or even notice if you hold your hands up now and say, No, sorry, I was wrong, I can't do this, thank you and good night.

Seeing me stall with fright in the middle of the room, the gallery girl leaned forward on her counter and kindly prompted me with an encouraging smile. I saw her watching me expectantly. I saw her gaze sealing off the only exit. I looked down at the floor and my feet and saw that, if I ran away now, then her disappointment and my cowardice would chase me all the way home and sit outside my door for days.

I walked up to the first photograph. I faced the first photograph. Faced it. Was face to face with it. With a face. My face. Yes. That inky shadow pattern that swooped under deep-set eyes and scribbled around a shaky smile was like a signature, and unmistakably mine.

Hello, I thought.

Hello, the face thought back, in a way that was stiff but not unfriendly.

Angela, the title card quietly added, and then the introduction was complete.

I moved a little closer now, and as I did so, I felt the image subtly retreat; edge away from me and back in time. I am two years younger than you, the photo-girl said, calling on the details of her face for confirmation. It's true, said the hospital-white skin. See? See? This is where you have just come from. Yes, said the black eyes. Do you see now? This is how you have been feeling. And look, look, the mouth told me, showing off a new, soft smile, one of my first gifts from Eddie; look who you've just met.

The second photograph called to me before this first one had really finished its chatting.

Hey, you! Come here! Come over here and remember!

I stood before the polished glass and breathed deeply. Slowly, as my reflection and fears faded, I began to see a sunny, summery day emerge. Oh. That's nice. Look, it's just nice.

This picture showed a seaside scene from a day trip we'd had some time ago. There was grainy-grey sand, dark-grey freckles that had raised like spirits beneath a white-hot sky, and a background wash of sparkling sea that defied the monochrome film to make it seem anything other than blue. And in the foreground, in sharp focus, there was a good-looking young couple, head to head and smiling brightly at the camera they held in their outstretched hands.

No, wait. They weren't really so good-looking. The man's face could not by any stretch of the imagination be called handsome; it was far too large and rubbery for that. And the young woman, well, she wasn't so pretty either, not caught at this funny angle, frozen in a hiccup

255

of happiness that made her eyes squint and her chin double. And yet, together, they had something. Together they were powerful, and knew it. Smugness settled around their wrapped, easy limbs. Their pale lips pulled softly and kindly over laughs that said to the world, We know we are lucky, we know we are lovely.

Angela and me. This photo was called Angela and me.

I could have stared for hours at that nice picture, but after five minutes or so, stripes and squiggles began to intrude at the corner of my vision, rolling and persistent, like drumming fingers. It was the next photograph. It was waiting and impatient and, reluctantly, I moved on.

This one was darker. I saw that immediately. Oh, the tones were very similar, and the lighting within the shot, well, that was pretty much the same too. Even the outfit that this female figure wore seemed identical to the one in the previous picture, and I realized now that they must in fact have both been taken on the same day. Strange then that they should be so different. This one was definitely darker.

The girl sat on an iron-grey bench. She was at the deserted end of a promenade. A broken street lamp loomed overhead and, from behind, a thirsty black bush was creeping up on her like a depression. The glorious smile and the lovely man were gone, replaced by a face full of brittle shadows and a dark, thin dog who grimaced with pain as the girl's leg jutted suddenly out; as her thick-soled, hard-toed boot connected brutally with its soft side.

Angela and a dog.

I sank a deep net into my memory, trawling my muddy past for some recollection of this moment, but I found nothing. I didn't remember this. I didn't remember doing this to Burroughs. I just hadn't thought it important enough to record, I suppose; although, clearly, Eddie had.

Smashing. Angela, smashing. That's what the next photograph was called. It showed me, smashing up a room.

It was Eddie's room, and he was in it, but the moment was mine and he generously stayed a background detail as I strode forward to kick this table, swipe those ornaments, hog the camera. The camera. If Eddie was in this shot, then where was the camera? Hastily, I reconstructed that day and that scene. The lens was pointing in at me from the back wall, from a height that would match a low bookshelf there, and I realized suddenly that Eddie must have set me up; must have fixed the camera to start its automatic shooting just as the trouble had begun. I wouldn't have seen him do it, not through the haze of fury and cushion feathers. I wouldn't have heard the machine's clicking disapproval beneath the sound of splintering personality and wood.

I gazed at the image with recognition and horror, as I watched myself lunging forward with a mad woman's slurred shriek and a mad father's blurred, black eyes. Is that what I looked like? How did I get to look like that, as awful and as ugly and as familiar as that?

Another photo. Another me. Me in a dress, in a street, in a fight with a tattooed girl. In my hand, there was a squeezed white roll of her flesh. On my shoulder, a small smudge of my own blood. On my face, an expression that was more unsightly than any scowl: a look of pure bliss as the girl's pain shot up my arms and settled like morphine in the brain.

I took a breath and a step and moved on, but things did not get any better.

There was me, in another street, in another stupid fight, this time with an idiot traffic warden. I was slapping her face, slapping hard, and now my own cheeks burned with shame at the memory. She looked frightened, ready to apologize. Oh, there was really no excuse for this. I did not even own a vehicle, so there was really no excuse for it.

There was me, in my bedroom, slashing a canvas that had upset me, allowing the blade to create what the brush could not; long and deeply satisfying gashes of nothingness, where before there had only been a gentle eye, a soft cheek.

Me in Eddie's bedroom. Stooped over in a dark corner with something sharp pointing at my arm. I looked pale. I looked feverish. I looked just like a junkie, except that I was after letting some demon out rather than shooting it in.

I moved on to the main wall, and now the exhibition and the trouble really got into its stride.

Another picture, another me, only not only me this time. Me and a man. Angela and a man. Now there was a man with prominent features forcing his way into the picture, pressing me hard up against a dirty wall. He was a tall, dark, pushy man whom I remembered but did not recognize; seen through Eddie's eyes, both the evening and the lover looked far uglier than they'd seemed at the time.

Next, a grey photograph of an overcast day. Park. Clouds. Puffy breaths. Me pale, but warm enough, wrapped up tight in a man who wasn't Eddie. A tongue and a breast poked recklessly out into the chilly air. A thin bush curled up to try and cover our shame and a squirrel turned away in disgust.

Next, a shot of a scruffy backyard. A graffiti'd wall. A soiled evening sky. A girl with a wrinkled skirt and a big man with a big arm up a wrinkled skirt.

More pictures, more men, more and more and more. A dozen, fifteen, twenty maybe, on and on and on. Even the white wall spaces between the pictures offered no rest for my throbbing eyes; I'd shift my gaze from the faces of the lovers that Eddie had seen, only to find myself filling the blanks beside them with the faces of those that he had not.

'Excuse me. Sorry. Miss? Are you OK?'

The counter girl had left her counter and now her soft shoes were padding tactfully across the room towards me.

'No. I'm feeling strange. I mean, faint.'

'Yes. It can get quite warm in this room sometimes,' she said kindly, finally providing me with the excuse that might actually get me out of there. 'Look, there's a washroom in the back. Would you like to go through and freshen up?'

I looked for the door, looked around the gallery. At the other side of the room, a woman was pointing out my left breast to her friend. Elsewhere, a man was lunging forwards to stare at my framed face. Right beside me, a young couple held hands and discussed my violence and promiscuity.

'There's also an emergency exit out there,' the assistant gently added. 'You know. In case of emergencies.'

'Yes. Yes. Thank you.'

A few moments later, I found myself in a room with probing white lights and walls that were mirrored from top to bottom; a cold, cold room that had no comfort at all to offer a person already sick of the sight of themselves.

I threw up quickly in a toilet and then moved over to a sink and stood there for some minutes, frozen before a stiff, pale reflection. The fluorescent lights overhead had stripped most of the copper from my hair. Shock and vomiting had drained the colour from my cheeks and the strength from my limbs, and now this new monochrome image hung starkly and silently before me, as if it were the final picture that Eddie had wanted to show me.

I looked carefully. I looked empty. I looked very clear and naked and open and empty. I knew now that there was nowhere to hide, and nothing left to hide; everything was already out there for everyone to see. Eddie, with his sharp, true eyes, had seen it all along, and had still loved me. My head reeled at the thought of this. It seemed too good to be true. It seemed that I had been the special project that he'd been working on all year with such dedication and care, snapping up tiny moments and fleeting expressions so that he could one day bring me face to face with the ugly truth. Well, I told you that he was a good photographer. He'd found a way to photograph madness. He'd found a way to photograph sickness and sadness. He'd found a way to capture and expose ghosts, and that is not an easy thing to do.

December's letter came the very next morning but, although it was the very nastiest I'd received to date, it didn't bother me at all.

The tone was desperate and indecisive, a mixture of sick gloating at my recent illness and terrible, spluttering anger at my recent recovery. There were disgusting doodles. Startling strings of swear-words. Curses and promises and massive threats; quite enough to terrify a small woman on her own. Alone in my quiet kitchen, I just smiled down calmly at the wretched scrawl, sensing from his almost illegible fury that my pen-friend had just realized that he'd missed his best chance to finish me off. That wasn't the only reason for my smile; I was also beginning to suspect, you see, that fate might have reached a similar conclusion. Over the years, my heart and I had had every opportunity to break; we *should* have broken, and yet we hadn't, and now I felt my body filling up with the rude health and good luck of a hardy, if somewhat surprised, survivor.

The letter finished by reminding me that the year would soon be over, but now I felt that it was *his* time that was running out. December would end, and I would not. The man who had found my fear so entertaining all year would be forced to admit that the game was over, and no wonder his final outburst sounded so hysterical and brattish, like a small child ordered to clear up his toys and put them away.

I scrunched that last letter and threw it out of my sight. I'd had enough of him. I had no time for all that. Today, I had a letter of my own to write.

Ring, ring.

Silence.

Knock, knock.

Silence.

RING! RING! KNOCK! KNOCK! RING!

'Yes? What?'

Some funny-looking girl opened the door and gave me a funny look.

'Hello. Can I see Jimmy, please?'

'What?'

'Jimmy. Can I see him?'

The girl peered at me coldly through the drizzly grey night and a long black fringe.

'No,' she said.

'No?'

'No.'

'Oh. Why's that?'

She sighed sulkily and grudgingly explained, 'He isn't in.'

'Right. And where do you think he might be?'

I asked this nicely, still not sure whether she was very rude or just a little stupid.

'Well, if he isn't in, then he must be out,' the girl replied sarcastically, and then there was no doubt.

'Yes,' I said.

'*Yes*,' she mimicked.

'So do you know when—'

'No.'

'Could I possibly—'

'No.'

'Oh. Right. Right.'

I shuffled my damp feet, grinned inappropriately; confused to find myself standing there so wet and unwelcome on such a familiar doorstep.

The girl thickened her displeasure and now I felt a shiver of frustration as I peered over her shoulder and into the warm orange hallway beyond. Look, I've been up and down those stairs a thousand times, I wanted to tell her. I've vacuumed this carpet. I've polished those banisters. I still have my own key to this very door, for heaven's sake, and am used to it shielding me in, not out. I wanted to explain that this was all the wrong way round, but I didn't get the chance.

'He's not here,' the girl said suddenly, roughly. 'Get lost, eh?'

I was aware of my muscles tightening in response to her hostility. Felt my face colouring up. Saw a hand fly out to press against the dark wood that she was trying to slam in my face. She pushed hard, but I'd had enough of closed doors and was very firm as I leaned forward and told her, 'Don't do that. Don't be unpleasant, let's not be unpleasant. I don't know who you are or what your problem is and I don't much care. I just know that I've come to see Jimmy and that I am going to see him. I'll see him and then I'll leave and then everyone will be happy. OK? That's the way it's going to be. OK? OK?'

The girl's arms gave way. Her face opened.

'I'm Jimmy's girlfriend,' she said weakly, and at that my own muscles relaxed. She was Jimmy's girlfriend, and now everything was explained. She was Jimmy's girlfriend, and probably had good reason to be unfriendly, unpleasant, unhappy. I let go of the door. I didn't want her silly door, so I let go, let her have it, watched her hug it possessively.

'Look,' I said gently. 'I just want to give him something. A letter. See? Just a letter, to pass on to someone I know. A mutual friend that I've lost touch with, that's all. That's all.'

Her angles softened slightly. She seemed pleased with my explanation.

'I suppose you could, you know, come in and wait.'

'Thanks. Thanks very much.'

I stepped quickly over the welcome mat and sighed with relief. I was in. I was very pleased. I'd stayed calm, no-one had got hurt, and now I was in.

The smell of the place hit me immediately, took my breath away. I know that smell, I thought. That is Eddie's smell. That is the smell that says that Eddie lives here, and that he cooks a lot of spicy food on an old gas stove, and that he shares the house with stupid neighbours who burn incense every night to hide their dopey smell, and that he has an occasional rolled cigarette, and that he once had a dog. You know us, the smells said, as I moved through the hallway and back in time. You remember us and him, don't you? No, stop it, no, I said to myself as I started up the stairs. No, they're not Eddie's smells any more, they're Jimmy's; he has inherited the flat and stove and neighbours, and now they're his. Not Eddie's smells, I repeated several times, but I couldn't stop myself from breathing deeply all the same; breathing them up my nose, down to my lungs, into my bloodstream and around to my heart.

'I'm Ellen,' said Ellen. 'You're soaked. Come up.'

I let her lead me to the top of the stairs, then around the corner, past the mirror and through the butterfly door.

I noticed in passing that Jimmy had repainted the entrance hall of the flat green. Green! That was my first impression, *green*; not what I would have picked if it had been any of my business. It's a colour you have to be careful of. You start out thinking of meadows and pine freshness, but you can all too easily end up with bad luck, envy, headaches.

'He's gone to get some beers. Won't be long. Come through.'

'Right. Thanks.'

Kitchen. Wonky tin-opener on the wall. Cracked tiles hidden beneath that mat. Sticky cupboard door. I sat at the wooden table that Eddie and I had bought together and watched Ellen moving about in the room, at home in there, knowing where everything was without having to ask once. It looked strange. A stranger in the kitchen. No, that was me, wasn't it?

'Sorry I was funny before,' Ellen was saying. 'Wasn't expecting anyone. Coffee? Tea?'

'Yes, tea, ta.'

'Milk and sugar?'

'Oh, yeah, both.'

'So do you live nearby?'

'Yeah, fairly near.'

'And have you known Jimmy long?'

'Yes, a few years.'

At this, Ellen's friendly questions dried up suddenly and some of the stiffness returned to her hair and eyes.

'But not all that well,' I added quickly. 'It's just this mutual friend. No, I don't know Jimmy very well at all, really.'

I shuffled in my chair, crossed my legs. It was a lie,

and I didn't want to lie to Ellen, I really didn't, but I also didn't want to mention the hand-holding and the secret-swapping and the *closeness* that had passed between Jimmy and me; felt that it would only mislead her, as it had me.

We made a bit more small-talk chit-chat, but it was hard for me to concentrate properly because curiosity kept dragging my attention off around the flat. Eddie's flat. Jimmy's flat. Jimmy's home.

Well, it doesn't look very homely, I realized slowly, noticing with some satisfaction the jangling disharmony of the things around me.

Jimmy had bought some new bits of kitchenware for the room; smart, well-designed pieces that few people can afford but many seem to like. The sensible kitchen, though, did not like them at all, and was doing its best to make the expensive black-and-gold intruders feel flashy and overdressed. Elsewhere, other new items were having similar problems settling in. On the drying rack, a couple of sophisticated china cups were being jostled indelicately by a crowd of earthy old mugs. By my feet, a fancy rug that Jimmy had forced the plain tiles to wear had become very badly crumpled and rucked across its length, as if the floor were constantly trying to shrug it off. At the other side of the room, the cooker had shown its disgust at a revolting display of tastefully naked women by spitting gobs of grease all over the calendar's bottom, and, right in front of me, Eddie's cracked cow jug was smiling serenely and mischievously as it prepared to leak a milky stain onto the pristine designer tablecloth.

No. This is not Jimmy's flat, I concluded with delight. You could just tell that it hadn't taken to the man and his ugly changes.

'The flat belongs to someone else,' Ellen informed me. 'But he moved away.'

265

'Oh. Yes,' I said soberly, remembering that the place had good reason to dislike me too. I couldn't be smug. I was, after all, the one who had *made* Eddie move away and so the rooms that missed him now should really hate me most of all. And yet, I didn't feel hated. Sitting there that night, I felt quite, quite comfortable. Warm. Nice. Almost at home. Almost as if I'd never left. And perhaps I hadn't, I realized suddenly. Eddie and Jimmy might have thrown me out several times between them, but perhaps part of me had never left.

Ellen caught me looking around, snooping for memories, and asked me if I'd been here before. I am still here, I wanted to reply, and this urge was accompanied by a strong desire to dive into cupboards and corners, searching for proof. Bits of me are still here, I was sure of it. I could find them if only I looked hard enough. There would be my name, doodled on the closed pages of the telephone directory, an old sock nestling quietly behind a wardrobe, a magazine of mine hiding undercover on the shelves. My things, mine. And even if these small things had been hunted down and herded out, then there would be other, smaller things. Fingerprints. Toenails. Maybe a few hairs caught deep down a plug hole, or the descendants of my germs breeding away beneath the toilet rim. And if even these things had been scoured away, well, I would still be around somewhere. I would be there, at the edge of the carpets, tiny particles of my skin in the dust where the vac can't vac. I would at least be there. You cannot get rid of a person as easily as you might think. I knew this for a fact, and it was a comfort now. It is not so easy to get rid of every last bit of a person.

'Listen, the fire's on in there,' Ellen said as she saw me shiver. 'I've got to start making Jimmy's tea, but why don't you go through? Go on, go in and get yourself warm, that's it.'

She smiled and then pointed me off in the direction of the living-room.

'Someone to see Jimmy!' she called over my head.

'Oh no, have I called at a bad time? You've got friends here? Sorry. I don't want to interrupt.'

Oh no. I don't want to see Jimmy's friends. I don't even want to see Jimmy, really, I thought. It's just this letter. I've got to make sure he gets this letter. Maybe I could leave it with Ellen, after all. I like her now. I'm sure she'd understand. It's just this letter, see?

'No, don't worry,' she said at my hesitation. 'Go on through. It's only Jimmy's brother.'

My head and body lost some of their weight, started floating higher and higher as her words sank in.

I stumbled, put out a hand, grabbed a wall. My eyes clenched around a heavy bookcase, a sturdy table. I felt my toes clutch at my shoes and my shoes clutch at the carpet as the ceiling beckoned, but nothing I did seemed to stop that upward drift.

I knew this feeling. I remembered this feeling. I was suddenly terrified of this feeling. The last time I had climbed out of myself in this way, it had taken a good friend and many weeks to talk me back down again. Stop it! Stop this! This was no good. I could not keep leaving myself just when I needed myself most.

Eddie. All right. So it's Eddie. That's all right.

All right, all right, all right, I chanted. This just means that you can give the letter straight to him now, that's all. That's the only thing that's really changed here. Apart from your blood pressure, that's the only thing that's changed. All right. We can do this. Let's go.

My courage moved forward, but my legs did not, and then I had to stay chanting and planning for a little longer.

All right, I told myself. Here's what we'll do. We will go in. We won't panic. We will breathe. We won't stay.

No, we won't stay. Can't stay, we'll tell him brightly, then we'll hand him the letter, then we'll walk away, and then it will all be over, thank you and good night. All right. All right.

'All right?' Ellen said, seeing me stuck in the hallway; said it sharply, like a nudge in the back, and at last I was on my way.

I walked into the room. Peered into the room. There he was. He was there. Eddie. Eddie was there, there was Eddie; in his living-room, in his armchair, in all his glory.

He was on his own. He did seem to be on his own, although I couldn't be sure of this at first because the lighting was very low and my eyes were doing special effects, blurring and spinning the picture at the edges. But it was definitely him. I was definitely aware of that. Right then, it was all that I was aware of. His wide face. His long, long legs. His straight, broad shoulders. His giant, heaving chest that seemed to pull the walls in and out as he breathed. I almost gasped out loud, impressed anew by the sheer size and presence of the man. I had forgotten how Eddie could just *fill* a room like that.

Eddie, I thought. Eddie is there. Here. And so am I. I am in the room and he is in the room, and we are in the same room. Together. My head spun wildly. His turned, slowly. And then he saw me. And then he nodded. And then he smiled. He did. He smiled at me. Not only that, he spoke too.

'Hello,' he said.

'Hello,' I said.

I didn't move. I didn't move. I was aware that I probably should, and tried briefly to force a leg forward, but it trembled so badly that I realized I was fortunate to be still standing, and had better not push my luck. I did not move.

'Hello,' Eddie repeated eventually, a cue for me to

begin my explaining and my letter-giving and my not staying, but I couldn't seem to do any of that just yet. All I could manage at that moment was a giggle: a sudden, high-pitched, nervous giggle that rippled out of me and made me instantly ashamed. In these serious circumstances, it seemed the rudest sound in the world, and now I covered my mouth and blushed deeply.

Some minutes passed. Nothing happened. I didn't faint or cry or say something stupid. Eddie didn't shout or curse or throw ornaments or accusations. This was going better than expected. They were peaceful minutes, and I savoured every one.

And then the trouble started. As Eddie looked me up and down, I started to twitch and itch and feel very uncomfortable in my body and clothes. Running my attention over myself, I suddenly realized why. I was wearing a short pink dress that Eddie had chosen and paid for, and a furry coat that always made him want to stroke me. My hair was loose, the way that Eddie and his fingers liked it, and my face was naked of make-up, the way that he and his kisses preferred. My perfume smelled of sweeties and bed and two years and us.

'I didn't know you'd be here!' I blurted out, terrified that he'd think me tempting and sly.

'No.'

'I didn't.'

'OK.'

'Honestly I didn't.'

'Yeah.'

'Do you believe me?'

Eddie smiled sadly and said, 'Would you lie to me?'

I winced inside from the stab of his sarcasm, but I didn't let it show on my face. I had already decided that if he was going to make me suffer, then I was not going to make it hard for him.

'Have a seat,' he told me now, and I did as I was told.

I moved shakily over to the chair opposite him and lowered myself into it, but remained careful all the time to stay perched uncomfortably on the very edge of the cushion; wanted to make it clear that I knew I didn't really belong here, that I was just passing through.

'You don't seem surprised to see me,' I said.

Eddie smiled again.

'Were you expecting me?' I said.

He shrugged.

'I suppose we should talk,' I said, but Eddie just shook his head at that; leaned back in his chair and closed his eyes, and now I didn't know what to do.

In the end there seemed to be nothing for it but to just sit and wait. So I sat and I waited. I sat and I waited and I stared at him. I can just sit and stare at him! I realized suddenly, and this cheered me up no end. A few weeks ago I'd have walked the length of the country for this opportunity, and I was determined not to waste it now.

The soft lamplight was making hard shadows on Eddie's face. It did not take much doing. Eddie had always had a hard face. His head was so square that it seemed to have corners. His nose had never been broken, but it had that same smashed quality. His skin was rough and his hair was brutally shorn and his brow hung so low that his eyes were often in shadow and would blink out at you like wild creatures in a cave. Look at him, I thought, as he shrugged his fat shoulders and scratched at an old scar on his cheek, a memento from an ugly old fight with Jimmy. Look at him. He's beautiful.

A fierce wind gusted up suddenly outside the house, making me and the windows shudder. I heard tough rain beating at the glass, and the sound made me cower in my chair, and draw the room a little more tightly around me.

I twiddled my fingers. I bit my lip. I looked around.

Everything was very still. Everything was very still and very calm. Cosy. It seemed cosy. Warm air draped itself over the room like thick blankets, and the lighting was quiet and dim; the blinds had rolled down like eyelids over the two wide windows and only one small lamp hummed softly in a discreet corner. In front of me, the long rug stretched like a cat before the purring gas fire. Across the old sofa by my side, plump cushions sagged like tired children and, elsewhere, several fat and boring books lay wide open, mid-yawn on the floor.

I wondered what to do. I wondered how long this quietness would go on for. I counted seconds like sheep, and soon I was aware of five minutes passing and of my own eyelids and good intentions beginning to droop.

I've got this letter, I reminded myself. I've got this letter and I've got to give it to him. I pulled the envelope out of my pocket, and then I pushed it back in. This wasn't the time. Eddie still had his eyes closed. He was still wrapped up in his own thoughts, wanting nothing from me.

I looked around the room again. I remembered everything about this room. Everything. Normally, I had no eye or patience for detail, but this was different. This was like the contours of a dad's face, or a boyfriend's last words; particulars that you have taken in so deep that you could not get them out again even if you tried. I remembered this. I remembered all of this.

And in its own way, the room remembered me too. Look, over there: a cigarette burn on the curtain. And over here, a bandage on the dining-room table, from where I broke its leg more than a year ago. Behind me, a boot-scar on the door, and before me, the rug: look, the pretty green hearthrug still bore the mark of my messy preparations for that date with the clumsy postman.

The big cushion on the settee had a wide bald patch

at its top, from where I'd torn out its tufts in a fit of anxiety one night, and now I flushed velvet-red as I looked at it. I did that, I thought, stiffening with shame, but to my surprise, when I leaned across sorrily to stroke the cushion's plumpness, I found it tingling pleasantly and yielding softly beneath my fingers, as if to say, No hard feelings, eh?

Minutes passed. The lamplight flattered me. The heat from the fire patted me on the shoulder like a buddy, and now I had a new idea. Now I imagined that the chair beneath me was making a definite effort to make me more comfortable; that it was recalling my shape, fitting me in, welcoming me back. The stern mantelpiece clock was still tutting and tutting, but it suddenly began to seem as if the sound might be a little softer than before, more like the clacking of a mother's tongue, disapproving but fond; ready to consider that maybe I had been punished enough.

The rain slapped very hard again against the windows, Smack! Thwack! Slap! as if to bring me to my senses, but I could no longer be reached. I was too deeply sunk now in cushions and memories. I was in a home, in comfort, in peace, in love, and I just didn't want to be reached. After all, I thought, as the black weather raged on, who in their right minds would want to be out on a terrible night like this?

'Why did you come?' said Eddie quietly.

It was a reasonable question, gently asked, but it knocked the peace out of me as sure as any fist could do.

Eddie's eyes were wide open. His face was alert. He was awake now and I felt the room start to stir around his roused body. Cold rain knocked once more at the window behind him, hard, harder than before. The world I'd come from, the world of harsh realities, was calling me back.

'I won't stay,' I said curtly. 'Don't worry, I won't stay. I just came to give you this letter. I mean, to get Jimmy to give it to you. But anyway, you're here now. So. It's just a short letter. I wrote it this morning. It seems daft now. It was probably a bad idea. Yeah. Well, I feel like an idiot. So. Anyway.'

Eddie breathed deeply as I chattered on. When he spoke, his voice was as soft and smooth as the gas fire, but considerably cooler.

'Don't you think we might all have had enough of letters by now.'

'Ha. Yes. Good point, that's a good point,' I gabbled. 'Yeah, you probably don't want it? Do you want it? Probably not. Sorry. OK. I don't know what to do with it now. Would you like to see it? Or not? Or what?'

'Yes. I'd like to see it.'

I laid the envelope down slowly onto the table between us, then pushed it towards him like a hostage.

'Well, that's that, then,' I said. 'That's that.'

That was that. I had given him the letter, and had nothing left to bargain for his interest with, and so I got to my feet, planned my escape.

'Wait,' said Eddie sharply. He was not going to let me get away as easily as that. 'Sit down.'

I sat down. He picked up the letter, then didn't speak for some time; just kept turning and turning the envelope carefully between his fingers, as if the contents might be dangerous and he was wondering if it was worth the risk.

While I waited for his decision, I made an effort to calm down and tidy up.

I was a mess. I had a snag in my tights from where I'd fallen in the hall. The dirty rain on my cheeks had dried as stiff as tearstains. My hands were trembling uncontrollably and my features had shrunk unattractively and my wind-whipped hair was standing off all

273

around my head in the style of a person in a rock band or shock. I was a mess. The evening had made a mess of me.

'Jimmy says that good underwear is important on a woman,' Eddie muttered, as he caught me adjusting my nerves and my bra straps.

'What?'

'He says that it shows she has her body under control.'

'Oh. Really. Right.'

Eddie sat back suddenly and straightened up in his chair. He looked big. He looked powerful. He looked at me steadily.

'So,' he said. 'Are you going to tell me why?'

'Why?'

I shied away from him a little now, intimidated by the breadth of his question.

'Why you've written me a letter,' he specified.

'Oh. That. Well. You know. Thought I'd say some things. You know. Stuff.'

'Yeah.'

'I mean, I wanted to say . . . sorry. And all that.'

'Yeah.'

'I mean, I wanted to tell you that you did . . . everything. That it was all me. That you were . . . everything. And I wanted to say that I know you can't forgive me—'

'And that you never meant to hurt me,' Eddie interjected quietly.

'What? Oh. Yeah. Of course. That I never meant to hurt you. And that I'm trying to figure out why, I mean, what—'

'And that you know what a fool you've been.'

'Eh? Yeah. That as well.'

'And that you always loved me, and that the other men never meant anything, and that if only you could turn back time.'

'Yeah.'

'Is that what your letter says, more or less?'

'Yeah. Yes,' I said glumly. 'How did you know?'

'Haven't you realized yet?' he said, turning his face away and sagging suddenly. 'I know everything, me.'

I let some minutes pass. I let Eddie drift off back into his own world. I stared at him again, but this time I saw things differently. No. Wait. Perhaps it was not my look that was different; perhaps it was him. Yes. See? I peered more closely. Yes. Eddie was different. And thinner. A lot thinner. How could I not have noticed it before?

The generous expanses of brawn and flesh had been replaced by a compact firmness that I did not recognize and did not like. His long and sprawling limbs were not as long and sprawling as they used to be; seemed to have been drawn back into his body, pulled back from the world like burned fingers. The sharpened bones of his cheeks jabbed at his skin in a way that made me wince with pain and guilt.

I looked closer. Closer.

His big stomach was almost entirely gone, just gone, just like that, just as if someone had come along and lopped it cleanly off with a cleaver. His colour seemed to have disappeared too, and in a similarly dramatic fashion; beneath the orange light and the grey stubble, I could clearly see or sense the sucked whiteness of his thin skin. Clearly, the last few months had taken much from him and now I had to lean away from my Eddie and my thoughts, for fear that I would start to feel his meat in my hands, his blood on my lips.

'I know about Jimmy,' Eddie said quietly.

'What? Pardon?'

'I said, I know about Jimmy. That's one of the things that I know about. You and Jimmy.'

'Oh.'

'Don't worry. I know that you didn't sleep with him.

275

I was watching. I was hoping that you wouldn't sleep with him. And you didn't.'

'No.'

'No.'

'I didn't do that.'

'No.'

Eddie slowly nodded his head, and now I got brave or reckless and leaned forward and said, 'Eddie. Why did you start watching me? When did you start watching me?'

'Watching over you,' he corrected.

'Watching over me.'

He shrugged.

'When I found those letters in your cupboard. They were nasty letters. I couldn't believe how nasty they were. So I waited for you to tell me what was going on. That's all I ever wanted you to do. But in the meantime, I had to see that no harm would come to you, didn't I? Only, of course, as it turned out, I ended up seeing a lot more than I ever wanted to.'

He chuckled now and the sound made me awkward and tense. I wasn't prepared for chuckles, you see. I wasn't expecting to have to chuckle. I looked at him uncertainly, as if this might be a trick, like when someone gets you laughing with them just so that they can stop suddenly and leave you foolish and gaping, like a stranded fish.

'Don't look so scared,' Eddie said, softening his voice as he saw my defences stiffen. 'There's no need to be scared.'

'No.'

'Didn't I try to tell you once that there was no need to be scared?'

'Yes.'

'I was always looking out for you. Keeping an eye on things.'

'But why?'

There was a terrifying pause. The room held its breath. A tightrope walker wobbled in my head, and then Eddie quietly said, 'Because that's what I do. Because I love you.'

Well, I was not expecting that either. That threw me right off balance. The thought that Eddie might still want me was suddenly just too much to take, and now I panicked and pushed the overwhelming idea of love away by abruptly turning the conversation to hate.

'No! You must hate me,' I told him.

'What?'

'After all the things I've done. After everything you've seen. It's only natural. You *should* hate me.'

'Well, I don't.'

'You must hate me more than you've ever hated anyone before,' I went on, waving my hands now, getting a little carried away.

'No.'

'More than you'll ever hate anyone again.'

'No.'

'I'm evil. I'm terrible. I'm like your worst enemy.'

'Angel,' Eddie said patiently, staring into the fire and sighing along with its gassy flames. 'I don't hate you. Don't you know that yet? Haven't you worked it out yet? You're not my enemy, and I'm not yours.'

There was some silence. And then there was some noise. Slamming. Stomping. Shouting. And then the main lights flicked suddenly, harshly on and then the living-room door behind us was flung open wide.

'What the fuck is she doing here?' bellowed Jimmy.

Jimmy. It was Jimmy.

'What the fuck is *that* doing here?' he repeated, prodding his gaze at me as scornfully as if I were some flea-bitten dog who had just sneaked in off the streets;

a bedraggled, unwanted mongrel with no breeding and no feelings.

'Sorry. I let her in,' said Ellen, and now I felt the cold draught of Jimmy's rage as he spun around to blast at the girlfriend in the doorway.

'Fucking great. You stupid woman!'

'I'm sorry. What have I done wrong?'

'Stupid! You stupid woman!'

Jimmy didn't say exactly what she had done wrong or exactly why she was stupid, but his enunciation was so forceful that Ellen believed him immediately, and immediately began stuttering and stammering like an idiot.

My anger leapt across the room towards Jimmy and Ellen and wedged itself between them, and then Jimmy looked at me as if I were stupid too, only I wasn't, not any more.

I understood everything suddenly.

Why hadn't I seen it before?

Now the expression that Jimmy addressed to me was speaking like words and it was clearly saying, Who do you think you are woman you are nobody slut just nobody and nothing you are just a slag bitch whore.

Jimmy saw that I had seen the light and his eyes flashed with menace and fright. Our stares gripped each other's bodies like hands around necks. Fury flew across the long pause between us, making crackles and sparks where it met in the middle.

I looked at him. He looked sickeningly well, standing there in the doorway like that, with his hair gleaming blackly from the rainy night, with his dark, expensive clothes making fine shapes of his trim torso and the new meat wrapped around his lean limbs. He looked better than the last time I'd seen him. Better and bigger. Yes, much bigger, I realized nauseously, as I noted that his growth seemed to be of similar proportions to that of his brother's shrinkage, as if those missing bits of Eddie's flesh had been applied direct to Jimmy's shoulders and chest.

Jimmy looked at me, sized me up carefully, ran his eyes like a tape-measure over my wild hair and skinny body and smudged, staring face. He took a moment or two to note down the extent of my weakness and strangeness and the limit of my credibility, and then he visibly relaxed. His shoulders dropped. His anger slackened. The fear went back behind the scenes of his face and a cocky smile strutted onto centre stage.

'So it's Angela, is it? Angela's come to see us. How nice.'

He swaggered slowly across the room to stand right in front of me.

'Well, this is cosy, Ed. No, really, this is nice. The woman destroys your life and you invite her in for a cup of tea.'

He threw a pack of beers roughly down onto the settee. The cushions winced, but I did not.

'I heard she had a breakdown, you know. Oh, it is a shame, but it has a certain symmetry; now she's mad as well as bad. The perfect guest. This is lovely. This is great.'

Jimmy scowled darkly and fumbled in his coat. His hand made a gun shape in his pocket and he pointed this at me for a few seconds, and then he pulled out his cigarettes and turned around to face the others.

'Let's see. What have we got? Well, she's a liar. She's a slut. She's handy with a knife. That's just fine. She humiliates my brother? No problem. Let her in, why not? Let's forgive her and welcome her in so that she can do it all over again.'

The back of Jimmy's head smirked at me while he was saying this, and then, when he'd finished, he turned around and smirked at me with the front of his head too. It doesn't look good for you, his eyes said, full of black and glee, poking and pulling at my wild hair and tarty dress and the torn tights on my skinny legs, trying to yank the confidence out from under me. He was composed and I was a mess, it's true. Eyes darted backwards and forwards between us and the judgement of the room seemed to be swinging in his favour and now he shrugged loosely, wrapped himself in smooth cigarette smoke and said silently, Ha! You can't touch me now, silly smart bitch! What are you going to do now, silly smart bitch whore? Look at you. Ha ha! They'll never listen to you!

Well, of course, I wanted to kill him now. That's what I wanted to do. I wanted to destroy him as he'd tried to destroy Eddie and me. I felt my muscles fill with strength and ache with this swelling desire to inflict terror and pain on the smiling Jimmy. The silly man. He should have finished me off while he had the chance, while I was weak. At certain points over the last few months, I couldn't have fought back and wouldn't even have really minded if he'd sneaked into my empty flat one night to put me out of my misery. He should have done it then. It was a bad mistake of his not to have done it then, not to have kicked me while I was down, because now I was up again and getting stronger all the time.

Jimmy chuckled slowly and now I made my move, and it took everyone by surprise, including me. I remained in my chair. My fists stayed in my lap. Only my lips were moving, and not threateningly; they smiled in a way that was strange and nice and then they started to quietly recite the names of several harmless-sounding towns in the south-east and south-west regions of the country.

For a few moments, it seemed as if Jimmy had been right after all: I was quite mad. What was I doing? It sounded crazy, but I just carried on with my little list: three names, five names, ten names, and then, when I reached the twelfth, I stopped and Ellen visibly started. She frowned. She remembered something about that last one. Perhaps Jimmy had taken her there just this week; driven her out in his fast car to browse around shops, to visit landmarks, to find a postbox.

'These are the twelve places you sent the letters from. You sent me twelve hate letters, didn't you, Jimmy?' I said calmly, rationally. 'It wasn't who I thought it was. It was you. You sent me drawings of women with their heads chopped off. You told me that I'd be dead soon. It was you. I know it was you.'

And now the atmosphere in the room changed. Somehow, you could just tell that I was telling the truth. *I* could tell, could feel its power like a charge of electricity in the quiet air. Jimmy could feel it too and jumped, then paled, from the shock.

Relieved, I sighed heavily and leaned back in my chair, rested my case. Frightened, Ellen moved across the room to stand by my side. Eddie, who had been watching all of this silently, waiting to see what I would do, now sent me a brief glance of satisfaction and pride.

'Eddie!' said Jimmy.

'Jimmy,' said Eddie, and then the two brothers fell into a moment of intense silence, eyeing each other through the smoky air like poker players with much at stake.

'I don't know what she's on about,' Jimmy said eventually, trying a bluff. 'This is stupid. This is very stupid. I'm not even going to discuss this.'

Eddie said nothing, gave nothing away.

'The girl is mad. She'd say anything. You can't listen to her. Clearly, she's mad.'

'No, I'm not mad,' I interrupted. 'I was a bit funny for a while, but I'm not mad.'

'And she's a slag,' Jimmy went on. 'You can't trust a person like that. Unfaithful. Untrustworthy. Dirty. Hello, Angela, will you have sex with me? Yes, of course mister. That's what she's like. That's what she does.'

'No I don't. I don't do that any more!'

'I can't believe that you'd believe her. I'm your brother. Who's she? Some lying little bitch, that's all. She's such a liar. Come on, Eddie! She lies and lies, you know that.'

Jimmy ran out of words and breath and stooped feebly before his brother.

Eddie stood up slowly, rolled his shoulders and then drew himself up to his full height and strength. Weakened as he was, he was still a mighty man, and now the people and the air in the room shuffled back a little to make space for what he had to say.

'No,' Eddie muttered quietly. 'I don't think she does that any more either.'

Jimmy looked startled. He wasn't the only one. Until I'd heard Eddie say this out loud, I myself hadn't realized that it was true.

'What? What?' Jimmy stammered, but Eddie did not repeat himself. He didn't need to; the atmosphere was so thick by now that his words would not disperse, and just hung there before him for some time, like sky-writing, for all to see.

I held my breath and wondered what Jimmy would do now. I wondered what he could do, and rummaged around deeply in my own, old bag of tricks, digging, digging for a way out of this. I came up with just one solution, and this was at the very bottom of the pile; was the liar's very last resort, only to be used in desperate circumstances like these, when the truth has hemmed you in on all sides and the walls of hard facts are pressing in like a shrinking room. He had to confess. That was his only chance. He had to confess, but he had

282

to do it really soon; any second now, those walls and Eddie's fingers might be squeezing the confession from him, and by then it would be too late. He had to do it now. Now!

'All right,' Jimmy muttered. 'I did send her some letters. What do you want me to say? I sent her some letters. I admit it. And I'm sorry, OK?'

There was a long, long pause, and then Jimmy rubbed his face and said, 'All right. So I was jealous, Ed. Is that what you want to hear? I've always been jealous of you and everything you had, and in the end it might have sent me a bit mad. OK? OK?'

There was a sigh. Another pause. Another sigh.

'So I tried to take Angela away from you. Last year. Last Christmas. I just gave it a try. I thought it might make me feel better. Only it didn't, because she didn't want me, you see, and that made me even madder. And that's when I started with the letters. Making threats. Calling her a whore and a slag. Later, of course, I found out that she really was a slag. Ha. It had just been a lucky guess, that. Turns out that she really would go with anyone. Yeah. But she still wouldn't have me, would she? Ha. It's funny, really. If you look at it a certain way, its quite funny. I mean, I wouldn't really have hurt her. I wouldn't. I just wanted to upset things, that's all. Just wanted to spoil things for you both. Look, I know how bad this sounds. It is bad, I know that. What can I say? All I can do now is tell you the truth, and the truth is that I'm sorry. I am very sorry. I am. I really am.'

Jimmy lowered his head and waited to be forgiven. When nothing happened, he waited some more and then apologized again; thought that would be enough. Across the room, I lowered my head too and thought about what Jimmy had said. I thought about the letters. I thought about the fire. I thought about Jimmy's two attempts to take me away from Eddie. I thought about

Burroughs, and felt sadness move through me like a ghost.

'Look, I'll tell you the truth now. I did some other stuff too. I admit it. I'm admitting it all. What else can I do? Do you want me to beg for forgiveness? Do you want a fight? A drink? Or what? Come on, Eddie, give me a clue. Say something. Do something. Come on, mate!'

But Eddie did nothing, nothing at all, and this was when the first sign of panic appeared. I saw it coming from way off: a small, blazing light way back in Jimmy's eyes, like a fast car hurtling towards you.

'I know I'm crap! Do you think I don't know that? I'm crap and I think that you should beat the shit out of me now, Ed. Go on, go on, I've got plenty more where that came from!'

Hot sweat began to appear on Jimmy's smooth face. It looked bad, smelled yellow.

'I mean, if you don't forgive me and help me, who will? I'm ill, you see, and I need your help. I've got nobody but you. I've got fucking nobody and nothing but you! Eddie! You're my brother. You can't do this to me. We're family!'

Flap! Flap! went Jimmy's arms and lips and insides. Flap! Flap! Flap! over and over and all over the place, but it was no use; the wilder the one brother got, the steadier the other seemed until finally, realizing that Eddie was not going to be moved no matter what, Jimmy sighed and gave up and let his arms and apologies fall limply to his sides.

It hasn't worked, I said to myself. He'd given it a good try, but it just hadn't been good enough; Jimmy was not after all as clever and cunning and extraordinary as I'd believed him to be. That's what I thought as I heard the silence coming into the room to finish Jimmy off, but I was wrong, wasn't I, because the very next moment, Jimmy did something amazing.

Time and us stopped what we were doing to stare at the unnatural sight in our midst. Jimmy. Crying. Jimmy, *crying*. It just looked so strange, you see. This hard man was turning to mush before our very eyes, and now I gaped as if at a miracle; as if he were wringing water from rocks right in front of us.

Oh, the first few drops were fake enough, don't misunderstand. To begin with it was no more than a cheap trick. Tears conjured up by will power and desperation. Tears pulled from the eyes like a string of scarves; a colourful dramatic gesture to save the show. He would cry, and then he would stop crying, and then we would all applaud his efforts with sighs and sympathy and that would be that.

But then, just as I was thinking this, I noticed something odd. There. See? He's not stopping. The moment of perfect timing came and went like a missed cue. The flashy diamond drops were replaced by crude red swellings and ugly green snot, and then the fetching little sniffs gave way to tremulous sobs that left both him and me badly shaken. This is real now, I realized to my horror. Jimmy was properly crying, definitely distraught. Perhaps the pity was only for himself, but it was genuine pity none the less and now I had to consider the possibility that Jimmy was, as he kept on insisting through hiccups of misery, really, *really*, sorry.

I glanced nervously over at Eddie, for some confirmation of what I seemed to be seeing and thinking. He caught my eye and nodded across, stiffly, sadly. Yes. Look. Eddie thinks that this is real too, and he knows everything.

Jimmy carried on crying. I started softening. Ellen wept quietly and then I saw that Eddie too had fat tears queueing in his eyes as he leaned forward and put his great, steady arms around his younger brother's shuddering shoulders. I watched him pull Jimmy close.

I saw him sob once. And then I heard him whisper softly, almost tenderly, 'We're finished, you and me, Jimmy. So shut up. So just get out of my sight. Get your things and get out and don't come back, ever. You won't change. I can't help you. I've tried to help you and now I'm going to stop. That's it. It's over. Family or not, we're finished, so just get lost. Go on. Go on. Goodbye. Go on! Fuck off!'

Jimmy's bottom jaw dropped open when the full meaning of these words hit him. His face turned blank, then flabby. Tears that had already been sent on their way chugged obediently down his cheeks, but he wasn't crying any more. He wasn't doing anything any more, didn't seem able to, as if some vital connection in his body had been suddenly severed.

And then, slowly, a new energy began to flow into him. I saw it happen. His eyes filled with it. His hands trembled with it. Finally, his whole body shook with this powerful force and then he was suddenly screaming and buzzing and jerking on the spot, like a machine that's been wired all wrong.

Ellen moved forward to grab her boyfriend's arm, but it was a terrible mistake to touch a man in this state. Eyes sparking, he flicked her off, set her trembling too.

I watched Jimmy swoop away around the room, out of control. I watched his long fingers ripping at the air and his own clothes. I watched strong legs kicking out at anything he came across, as if to pass on the fear and pain which now swelled in his face.

Oh, I'd thought he was beautiful once, I remembered now as I stared at the ugliness erupting from him. How had that happened? How had he managed to get in my head and fiddle with my eyes like that?

'FFFUUUCCCKKK . . .' yelled Jimmy, running from the room.

'Jimmy!' called Ellen, heading for the door.

'Ellen!' I said, but it was too late, she'd already gone; she loved the man, you see, and wanted to help, thought that she could help.

There was the sound of crashing lamps and fury. Jimmy punched a wall, battered the wardrobe, assaulted the bed, hating and punishing these things just because they were Eddie's. At some point, I heard him yell my name, hating me in the same way, and for the same reason.

Around the sound of the man's thumping madness, the house shook, or was that me?

There were more thuds. There was more damage, more swear-words and more breakages and then, two horrible screams and one almighty crash. Eddie and I dashed into the hallway to find a terrible mess before us: a wreck of shelves and magazines and books, with Ellen in the middle of it all, splayed out on the floor in the awkward position into which she'd been tossed, like some cheap paperback, broken-spined on the floor.

Eddie groaned and stooped over to try and fold Ellen back together, as Jimmy stomped away, cursing and raving. He swiped wildly at a mirror on the wall, like an animal startled by a reflection it can't understand. He hit out at the coats which hung in his way, landing a creasing punch into the back of Eddie's old jacket. He kicked the door, then opened it, then slammed it, then smashed its beautiful butterfly panel with one ugly backward jab of his elbow.

'Leave it,' Eddie said as he saw me go over to finger the door's jagged edges.

'Leave it. Let him go,' he advised, but I couldn't, not just yet. I'd spotted blood on the glass, you see. There was blood on the glass and blood on the floor and a line of pebble-sized blood dots running away down the stairs; a trail of red that instinct forced me to follow.

I reached the bottom stair just as Jimmy was leaving the house. The door swung open behind him, creaking painfully. The hallway table tottered feebly, like an old lady harassed in passing. I saw Jimmy kick out at milk bottles and then a scared cat. I saw him stamp down the front steps and wrench the stiff gate violently open. I saw Jimmy overturn a bin and then thump a parked car and then I did not see Jimmy any more; he disappeared suddenly out of sight, stormed away into the black weather, yelling at the night as the darkness engulfed him.

Jimmy didn't look back and he didn't come back. I knew this because I stayed there at the open front door for a long time, gazing at nothing, waiting for something, thinking about the missing man and the trail of broken things that he'd left behind.

Before me, Decemberness roared and swirled powerfully, hypnotically. The wind tugged and tugged at my hair, spoiling for a fight. I got cold. Very cold. So cold that the blood seemed to set like jelly in my veins; not pulsing, not flowing, just wobbling every now and then from the deep tremble at the core of me. As the minutes passed, I found myself feeling all sorts of painful feelings and thinking all kinds of strange thoughts. For an instant, I even thought that I might follow Jimmy, go after him, go with him, pulled along the bleak street in his wake as if still attached by invisible cords to that dangerous man and life. But then I heard Eddie. Eddie was calling my name and his voice was very strong and kind and then everything was all right. On the threshold, I shivered once and violently, as if to shrug off an old habit, and then I gently closed the door and went back inside.

THE END